CARY HART

COPYRIGHT

Disclaimer. This is a work of fiction. Names, characters, places, brands, media, and incidents are either a product of the author's imagination or are used fictitiously; any resemblance to actual persons living or dead, business establishments, events or locations is entirely coincidental.

The author acknowledges the trademarked status and trademark owners of various products referenced in this work of fiction. Any trademarks, service marks, product names or named features are assumed to be the property of their respective owners and are used only for reference. There is no implied endorsement.

This book contains material protected under the International and Federal Copyright Laws and Treaties. Any unauthorized reprint or use of the material is prohibited. No part of this book may be reproduced, stored in a retrieval system, or transmitted in any form, or by any means, electronic, mechanical, photocopying, recording or otherwise, without prior permission of the author. For more information regarding permission email caryhartbooks@gmail.com

Editing provided by Word Nerd Editing
Proofreading provided by Proofing with Style
Interior Design provided by Cary Hart

Publication Date: June 2019
UnLucky in Love (Hotline Collection, Book #1)
Paperback ISBN: 9781078475631
Copyright ©Cary Hart 2019
All rights reserved.

BOOKS BY CARY HART

THE HOTLINE COLLECTION

UnLucky in Love

BATTLEFIELD OF LOVE SERIES

Love War

Love Divide

Love Conquer

SPOTLIGHT COLLECTION

Play Me

Protect Me

Make Me (Coming 2019)

Own Me (Coming 2019)

THE FOREVER SERIES

Building Forever

Saving Forever

Broken Forever

STANDALONES

Honeymoon Hideaway

PLAYLIST

Better Luck Next Time by Kelsea Ballerini
Bitter Love by Pia Mia
Voices in My Head by Ashley Tisdale
Love Myself by Olivia O'Brien
Last Kiss by Taylor Swift
If We Never Met by John.k
How Can I Forget by MKTO
Best Damn Thing by Alexander Stewart
I Don't Care by Ed Sheeran w/Justin Bieber
Sucker by Jonas Brothers
Just Friends by JORDY
Fight For You by Grayson Reed
Wait For You by Jake Miller
Look What God Gave Her by Thomas Rhett
Forever Right Now by Conor Matthews
Incredible by James TW
Falling Like The Stars by James Arthur
You Feel Like Home by Hills x Hills

DEDICATION

Ceej — I started this book to make you laugh and finished it so I could smile. I miss you!

CHAPTER ONE

CLOVER

"He didn't?"

"Oh, he did! Clover, I'm telling you," CJ, one of my best friends and New York's sassiest socialite, groans over the hands-free system, "every—single—sense was in over-freakin'-load."

"So, the blindfold didn't scare you?"

It's a reasonable question, right? I know I'm not as adventurous in the bedroom as CJ, but a blindfold? That seems kind of creepy and definitely requires a little more "research"—and when I say "research," I mean Google.

Don't judge. You know I'm right! Google…knows it all!

Need to get lipstick out of the carpet? *You Google.*

Need a quick and easy recipe? *You Google.*

Need a quick background check? *You Google.*

Need to figure out what exactly your best friend is doing with her latest boy-toy, Mr. Do-It-All-Night-Long? *You Google.*

So, is there really a question as to what I'm going to do? Of course not! I'm going to pull over to the side of the road and park.

"Are you being serious right now?" CJ stalls, waiting for me to reply.

She's onto me.

If I tell her I have no clue what she's talking about, I'll get the whole "spice up your life" speech delivered in the form of a Spice Girls tune.

"It's a reasonable question." I give her a quick answer to buy myself some time until I can figure out what in the hell she's talking about.

It's not like I don't have sex, I do. I have it all the time. Every single Friday from five to six, after Jeffery gets home from work. We both agreed too much sex could complicate our relationship. Make it messy.

At first, I thought maybe he just wasn't into me because what guy wouldn't want it all the time? But Jeffery is different. He has a plan—a plan I can respect.

"Hell no! That's the whole point of sensory deprivation."

There it is! The clue I was looking for!

Pressing the speaker button, I pull up the Google app and search for the newest kink trend. At least, I'm sure it's a trend. Something new everyone is trying. Well…everyone who isn't in a lasting relationship like myself.

Ugh! The blue-line of death. Are you kidding me? This is supposed to be the largest 4G network in America.

"Why is this thing so slow?" I mumble.

"Well, yeah. Sometimes he went slow, and other times it was so quick and hard, it had me jumping off the table."

Did she just say table? What did she get herself into? Finally, Google comes to life and gives me the answer I'm looking for.

SENSORY DEPRIVATION: a process by which someone is deprived of normal external stimuli such as sight and sound for an extended period of time, especially as an experimental technique in psychology.

Okay, this isn't nearly enough. I need to see what this is about. Time to mute CJ and head for the videos.

"When you're blindfolded, you have no idea when or where you're going to be touched. The wait—the anticipation *alone*—is orgasmic," CJ rambles on. "Then, when your partner, or as I like to call him, Sex God Extraordinaire, removes two or more senses? BEST ORGASM EVER!" she shouts.

CJ carries on, giving me a play-by-play of her sexcapade as my fingers work to find something to explain this madness.

Here we go!

A scene from that movie everyone was talking about. The suit who just so happens to be a dom fell in love with a virgin college graduate starting her career. Insert a contract, she becomes his sub, and hello red room full of whips, battery-operated devices, and…*blindfolds.*

"Clover? Are you even listening?" CJ seems a little annoyed.

Oops! I quickly take it off mute. "Of course. I was just taking it all in."

"Clover Kelley, don't you lie to me. You Googled!"

She says the word like I should be ashamed.

"It's a search engine, not some dirty little secret." I take the phone off speaker and hold it up to my ear. "I have nothing to be ashamed of." I look around, then whisper into the phone. "You, on the other hand," I deepen my voice even more, "are into BDSM."

"Wh-What?" CJ laughs out. "I'm not."

"Don't lie to me," I interrupt. "Right here. It says, and I quote. 'Sensory deprivation is commonly used in BDSM.' What do you have to say for yourself, missy." I twist in my seat, feeling a tad uncomfortable while turning fifty shades of red.

"I knew it! You totally Googled!" She must have slammed her hand down on the steering wheel because the horn honks and CJ lets out a curse.

"Don't change the subject about how Mr. Do-It-All-Night-Long, or Mr. Sex God Extraordinaire, or whatever you call him totally Christian Grey-ed you."

She laughs.

I don't.

"Did you just make Christian Grey into a verb?"

"Don't turn this around on me. This…" I wave my hands around in the air, looking like a crazed lunatic to the passersby, I'm sure, "is serious, CJ. First, it's this sensory thing. Next, it will be those underground sex clubs where you participate in group orgies. Then, before all is said and done, you will end up in one of those polygamist relationships."

"Clover!" CJ laughs out. "You really need to chill. I had great sex. Nothing more. Nothing less."

"You say that now." I close my eyes and think about what could happen. *Next up on Dateline: The Death of NYC Socialite, Carly Jane Collins.*

"In all seriousness, Clo, you need to let loose once in a while. You know, like, live a little and *orgasm* a lot."

"That's your solution for everything, isn't it?" I roll my eyes.

I know she's right. I've lived my entire life for my future—not the now. It's not like it's something new, though. I've mapped it all out—every goal, ambition, and what I have to do to make it all happen. If it didn't, I didn't do it.

"Then come have a snow cone with me," CJ dares.

I grumble. "Seriously?"

She knows I'm going to say no. Why? Because of a simple little stain. You know, the ones you get from sloshing the cup around or missing your mouth because of a sudden brain freeze? Yup, I avoided those at all costs, which means I've also never had a snow cone—*ever.*

"You are twenty-seven years old. I promise you—no stains," she pleads. "We can even get you a coconut cream one. It's white. No stains."

CJ is trying to get me to get out there more, but I'm happy with the way things are now.

I have the *perfect* job.

The *perfect* home.

The *perfect* boyfriend.

The *perfect* life.

Why would I mess with *perfect?*

"It's not about the stains," I lie. It's totally about the stains. My parents worked hard to provide me and my brother with nice things.

I wasn't about to ruin my new dress by having a stupid, cold, but very tempting, icy treat tumble down the front of me.

My brother, on the other hand, couldn't help himself, and my parents constantly had to replace his clothes. So, I played it safe. I became the rule follower, the good girl.

"Whatever. I'll forget the snow cone for now because I'm pretty sure that's going to take a therapy session," CJ mumbles. "Or ten."

I roll my eyes. "I don't need therapy."

"You're right," she admits.

"I-I'm right?" I question as I take a sip of my Diet Dr. Pepper. I'm never right when it comes to CJ.

"Yes, you are a hundred percent right," she confesses. "You need an orgasm."

Soda spews everywhere. "Carly Jane Collins," I choke out her full name while pulling one of my special *oops moment* towelettes and frantically wipe the dashboard before the stickiness sets in.

"Oh, hell no! I'm going to pretend you didn't just call me that. You know how I hate—"

"What CJ?" I interrupt, a little upset she's snooping in my sex life again. "You brought it on by telling me I need to—that I should—well...you know."

"What? Orgasm?" She laughs out. "You can't even say the word. I'm willing to bet you haven't even—"

"I orgasm just fine," I interject.

"Really? Come on, Clover. Someone who has great sex doesn't orgasm *just fine.* It's amazing, explosive, life altering, it's anything other than *fine.*" CJ snickers. "So—tell me, *Clover...*" she draws out my name.

This can't be good.

"When is the last time you orgasmed?" I can almost envision her red-lipped smirk knowing she has me backed into the corner.

I could lie and say it was last night, but why? Why does a woman have to orgasm to prove her love life is perfectly fine? Jeffery, my boyfriend of the past six years, is absolutely amazing, even if our sex life is anything but stellar. I don't need to defend him—or myself, for that matter. Orgasms don't strengthen a relationship. They can actually distract you into believing what you feel is love when in all reality it's lust.

Our relationship is built on happiness, communication, trust, enjoying each other's company. Not whether or not we are compatible in bed. Sex is a distraction that complicates a relationship. One I'm not willing to risk. I have a plan, and that plan is to get married and have kids before the age of thirty. I have too much time invested in this relationship to risk it all by suggesting we get a little risky in bed.

So, I do what any woman would do with a need to release the tension—I break out the Satisfy Pro. A trusty little gadget that doesn't make me feel like I'm cheating, but helps me unwind after a rough day before Jeffery gets home.

"I'm waiting," CJ persists, and will keep on until I finally answer.

So, I finally answer somewhat honestly. "A couple days ago."

"Ha! Liar!" She calls me out, but I'm not going to back down.

"Were you there?" I give her half a second to answer, then keep going. "I *did* indeed get off on Wednesday, right after work, and it was glorious."

"Oh, jeez. Are you being serious right now?" CJ calls me out on the BS I just gave her. "Jeffery doesn't even get home till six. So what you're telling me is the *only* way you get off is by fingerbating? Come on, Clover, you have to know this is not okay."

I gasp.

"Yes, you know exactly what I'm talking about. Fingerbating, muffin' buffin', saucin' the taco, clubbing the clam, polishing the pearl—I could keep going if you want me to, but something tells me you know exactly what I'm talking about."

"Stop!" I shout, and CJ lets out a chuckle. "Stop laughing. It's not funny."

"I'm not trying to ruffle your feathers, Clover. You are my best friend and I hate that you aren't getting the most out of your relationship. Jeffery Dahmer should be making sure you…"

"Stop calling him that," I demand.

"Dahmer, Dalton…all the same," CJ jokes.

"No, not really. Dahmer eats people," I point out the obvious.

"And Dalton should be eating you."

"Touché." I cave, admitting the truth, though I still stick by my theory that sex complicates things.

"Now we are getting somewhere," CJ huffs out. "Clover, why do you think I go into detail about all my adventures?" CJ pauses but doesn't give me time to answer. "It's because I'm hoping to trip your trigger so you don't have to flip your *own* switch." She giggles. "Sorry, I totally couldn't help myself. The moral of the story…I want you to have your dream."

"I do," I whisper.

"But, sweetie, you don't. You are stuck on autopilot when you should be shifting gears."

"Autopilot isn't so bad, is it? I mean, it gets you there, right?" I try to convince myself more than her.

"Of course not, but even on autopilot you have to refill, and you, my sweet, wonderful, kind of OCD, refuses-to-have-a-snow-cone-with-me friend—have been running on empty."

Leaning my head against the soft leather, I let out a sigh. I know she's right, I'm just not sure how to fix it. I have worked too hard to make our relationship work. If I give up now, what does that say about me?

"I'm sorry to throw this all at you at once, but it seemed like it was heading there, so I went there."

CJ seems almost apologetic, which she shouldn't be. It's not her fault my sex life sucks. There, I admit it.

I, Clover Kelly, am sexually deprived.

I take a few deep breaths and say what I know she's thinking. "I can't leave him."

"I'm going to ignore the fact that you said can't and not won't, and yes that was a little seed I just planted right now, but ignore it. It's a seed. It will eventually grow…"

"Spit it out, CJ," I bark.

"Fine. Chill, girl. I'm not saying you need to make any drastic changes in your relationship status. I'm just saying take it from vanilla to french vanilla. Test the waters a little bit. Beat Jeffery home, freshen up, undo a few buttons, hike up your skirt, and ravage your man. Sweet talk, dirty talk, or whatever you're into, and greet him at the door. Make sure he has no choice but to take you right then and there."

Everything she's saying makes sense. Our relationship is fine. It has a sturdy foundation, the walls are up, we just need to change the color.

"I hate it when you're—" A beep interrupts. Holding the phone away, I see it's the man of the hour. "Hey, Jeffery is calling, give me one second."

"Wait! Tellmewhatyouweregoing—" she says in one breath, trying to get it out before I switch over.

"Hold please," I cut her off with a smile and answer Jeffery. "Hey, honey. What's going on?"

"Where are you at?" His deep voice rumbles through the speaker. "I need to talk to you."

"I made a quick stop on my way home. Is everything okay?" My forehead scrunches. Something seems wrong. Very wrong. Jeffery isn't a talker, more of a head nodder. Don't get me wrong, we have our conversations about what's going on in the world, but when it has to do with menial things like what's for dinner, movies, or even work, he tends to nod.

"Oh—um—yeah, it's fine." He stumbles over his words. "I'm almost home. This *needs* to happen in person. So, meet me there," he commands as my phone beeps. I roll my eyes as CJ's name flashes across the screen. I must have accidentally hung up on her. *Oops*!

"Okay, I'm about twenty minutes away. I'll see you soon."

"Perfect. When you get home, don't go into the bedroom. Wait for me," Jeffery insists.

I perk up at the request. This can only mean one thing.

"If you say so." I smile.

"I do." He ends the call, and CJ rings in. "I didn't mean to hang—"

"Never mind that," she cuts in. "What did Dahmer want that had you hanging up on me?"

"CJ!" I shout, ignoring the obvious insult. "I think Jeffery is *finally* going to pop the question," I blurt while bouncing in my seat.

"Wh-Wh-What?" CJ chokes out. "You have been dating for over six years and every time we get together for a girl's night, you complain about him never asking, yet he calls for five minutes—"

"Five *very* long minutes," I butt in.

"Yeah, it did seem like forever, but…it wasn't."

"I know, but Jeffery and I have a plan. Do you know he asked me how I wanted to be proposed to?"

"Are you kidding me right now? Clover, listen to yourself. He had to ask you how you wanted to be proposed to. That doesn't sound like a man you should be marrying."

"Jeez, mood killer. Can't you be happy for me?"

To most people, this would seem like an insincere gesture, but my Jeffery knows me. He knows I have a plan, and that plan includes a rose petal trail that leads to a bedroom glowing with hundreds of candles and him on one knee with a tiny blue box from Tiffany's. It's a day I have been dreaming of since forever—and it's finally here.

CJ sighs. "Listen, Clo, I know you have a plan, but I don't think—"

"I know you don't like him, but I have waited all my life for this moment," I plead with her.

Jeffery isn't the easiest person to be around, but I need my friends to understand this is forever. I mean, it's been six years and he hasn't gone anywhere yet.

"Your plan," she whispers.

"My plan," I agree.

"Then shut up, hurry home, and make french vanilla with your man. Clover Kelley has a plan!"

"That's right! I'm getting married!"

Or so I thought…

CHAPTER TWO

CLOVER

This isn't so bad…

Red lip—*check*.

Girls front and center—*check, check*.

I went from uptight real estate agent selling houses to a sexy seductress glamming it up for my very own open house—if you know what I mean.

"Clover?" Jeffery hollers out from the front room.

"In the bathroom. Give me a minute."

Shaking off the nerves, I stare at my reflection.

Hair down?

Bright lips?

Unbuttoned blouse?

Hiked up skirt?

This isn't me, but I thought maybe CJ was right—maybe I *did* need to spice it up a little. This, though…this is a far cry from french vanilla. This is more like a Mexican vanilla with a little too much chili powder. It was ridiculous for me to think Jeffery would be into this. After six years, you tend to know someone.

"He loves you…for *you*," I whisper to myself as I reach for the makeup remover towelette and swipe at my lips, careful to not smear the Russian red stain. "You are enough," I remind myself as I toss the wipe in the trash and smile.

I know Jeffery Dalton, my future fiancé, better than anyone. I'm his perfect as he's mine.

"Clover, we really need to talk." Jeffery's voice vibrates down the hall.

"Coming!" I hurry to button up my white charmeuse silk blouse and smooth down the black and gray pin-striped pencil skirt.

"Clover?" The door swings open, and in this moment, I have two choices: stand there, eyes wide, like a moron, or jump into his arms and start this proposal off with a bang. I opt for neither.

There's nothing for me to worry about. These nerves…they're normal. Taking a deep breath, I step forward and wrap my arms, one by one, around Jeffery's neck, welcoming him home.

"Looking for me?" I whisper across his lips.

"We need to talk," he demands.

Hmm? This is new. Jeffery isn't really a demanding guy. Assertive, yes—but demanding? Not so much. Maybe he's as nervous as I am? I mean, we are talking forever here.

"You don't say?" I flirt back, trying to ease his mind.

"Clover, we've been together for six wonderful years…"

Oh my God!

Here it comes. The moment I've been waiting for. Just me and my dream guy standing right—in the middle of the—wait…we're in the middle of the bathroom. Okay, it's not *excactly* how I pictured it, but when you can't wait, you can't wait.

"Yes, it's a long time," I cut in, practically bouncing from foot to foot, waiting for him to say those four glorious words.

"Agreed." He nods as he reaches up behind his neck and pulls one hand down, then the other.

I hold my breath, afraid I'm going to interrupt this magical moment.

Here it comes.

"In six years, you should know whether it's going to lead to something more and, Clover, I think we should—"

"Yes! It's always yes!" I say at the same time he says, "Break up."

I hear the words, but they don't register. Instead, I drop his hands, fly into his arms, and feather kisses all over his face as I repeat the word *yes* over and over again.

"Clover…" Jeffery stiffens. "Did you hear what I said?"

"I love you so much, Jeffery. I have waited forever for you to say those—"

"Break up?" Jeffery questions as he lets out a nervous chuckle. "Thank God. Clover, you don't know how relieved I am you say that. After all these years, I thought you surely would have flipped out. I mean, you have spent your whole life following those rules for that ridiculous plan. Years and years of those stupid rules."

My plan?

Breakup?

Everything comes crashing down at once. The reality of his words sink in.

"Clover? Clover, can you hear me?" Jeffery's hands are firm on my shoulders as his brown eyes meet my blue. "Shit, Clover. You're turning blue. Breathe, honey."

I'm not sure what came over me in that moment, but when you are deprived of oxygen, your thoughts become screams. With each pounding pulse of my heartbeat, everything suddenly became clear. *It's over.*

I exhale and say the first thing that comes to mind. "You have shitty brown eyes."

"You scared me…wait—what did you say?" His face twists with confusion as he straightens.

This is where I should ignore his question and ask him why. Plead for him to stay. Convince Jeffery what he's feeling is normal. Instead, I let go. Every—single—annoying—quirk I've overlooked comes flooding—front and center.

Narrowing my eyes, I open my mouth and let the word vomit fly. "You heard me, jerk. You have shitty brown eyes," I throw a finger in his face and twirl it around, "and a unibrow. A big, fat, out-of-control, hairy unibrow."

"I do?" He turns to examine himself in the mirror.

Okay, maybe it's not a unibrow, but saying it made me feel good, and this is about me making him feel like shit so I can feel better. After all, he's the one who wasted six years of my life. Six freaking years!

Hmm…I wonder what it would feel like if I just took his head and bashed it against the mirror? Because I want to. So bad.

"What?" Jeffery snaps his head in my direction.

"Oops! Did I say that out loud?" I smirk.

"Clover, I know this is hard," he tries to continue, but why? What's the point? He already ripped my heart out, and now he wants to stomp all over it by telling me everything *I* did wrong? *Not happening, Buddy.*

"You don't get to go there, but I do. Jeffery, do you want to know what *is* hard?" I don't give him time to answer. "Wasting my love on you. For six years, I loved you. I gave you everything I had—and for what?" I throw my hands up. "For a head nod? A weekly romp in the sack?"

"Clover, it wasn't like…" he pleads.

"Wasn't like what, Jeffery? Because it *is* exactly like that. I gave you *everything* I am. *Everything.*" I tried to hold them back, but tears begin to fall. One by one, shedding over the life I'll never have.

"Honey, please don't cry." He reaches up to swipe the tears away.

"You don't get to do that." I slap his hand away. "You claimed my heart, you don't get to claim the tears." I reach up and wipe my own tears, ashamed I'm letting this man see me cry. "I dedicated myself to you."

"That's where you are wrong," he interrupts. "You dedicated yourself to that stupid binder of yours. You loved that plan more than you loved me and when—"

"Jeffery, are you okay in there?" A squeaky voice echoes in the foyer, and my head whips around to my asshole of an ex.

"Clover…" He holds his hands up. "It's not what you think."

My eyes dart between the doorway and Jeffery the jackoff. "It sounds like to me there is another woman in our house worried about you." I throw his hand down and rush out to find out who that annoying voice belongs to.

"Okay, so maybe it's exactly what you think, but I was trying to tell you…" Jeffery chases after me, but I refuse to let his words tackle me. "I didn't mean to fall in love with her…"

His confession makes me stumble, but I'm determined to keep going.

"It was only supposed to be one night," he continued as we rounded the corner. "But then one night turned into forever."

That did it. That last one is like a punch to the gut.

"What did you say?"

"Clover, she's pregnant," he admits as he walks right past me to the Victoria's Secret looking Angel standing in front of us.

"Hiyee." She waves to us both. "That's me. I'm the one with the bun in the oven." She smiles as if nothing is wrong. Like it's perfectly natural for the three of us to be standing here. Man, woman, and mistress.

You know that *Sesame Street* song "One of These Things (is Not Like the Other)." This is one of those times. Except I'm the one on the outside looking in.

"Is this really happening?" I look at the man I thought I knew whispering something to his baby momma. If I think of her any other way, I may lose my shit right here and now.

"Angel, can you give us a minute?" He nods over to the living room.

"Sure thing, Poogie Bear." She gives him a quick peck on the cheek just as Kramer decides to bark. "Oh-em-gee! You have a dog?" she squeals and skips into the other room.

"It's a barking cockatoo!" I yell after her before I turn and glare at Jeffery. "So, *Poogie Bear*, does your *Angel* have a name?"

"Her name *is* Angel."

"Of course it is."

"You know I don't do nicknames."

"No, I don't know that because everything I thought I knew isn't real," I spit back.

"Come on, Clover. That isn't fair."

"Not fair? Are you kidding me right now? What's not fair is that I'm standing here while your pregnant girlfriend is playing with *my* barking bird you bought me for *my* twenty-fifth birthday."

I hated that bird when Jeffery brought him home. Jeffery the Jackoff was allergic to dogs, and…well, I love them. So, I did what any loving girlfriend would do: I compromised. I found a hypoallergenic dog for us to adopt. I know they aren't really hypoallergenic, but paired with his meds and a controlled living space, Jeffery would have been fine. Except he didn't come home with the dog. Nope! He came home with a cockatoo the shelter owner was desperately trying to get rid of.

This bird would bark nonstop at the shelter dogs. You could only imagine what life was like for the owner, so when he saw Jeffery, a man allergic to every man's best friend, he pounced, convinced him it was the perfect solution. Needless to say, I wasn't too happy.

The dog was a part of my plan. You know, like *Marley and Me.* I wanted that life. I wanted the late nights, the run in the park, the chewed-up shoes…okay, maybe not the shoes, but a puppy is supposed to prepare you for parenthood.

Then Kramer and I bonded the next day. Jeffery was irritated at his new gift for keeping him up and slammed the door on the way out. I silently flipped him the bird, so to speak, and Kramer…well, he let out a slew of curse words that would make a sailor blush, then climbed up into my lap and nudged me to pet him.

So, yeah…Kramer is *mine.*

"Jeffery, can we quit pretending here?" I move to stand by the door, hand on the knob, ready to kick these two out.

"Fine. Let's get down to business." Coming to stand beside me, he pulls a piece of paper out of his pocket and hands it over. "I have packed most of your clothes and boxed up all of your belongings in the bedroom."

"Wh-What?" I stumble over the words. I was prepared to send him packing and forgot one major detail: Jeffery inherited this brownstone from his parents. I'm homeless.

"I know this is hard, but this list should help." He reaches over, running his finger along the little Post-It note that sums up our life together.

~~*Move out.*~~

Divide the business.

~~*Split the savings.*~~

~~*Sign over the car title.*~~

"Now, I assumed you would want to leave right away given the circumstance." *Oh, right! Baby momma.* "But if you need more time, I can grab a few things and stay at Angel's."

"Of course, you will."

He's taken care of everything. My whole life, I've planned for my happily ever after, and with a few swipes of a pen, he's destroyed it.

"I've signed over the title to you and transferred your half of the savings to your business account. I've also taken care of Lucky Listings."

"Jeffery, that's mine. I've made Lucky Listings what it is today. I'm the one who sells homes to families each and every day. I built that—not you."

I begin to panic. Lucky Listings has always been mine. Jeffery did put up the down payment and co-sign, but that was only to build my credit, and should have been a non-issue since we were supposed to spend forever together. What's mine is his and what's his should be mine. *Wrong.*

"Calm down, Clover. What kind of guy do you think I am? Dalton Enterprises is worth billions, I don't need your—"

"Do not finish that sentence, Jeffery. You are *only* worth billions because your daddy built that company with old money. With Lucky Listings, I can honestly say I built it from the ground up and made it what it is today," I snap back.

"Okay, I can see this isn't going as planned." Jeffery backs away and hollers for Angel before he continues. "As I said before, I'm sorry, but I took measures to protect you. The car is yours, the savings is yours, the business is yours, but the house…it's mine."

"And mine." Bleach blonde baby momma comes bouncing back in the room. "Poogie Bear, can we keep the bird? He's totes adorbs and has this cute little Mohawk. We can name him Spike."

"It's Kramer," I defend my little cockatoo.

"Spike is more fitting, don't you think?" Angel chimes in. "Like, I mean, he does have a Mohawk."

Listen, Barbie. Don't fuck with my bird.

"And, like, Kramer has, like, this totes crazy hair, which is why I totally named him that," I mock. Where did he find her?

"Who's Kramer?" She stands there, confused.

"He's from *Seinfeld*, that TV show about…" I begin, but realize she's already off, walking around the front room, looking and touching everything. "You know what? It doesn't matter, the bird is going with me."

I'm not sure how it happened, but I lost control of this conversation. Just an hour ago, I was in the car thinking I was going to become the future Mrs. Jeffery Michael Dalton, and now I'm standing here letting them tell me what I'm going to do with my life—how I'm going to proceed without him.

"So, when do you think you'll be moved out so I can let my decorator know?" baby momma blurts out, and I can't help but stand there dumbfounded at her statement. I don't know if I want to scream or smack some sense into her. The hands-on approach is very tempting.

"Angel, honey. Let's give Clover some space," Jeffery says as he pulls her in for an embrace. "Plus, I want to introduce you to Mr. Hawkins, your new neighbor."

She giggles.

I giggle and roll my eyes.

He side-eyes me.

I mentally flip him off and telepathically summon Kramer to spew all the bad things.

He doesn't.

"I'm sorry it's come to this, Clover. I never meant to hurt you." Jeffery opens the door and guides his baby momma out. "Please take as long as you need. The last thing I want is for you to feel pushed out of your home."

This isn't my home. It was only a temporary place for us until we settled down to start our family. The furniture, the décor…everything in this house is Jeffery. I tolerated it because it wasn't our forever home.

"I'll have my attorney send the documents over to your office Monday morning. Just sign the marked pages and Lucky Listings is yours."

"How gracious of you," I mumble.

"If you need anything, call the office, my secretary will get a hold of me." Jeffery throws me one little bone before he turns and walks out the door, but not before bimbo baby momma pipes up.

"That's me! Right, Pookie Bear?"

Jeffery grumbles something about later, and before I reach out and yank her back by her platinum extensions, I slam the door.

"Jeffery has a little dick. Little dick." Kramer finally gives his two cents as he bops up and down, ruffling his feathers.

"Shhh! Kramer, no. I told you that was our—" I stop myself. He's right. Jeffery has a small dick. Not as in teeny tiny, but as in pencil-thin. Actually, I'm pretty sure my vibrator is twice the size of it.

Running to my bedroom, I fling open the door and skid to a halt. Everything is packed up like he said. My bags are on the bed, the closet doors are open, and my clothes are gone. Jeffery never intended for me to stay for as long as I needed. He wanted me out. That's how much I meant to him. He wasn't trying to do me any favors by getting everything together and switched over. He was making it easy for me to leave and for baby momma to move in. Well, I'm not going to give them the satisfaction.

Forgetting everything, I reach into the nightstand, snag the velvet bag, and run back through the house and out the front door, trying to catch Jackoff and Bimbo Barbie before they leave.

"Hey, asshole!" I holler from the top step as Jeffery opens the door to his black, overpriced SUV. "If you want to keep this one, you may want to give her more than you're working with, if you know what I mean." I wink as I pull my very large, very pink vibrator and throw it his way. "Use this so you know how a real orgasm sounds."

"What in the…?" He coughs as his eyes scan the area to see who's watching.

"That's right. I faked every single one. You, my friend, have a teeny tiny baby dick. If you think what you have is enough to keep someone like her." I shrug. "Good luck."

"She's joking." Jeffery laughs nervously and points to me. "She's upset. You know how women are," he says to the neighbors, who have front row seats. "I have a…" He holds his hands wide, as if they care.

"Poogie Bear, let's go," Angel whines. "I'm hungry."

"Yeah, Poogie Bear, why don't you go?" I urge him along.

"Clover, I thought you were classier than this." He shakes his head as he rounds the vehicle.

"Yeah, I thought you were forever. Guess we were both wrong." I flash him my biggest go-to-hell smile before I turn to address the neighbors. "I'm so sorry. I guess I got carried away back there."

"Don't worry about it, sweetie." Mrs. Hawkins, who joined Mr. Hawkins halfway through my outburst, nods toward the road. "Looks like he had it coming."

"Yeah, I guess he did." I glance back to see Jeffery pulling away.

"It also looks like he took your advice." She giggles. "You didn't need that thing anyway."

"Nooo!" I twist to see the vibrator gone. "He didn't," I gasp.

"He really did." She winks as they both go inside.

I didn't plan to lose my shit on Jeffery, but one minute, we were perfect, and the next, he was standing next to his pregnant mistress introducing her to our neighbors. How was I supposed to know I was going to turn into a name-calling, dildo-slingin', crazy ex-girlfriend? I'm not sure there is an etiquette on breaking up.

Heading inside, I gather up the few things I do want to keep. My fuzzy blanket, my favorite whisk, and the picture of my parents. Everything else is just stuff.

Grabbing the suitcase with all the necessities, I throw in a couple outfits, shoes, and all my jewelry—everything I could possibly need to get me through the weekend until I can schedule a time to get Kramer and the rest of my things from Jeffery.

It's kind of funny how I'm almost thirty and everything I've worked for my entire life fits into one single suitcase.

How is that for planning?

CHAPTER THREE

CLOVER

I never thought I would find myself here, in the parking garage, at Austin Montgomery's apartment. Yet, here I am, staring at a cinderblock wall, wondering how I'm going to explain this. How do I say, *"You were right! Jeffery's a douche and now I'm homeless?"*

My "Girls Just Wanna Have Fun" ringtone, fills the car and drowns out the self-doubt. Scaring the bejeezus out of me.

Girls don't just want to have fun. They want to get married and live happily ever after. Fun is temporary. *Love is forever.*

"Um—hello?" I answer with a question, even though I know who it is, and brace myself for her celebratory verbal parade of questions.

"I'm going to forgive you for not calling right away because I get it," CJ blurts out, barely pausing to take a breath. "You probably got your french vanilla on after he popped the question, but come on, it's been like two hours and I'm pretty sure vanilla has a time limit."

"Ceej, we—"

"Oh-me-gee!" she gasps. "You sprinkled that shit up, didn't you? I mean, I always knew you had it in you, but I-I've just waited so long for this day." CJ begins to fake cry, bringing out all the dramatics. "Well done, grasshopper."

"CJ, we didn't sprinkle it up, we didn't even have french vanilla." I try to get through to her, but nothing seems to work.

"I've read about this," she carries on. "I think there was a Buzzfeed article or something about how some couples after they get engaged like to wait till after the wedding to relive the first time all over again. R-E-S-P-E-C-T, my friend. I couldn't do that, but to each their own."

"He left," I blurt out.

"Oooh! Then hurry and give me all the deets before he gets back," CJ pries.

I love my friend, but this is her trying too hard. She's never liked Jeffery, and now I'm beginning to understand why.

"CJ, you can stop pretending to be happy for me because there's nothing to be happy about. Jeffery left…for good."

"Fuuuuck!" CJ moans. "You were trying to tell me and here I am being all extra. Sometimes I wonder why you're even friends with me. I'm such an asshole."

"You're not an asshole."

"Yeah, I am. A big fat hairy non-bleached stinky asshole…with dingleberries." CJ laughs.

"Dingleberries?"

"Yeah, Google it."

"I'm not in a Google mood." I find myself whining.

"Gasp."

"I know."

"Why don't you come over? We can order takeout, braid each other's hair, make voodoo dolls…" CJ rambles on and on about drinking and playing dashboard confessionals with her new webcam and who knows what else before she finally realizes what this means for me. "Wait! Does this mean you're homeless?"

"Something like that."

"Shit, Clo. You can come live with—" A knock interrupts us. "Oh, good! I thought I would have to persuade you."

"I'm not—"

"Get your ass—oh? Wait…you're not…um…here?" She lowers her voice to a whisper. "This isn't you."

"Nope, it's not."

"Well, then, hold please." The background becomes muffled before her voice comes over the line again. "Okay, I'm back. As I was saying—"

"Ceej, as much as I love you for offering, I'm going to pass."

CJ lives in a one-bedroom loft apartment. Even though it's fairly open, there is no privacy, and right now, I need exactly that.

"Cheese'n'rice! You spoon a girl one time—one time!—and she holds it against you for the rest of her life. I told you, I can't help it what my feet do when I fall asleep." Her laugh vibrates through the phone.

I can't help but join in. It's the perfect medicine to forgetting. That night, we both had a little too much to drink and passed out on her very small full-size bed. When I woke up, CJ was spooning me and her big toe was using my leg as a scratching post. I'm pretty sure I still have the scars to prove it.

"It's not that," I reassure her. "It's just…at Austin's, I'll have my own space, and…well…"

"Mm-hmm. Is that the *only* reason," CJ teases. "Because that man talks like he has some skills."

"Ew—no! I told you it's not like that. He's like—"

"A brother," we say in unison.

"Blah, blah, blah. If he's like a brother, then let me hit that," CJ begs.

There is no way I'm going to let CJ hook up with my best friend. That is a line I'm not willing to let either of them cross, no matter how much they have in common or how good they could be together.

I've known Austin Montgomery since we were middle schoolers living in a small town in the Midwest when his parents moved in next door.

He was the geeky new kid, and I was the popular girl on the debate team. Just being friends with me gave him an instant in. However, in high school, our roles reversed. I was considered the nerdy girl with big glasses, and over the summer, he grew four inches and decided to try out for football. His popularity sky-rocketed while mine sank, and even though his friends tried to get him to ditch me, he wouldn't.

Austin and I…we've been through a lot together. His parents' divorce, my dog dying, car wreck, pregnancy scare—his girlfriend, not me—college, an injury…We did everything together and consulted each other about everything. Neither of us made a move without the other one.

That's how I ended up in New York. After he injured his knee, his football career was over and he started a campus podcast that talked about dating, sex, and anything real life. So, when Live Wire Radio came knocking and offered him his own satellite radio show, he took it, and I followed.

Neither of us could have imagined the way The Hotline Hookup with Dr. Feelgood would blow up. It became the number one talk show radio show in the nation. Men worshiped him. Women fell at his feet.

And me? I was always his constant. And he was mine. We never lost touch. We never crossed "the line." Everything *always* stayed the same—just how I liked it.

So, when I say we are like family, I mean it. There is no one I trust more than Austin Montgomery. It's why I'm sitting here. He's my go-to. My safe haven.

"I'm waiting?" CJ pries.

Even though CJ asks me all the time *why not her*, I know she doesn't really want Austin, but just the thought… Nope! Not doing it. Not going there.

"Hello? Are you there? CJ?" I hold the phone away, pretending it's cutting out. "I'm getting into the elevator…I think…" I pause for a brief second, hoping she buys my story. "I'm losing you."

"Clover Marie Kelley! You don't get to pull a CJ. I taught you—"

Click.

The line goes dead; I toss my phone into my purse and take a deep breath as I step into the elevator and wait for the big silver walls to beam me up.

Nothing.

"Ugh. Of course."

It's been a while since I've been here. Actually, the last time, I think I walked in on Austin doing yoga, bare-ass naked wearing only a charcoal facial mask. I guess having his face plastered on billboards and buses has Dr. Feelgood feeling a little under the microscope. Since then, we felt we should raise our boundaries a tad. I was allowed to keep my parking spot since he has a car service and my key as long as I promised to knock before entering.

Pulling out the card, I swipe it, waiting for the lift to automatically take me to the forty-ninth floor.

It doesn't matter how many levels separate me from Austin, there will never be enough time to prepare me for this—admitting the plan I came up with years ago failed, proving he was right, and I was painstakingly wrong.

The elevator slows to a stop, and the doors slide open.

This is why I should've called. Austin is standing in the doorway, shirtless, whispering God knows what to this bleach blonde hussy who looks more mid-west stripper than New York gentleman's club.

I clear my throat. "Sorry to interrupt, but…"

Austin stops what he's doing, a big Cheshire grin creeping over his lips, as his eyes slowly meet mine. "You know what they say, *there's no place like home.*" He winks as he smacks stripper girl on the butt, sending her on her way.

"Call me," she coos, blowing him a kiss.

"Speaking of home." He nods toward my single piece of luggage. "You moving back in?"

"Yeah…well, turns out there was a flaw in my plan." I step forward as Austin meets me halfway, reaching for my bag.

"You don't say?" His hand rests on my lower back, rubbing comforting circles as I struggle not to fall apart. The only man, I can really count on, takes my hand and leads me into his apartment.

"Apparently, I forgot to add in a 'don't knock up another woman' clause."

"Ahhh." He clicks his tongue. "That's a doozy." Austin shuts the door, sets the bag down, then wraps me in his arms.

"Austin, what's wrong with me?" Tears begin to fall as I cry over the life I ignored for the future I dreamed of. All that time invested was a complete waste.

"Hey now." Austin leans back to see how pitiful I look as he wipes away the sadness with his thumbs. "You are perfect. Dalton is a little bitch baby who doesn't deserve you." Austin gives me a few moments to suck it up before his lips curve up in a shit-eating grin. "If you're looking to forget for a few moments…" He eyes me up and down, licking his lips.

"You're an asshole!" I slap his hands away, irritation overtaking the sudden feeling of loss.

He throws his head back and laughs. "Have a seat. I have just what you need." Jogging into the kitchen, he pulls a carton of my favorite ice cream out of the freezer and grabs two spoons.

"I'm not sure if ice cream can fix this," I huff out, falling back into the couch. "Vanilla is what got me into trouble in the first place."

Hopping over the back of the couch, he settles in beside me and nudges my shoulder. "I call bullshit." Austin passes me the open container and hands over a spoon. "Vanilla is a classic. It's the base for every sundae." Austin stares at me staring at the carton.

"What does that have to do with my breakup?"

"Fuck, Clover. I'm trying to use metaphors to make this less awkward." Austin sighs, then pulls a bottle of chocolate syrup from behind his back and squirts it over the vanilla bean goodness. "Don't you see? It was up to dick face to bring the toppings." Austin sets the container down and reaches for his spoon, scooping up a huge bite.

"And up to you to see what *tastes* good." He nudges at my lips. "Try the flavors."

It's not that I don't like chocolate. I do. But chocolate melts, becomes messy, and is hard to get out. Why go to all the trouble for something that sticky when you'll just want to wash your hands? Total nonsense *and* goes against the plan.

And look how that turned out.

"Fine." I open wide and moan, losing myself in the flavor.

"In the words of another brilliant Austin, 'yeah, baby, yeah.'" He waggles his eyebrows as he shovels a huge spoonful into his mouth. "Fucking delicious!"

I shrug and smile, pretending it's no big deal.

I'm not sure how much time has passed, but it's long after we finished the carton of ice cream and I filled Austin in on everything from the moment I walked in through the doors to the moment I tossed my vibrator at Jeffery.

Austin leans back, taking it all in. Resting his arm against the edge of the loveseat, he signals for me to scoot closer. I rest my head on his shoulder as his words vibrate through me. "So, what's next?"

"Well, I guess I need to find a place to live," I admit, mentally adding it to my long list of things to do.

Get the rest of my things.

Kramer.

Search for a place.

Forward my mail.

Update my driver's license.

"You can stay here as long as you need." Austin glances down as I look up, kissing my forehead. "It'll be fun. I've missed having my wingman around."

I smack him on the chest, laughing. "You just miss having someone to clean up after your skanks."

"Nooo. That was an added perk." He smirks.

I narrow my eyes. "Speaking of which…" I take a deep breath and wrinkle my nose. Alcohol, smoke, baby oil, and a musky stench. Just as I thought—*strip club.*

"I'm going." He moves to stand.

"You're so gross."

"At least I'm trying the flavors." He turns around and flips me off as he walks backward to the bathroom.

"Last I checked, tuna wasn't a topping." I stick out my tongue. "Are you sure you didn't catch anything?"

"Nothing a shower won't cure!" Austin shouts, disappearing down the hall as my phone chimes.

CJ: Come out and play.

CJ: I called in reinforcements.

I begin to type out a message, declining the offer, but a pic begins to download.

CJ: <pic>

Great, CJ and Mallory, Austin's little sister, are together, drinking—which means news traveled fast and there's no way I'll be able to avoid this for much longer.

Me: Not tonight.

CJ: Aw!!! Mal says PLEAAAAASSSSE!

Me: I'm too tired. How about coffee in a couple days.

That should give me enough time to wrap my head around this whole situation.

CJ: Cuppa Joe.

CJ: Tomorrow.

That's not a couple days. I contemplate how I'm going to respond as I grab my things and head to the spare room. As soon as I reach the door, I freeze, staring at the bed with ruffled sheets. "Looks like someone went a couple rounds in here," I mumble, grossed out.

"Montgomery!" I call out. "Are you kidding me?"

"What's up?" He peeks his head out from behind his bedroom door, hair dripping wet.

"Did you have sex in *my* bed?"

"Nah! I fell asleep in there a couple days ago while I was waiting for my sheets to dry."

"Uh-huh. Before or after you showered," I grill.

"Jeez, Clover. After."

"You better not be lying."

"Get some sleep," Austin demands before he shuts his door, giving us both the privacy we need.

Plucking up the comforter with the tips of my fingers, I drag it down to the end of the bed. The smell of lavender-scented fabric softener fills my senses. *Okay, maybe he wasn't lying.*

Now that the bed is deemed safe, I plop down and begin to type out a reply to CJ, but quickly delete it as another rolls in.

CJ: Mal WILL NOT take no for an answer.

I have no choice. Tomorrow it is.

Me: Fine. 10 good?

CJ: YAY! We won! Make it 11. We may have hangovers.

CJ: Wish us luck. ;) xoxo

Me: Luck.

CJ: Clover, everything will be OK.

Me: I know.

CJ: Byeeee! <3

CJ is right. Everything *will* be okay.

Opening my bag, I pull out my very large, very detailed, twelve-by-twelve binder where my carefully constructed plans are laid out. It's all there. Every. Single. Detail. All in black and white. A simple design that should have led me to my happy ever after, but failed.

Now, to figure out where I went wrong.

CHAPTER FOUR

AUSTIN

I knew that fucking twat was never going to marry her, but when I tried to warn Clover, she defended his ass and reminded me all good things come to those who wait. Who in the *hell* made that shit up?

I'll tell you, probably some author of some bullshit motivational book who makes money off people waiting for their next release, teasing them when "*that time*" will come. I should know, my sister lives by those fuckers.

When those elevator doors slid open and Clover was standing there looking broken, I knew Candi—Cherry—or maybe it was Jessica?—fuck if I can remember, but she had to go.

Truth be told, I had no business bringing her home in the first place, but Owen, the producer of Hotline Hookup, had this idea about a strip club segment. And with our schedule, our time was limited. So, there we were, day drinking on the job having titties rubbed in our face. Not a bad day, if I do say so myself.

Blondie stood out. She seemed sweet and was kind enough to let us interview her with her manager's approval, of course. Come to find out, she just moved here from a small town in Kansas with unrealistic dreams of getting signed by a top modeling agency. Wrong move. And an expensive one at that. Her style and body type would have had better luck in LA.

Fast forward to a spilled drink and Blondie insisting to clean me up. Well, next thing I know, I'm back at my place, shirtless with her hands all over me—caught red-handed by Clover. Thank God.

Now, here it is, six the next morning, and I'm tired as fuck and a tad hungover, if I'm being honest. I could have slept in since I don't have to be at work until ten, but after talking to Clover last night, I have no choice but to get my ass up to take care of a few things.

If I want that prick to stay out of her life, I need to make sure she doesn't have to see him ever again. If that means I have to send for Kramer and her things, so be it.

I would go myself, but I'm not sure what I'll do to him. Punch his fucking teeth out? Grab him by the balls and swing him across the room? Hell, if I know. But instead of finding out, I pull out my phone and punch out a text to tell him to have everything ready for my driver late this afternoon. His response? *"Will do. No hard feelings?"*

Is he fucking crazy? Yes, all the fucking hard feelings, dick face. Clover truly believed that pencil dick was her Prince Charming and lived her life accordingly—so goddamn boring and accordingly.

There's a part of me that wants to burst the new little bubble he is living in. His so-called baby momma is Angel Anderson, a model for Harper Agency. That girl has slept her way to becoming one of the most sought-after models in that low-class agency. Hell, I even started to dip my stick in that pond until Owen informed me it was more a swamp.

My point is, that girl has been looking to trap someone who can provide her a lifestyle of the rich and famous. Jeffery, with his old money and successful investments, can do just that. Too bad the baby may not be his. So sorry, asshole.

He's wasted too much of Clover's time, and I refuse to let him waste anymore. This is a done deal.

The end.

Moving on.

See you fucking *never.*

Draining the rest of my coffee, I finish jotting down the list of things for Clover.

Clover—

Key is on the counter. Don't forget it.

Bird & the rest of your things are being delivered this afternoon.

Help yourself to whatever you need.

Don't cook. I'll bring home dinner.

See you later,

A—

Knowing her, she plans to get up and tackle the day, but hopefully, with everything I've done, she can sleep in and ignore the outside world.

Pushing open her door and tiptoeing in as quietly as someone of my physique can, I place the note on the nightstand beside her phone.

"Mmm…Jeffery, what time is it?" Clover moans as she rolls over and stretches—and when I say stretch, I mean the fucking covers fall off, revealing her smooth, creamy, and very *naked* body.

"Holy fuck!" I shout as I bring my fist up to my mouth.

"Huh? What?" Startled, Clover shoots up out of bed as my dick decides to salute her.

Down, boy.

Think bad thoughts.

Think bad thoughts.

Think bad thoughts.

I can't help but repeat those words in my head. Except for when I repeat it, I can't help but chase it with what that bad thought actually is.

Quickly turning, I grab a robe hanging on the back of the door and throw it over my shoulder. "Clover, I like naked day just as much as the next person, but today is not the day. Put this on."

"What's this…?" Realization sets in and she lets out a high-pitched squeal. "Austin! Oh my God! Get—out—now!"

"Seriously?" I spin around as she holds the robe together with both hands. "You want to get mad at me," I point to myself, "but you're the one who slept naked—in my bed—on my sheets—spread out for anyone to see?" I gulp. "Clover, I saw *everything*."

"Really? *Everything?*" she confirms.

"*Everything.*" I nod. "So, when did you get all that? Like, you didn't look like that when we went to the Hamptons last summer."

"Is that a bad thing?" She starts to fidget, doubt setting in because of me.

"Hell no. I mean—I just…" I begin to choke on my own words as I try to tell my friend she has a smokin' hot bod I can't unsee. "Obviously, you look great," I spit it out.

"Oh!" Clover smiles. "Thank you. I've been doing Pilates daily and hot yoga every other day…" Clover freezes, suddenly realizing what happened.

I.

Saw.

Clover.

Naked.

Our living arrangement is about to get awkward if I don't make light of this situation—stat.

"So, is this going to be one of those things—you show me yours, so I have to show you mine?" I tease with my hands on my belt. "I mean, I guess this was bound to happen since we never played house when we were kids."

Fire lit.

"Get over yourself. I forgot to grab some pajamas and only had an outfit for today and work clothes…" she rambles on.

Crisis adverted.

"Speaking of which, that's why I came in here." I signal over to the note. "I didn't want you to have to deal with jerk-off, so I made arrangements for Thomas to pick up the rest of your things and Kramer."

At the mention of the ex, Clover climbs back into bed and covers up.

"Listen, if you'd rather…"

"No!" she blurts, cutting me off. "I'm sorry. It's a lot still…you know."

"Well, that's why you're here. Now, let me do my job and take care of you." I walk over to the bed and tuck her in. "It's still early." I reach down and brush the hair out of her face, tucking it behind her ear. I haven't seen Clover this vulnerable since prom night when her date ditched her for refusing to hook up at this rundown hotel he could barely afford. "Why don't you take it easy today? If you decide to leave for whatever reason, just make sure you grab the new key off the counter. Maintenance had to change the locks for some reason."

"Oh?"

"Yeah, long story."

"Okay."

"I'll bring home dinner and we can binge-watch bad reality TV. Sound good?"

"Yeah."

Clover tries to smile, but it just doesn't tip in the right direction. *Fuck that asshole for taking her light.*

CHAPTER FIVE

CLOVER

Have you ever experienced a movie moment? You know, the kind where you think it only happens on the big screen until *you* actually experience. it.

That was me, this morning, when I flashed my goods to my best friend, who happens to be a guy and gorgeous. Oh! And my new roommate.

And it's also me, right now, at this very moment, as I rush into Cuppa Joe hollering to anyone and everyone who is willing to listen. "I'm so sorry I'm late. I've had the morning from hell."

Not movie enough for you? Well, insert someone turning with a coffee in hand, me with my binder in my arms, and a little head-on collision with a slo-mo effect, and you have yourself a classic rom-com coffee shop clip—thanks to yours truly.

Everyone is okay, the floor is a mess, and my binder…it's on life support, but given the situation it put me in, I'm not sure I want to resuscitate it.

CJ lowers her shades. "Dramatic much?"

"Shhh!" I scan around the room to see who's still watching. *Show's over, people.*

"You shhh!" Mal chimes in.

"No, you shhh!" CJ bites back, squinting as she shoves her Ray-bans back on. "Who let the sun in here anyway?"

"Seriously, Ceej. Are you that hungover the lights are bothering you?" I slam my binder on the metal high-top table, not giving two-shits whose head is pounding.

"I'm fine." CJ raises her cup and takes one long, drawn-out sip. Actually, I'm pretty sure she is gulping—no, downing—her latte before tossing it over her head and hitting the trash behind her. "Or I will be in ten minutes when this triple shot takes effect."

"How did you do that?" I ask CJ, quickly turning to Mal when she doesn't answer. "How does she do that?"

Mal shrugs.

CJ rests her head on the table.

I roll my eyes.

"I got this for you." She slides what looks like some kind of frozen frappe across the table.

"What's this?"

"It's The Britt." She holds up her hand. "Don't ask."

"Why did you have to say that?" I throw my hands in the air. "That is like tempting Eve with the apple. Of course, I want a bite."

"Finnnnnne." Mal exhales. "Monica, the barista, was waiting on this customer who wanted, I guess, a caramel crunch frappe, but she held the caramel, held the cookie, held the coffee, but added mocha."

"So, this is basically a chocolate shake?" I take a sip and gag. "No! Just no! This is definitely not a chocolate shake."

"Right! Well, I made the stupid mistake of ordering what *she* had. But I figured they would double the order and I would get my drink at the same time. Monica handed me my order and told me to enjoy *The Britt.* Needless to say, I ordered something else and it ended up taking twice as long," Mal throws her thumb in CJ's direction, "making this one even grouchier."

"Word," CJ pipes up, then rests her head back down on the table.

Even though both of my friends are severely hungover, I'm glad I came out. I needed this. I needed the distraction from the walls falling down around me.

"So…" Mal leans in, resting her chin on her hands as she prepares to hang on my every word, "how's it living with Austin again?" Her eyes widen. "Wait! First, tell me about Jeffery. Then my brother."

"There's nothing to say." CJ decides to speak, flipping up her shades and now investing herself in this conversation.

Mal and I just stare at her.

"Whaaaat?" She crosses her arms. "The coffee kicked in."

"That's rude, CJ. Don't you think we should give Clover the chance to tell us the whole story?"

Mal tries to defend my honor, but there's nothing to defend. There really isn't anything to say. I'm sure CJ filled Mallory in on Jeffery's baby momma, so why rehash it?

"She's right."

Both of their heads swing around, confused at my confession.

"I am?"

"She is?"

"Yeah." I nod. "She is." I pause, taking a sip of *The Britt*—not so much for the taste, more to wet my throat. "I want to blame Jeffery for everything. For leading me on. For wasting six years of my life. For cheating on me. For starting a family with that blonde bimbo, but most of all, I'm mad at myself for ignoring the signs."

There, I said it. I can be pissed at Jeffery all I want, but the truth is, we're like two puzzle pieces that don't fit. It doesn't matter how hard you try, if they aren't made to piece together, they won't. *We didn't.*

"Honey," Mal places her hand over mine, "don't blame yourself. You just wanted the fairy tale, like your parents."

"I'm beginning to think that doesn't exist." I pull my hand back and rub the front of my coffee-soaked binder.

Even though Mal is four years younger than Austin, she still remembers what it was like. Living next door, they got to experience everything we did: the family dinners, the dancing around the kitchen, finger food Friday, family game night…the list goes on.

"It does," CJ chokes out, like it was painful to say. Mal and I turn and stare. "What? Just because I like to have a good time doesn't mean I don't eventually want to settle down. I just want to make sure I try all the eggs, so to speak."

"Eggs?" Mal and I look at her like she just lost her marbles.

"It's the hangover." Mal slowly nods. "It has to be the hangover."

CJ leans forward. "Listen here, bitches. I'm not hungover."

I wince.

Mal holds up her fingers and pinches them together.

"Fine! Maybe a tad, but still…" CJ scoots her chair closer and folds her hands together. "I don't want to suffer from RBS. It's a very serious illness that is becoming an epidemic. It's super contagious, so beware."

"I thought we were talking about relationships, not STDs." Mal laughs, then winces. "Ouch."

"Who has the hangover now?" CJ smirks.

"Okay, tell me more." What do I have to lose? Even though CJ is a little crazy in her methods, she's usually right. "What is the RBS?"

"Runaway Bride Syndrome." She grabs my binder.

"Hey!" I yank it back.

"Jeezus, Clover. Learn to let go." CJ plays a visual game of chicken. Her stare is so intense, I have no choice but to hand it over. "Good choice." She winks.

"Be careful! The pages are wet from the coffee." I turn to look at Mal, hoping for a little backup, but she's just sitting there, sipping her coffee. "You're no help."

"What?" Her smile is wicked, hiding behind the lid of her latte. "I'm trying to follow along."

CJ clears her throat. "As I was saying, RBS is better known as Runaway Bride Syndrome. In the movie, Julia Roberts was known for ditching her man at the aisle due to a serious case of cold feet."

"Ohhh! I know where you're going with this," Mal cuts in, grinning from ear to ear. I give her the stink eye. How dare she side with CJ. "Buckle up, Clover. CJ is about to take you on one hell of a ride."

Shaking my head, I roll my eyes at them both.

"Kid, it's cute you want to back me up, but let me get this out so Clo can have her *ah-ha* moment." CJ eyes us both, daring us to speak. "Okay, good. So, Julia ran because with each man, she became unsure of who she was. She was a chameleon, changing colors to fit the guy she was with. Sure, everything was fine. They got along, had a wonderful time, but in all reality, she was falsely advertising the goods."

"Uhhh, what does this—?"

"Shut it, Clo," CJ interrupts. "Do you want me to get to the point or not? Because this shit is good."

"Hey, ladies, can I get you anything else?" Monica, the barista, walks up, picking the wrong time to interrupt.

"Holy hell! Can you all just let me finish?" CJ announces.

"Jeez, and here I thought Starbuck's customers were assholes," Monica mumbles as she quickly walks away.

"Shit! Did I just piss off my coffee chick?" CJ glances over her shoulder.

"You really shouldn't have done that." Mal shakes her head. "Pissing off the barista is like pissing off the IT guy. It should never happen. Never!"

"I'll find a way to make it up to her. Now, where was I?" CJ taps her fingers on my binder. "Oh! False advertising." She pauses, reaching across the table to take a sip of Mal's drink.

"Hey! Get your own!" Mal hollers.

"I would, but I pissed her off, and until I clear the air, I'm drinking this." CJ hands it back. "Okay, I'm good now. My point, Clo, is that Julia, or…well, her character, didn't know what she wanted so she took on the likes of whoever she was dating. If one liked omelets, she liked omelets. If the other liked over-medium, she liked over-medium. She was a fucking chameleon, taking on the personality of each of her grooms because it was easier than actually trying the eggs. Finally, Richard Gere's character knocked some sense into her by asking one simple question. "What kind of eggs do you like?" She had no clue. None what so ever!"

t wasn't until the end when Richard Gere pointed out that she was lying to herself that she had no clue who she was or what made her happy. He asked her what her favorite eggs were, and she didn't know."

"Okaaay…?"

"Jeez, Clo," CJ huffs, knocking on my head. "Anyone home? The point is, she was too busy making everyone else happy to live a life expected of her that she didn't take the time out to figure out what she really wanted. She never took the time out to try the eggs because she was too focused on the end instead of what gets you there."

"She tried the eggs," I whisper.

"She tried the eggs," CJ agreed. "Everything in this binder," she opens the coffee-soaked pages, flipping through as she continues, "this is what you thought you needed to get to the end. Your goal? The happy ever after. The problem? You forgot the happy."

CJ's right. I thought if I lived my life accordingly, followed all the rules, I could have exactly what my parents had.

"So, the real question is…what kind of eggs do you like?" Mal joins in.

"I don't know." I hang my head. The reality is, I fixed us what Jeffery liked: two eggs sunny-side up with a slice of bacon. "What I do know is I kind of hate sunny-side up," I admit.

"Jeffery's favorite?" CJ questions, though she already knows the answer.

"Yeah. Too yellow and way too runny." I make a face.

"Don't tolerate the eggs, taste them," Mal joins in.

"When she says eggs, she means dicks." CJ laughs.

Mal nods.

They both high-five.

"Speaking of dicks, look at this one." Mal swipes her phone to life and flashes us the screen.

"Who is that?" I can't help but blush.

"It's this guy I met through a dating app. Apparently, when I said let's chat, he took that as let me take a picture of my penis and send it to you." Mal chuckles. "Like, why he would do that?"

"Question is why would you keep it." I take the phone, examining the pic a little closer.

"Let me see." CJ yanks the phone from my hands, blowing the pic up to twice the size. "Just as I thought." She flashes us the screen. "It's a Google dick."

"A what?" Mal and I question.

"Clover, I'm disappointed in you." CJ hands Mal her phone back and grabs mine. "And you call yourself the Google queen…" After a quick search and a couple swipes, she flips the cell around. "Google dick: a picture of a dick found with a Google image search. Most often used for sexting," she whirls her finger in Mal's direction, "when you don't want to send a picture of your actual dick."

"So, that's not his dick?" It's Mal's turn to examine it. "I mean, I thought it was gross he sent it to me, but never thought it wasn't his."

"It's pixilated. Plus, if you zoom in, you can see a small border, which proves it's a screenshot." CJ points out.

"Wow! You can." Mal laughs, zooming in and out really fast, as she practically falls on the floor laughing. "Grower." Zoom out. "Shower." Zoom in. She repeats this a few times until she realizes we aren't at all amused. "Um…can I blame the lack of sleep?"

"No, you can't. However, we can go with lack of nutrition." CJ scoots her chair back. "Who's ready to move this gab-fest to the Shake Shack? I need to get some grease in me."

"Me!" Mal follows.

"Guys, I'm going to pass." I reach for my binder and stand. "You both have given me so much to think about."

"Going to try some eggs?" Mal flashes me a smile.

“Maybe, but first,” I hold the binder in front of me, “I’m going to—”

“Clo, that binder is holding you back. I thought we—” CJ reaches for it, and I hug it to my chest, then quickly turn.

“Let me finish,” I interrupt CJ interrupting me. “I’m going to learn to live a little and color this baby up.”

“That’s my girl.” CJ turns me around and smacks me on the butt. “Go get ’em.”

“Wait…” I purse my lips. “Are you not walking out with us?”

“I have to make up with Monica.” CJ throws her thumb over her shoulder. “I’ll probably need Mal’s help.”

“Good luck. You’ll need it.” I shake my head and laugh as I turn and head for the door.

This time, my exit is a little more graceful than it was before.

CHAPTER SIX

AUSTIN

I came to work early to get things done. To forget about *her.* And I was doing pretty damn good until it was time for Dr. Feelgood. When it's your job to talk about sex, you have no choice but to think about it—a lot.

Most guys wouldn't have an issue with this, but Clover is my best friend—hell, she's practically family—and this is a massive goddamn problem because here I am imagining what it would be like…

Fuck!

I'm being a little pussy. Mind over matter is all it will take. I'm a dude. It's easy to override our system. Just replace the data—and by data I mean the naked images of Clover imprinted on my brain.

I wish it was as simple as holding up a wand to forget it all, but that's only in the movies. This is actually more fun—adult show-and-tell, cell phone style.

Reaching for my phone, I swipe it to life and scroll through my contacts.

Abby — too clingy.

Bianca — too handsy.

Ciara — too hairy. It's the toes!

Jenny — too freaky.

Sexy Sierra. She's pretty fun, and if my memory serves correctly, she has a pretty sweet naughty nurse costume.

Me: Hey, beautiful.

Girls love it when you make them feel special. "Beautiful" hits all the right spots.

What do you know, we got dots…

Sexy Sierra: Hey, handsome. It's been a while.

If I were any Average Joe, this could possibly be a sticky situation to reply to. *It's been a while* could be code for "why in the hell are you messaging me?" or "the past is the past. Let's hook up." Good thing I'm Dr. Feelgood and I have an answer for everything. It's why men and women write, email, or call into me for advice. It's also why I have the number one talk show on satellite radio.

Me: It has. I was hoping you would call. I've missed you.

Sexy Sierra: Aw. <3 Does Dr. Feelgood need a naughty nurse?

And here it is. The perfect opportunity knocking on my door. *Clover who*?

Me: I was hoping for dinner. To catch up, but now that you mention it…

This is where she thinks the ball is in her court but in reality, I'm controlling the score.

Sexy Sierra: <pic>

Sexy Sierra: Maybe that will hold you over until tonight. ;)

That's what I'm talkin' about. I didn't just get a boob pic, I got a full-frontal of Sexy Sienna lying naked on her bed. Legs spread, waiting for…

Clover: I forgot my key. I'm near the office, can I swing by and get yours?

No! No! No! She doesn't get to invade my texts. Not when I was thinking about doing very naughty things to Sexy Sierra.

Me: Sure. TTYL.

Clover: Thx. B there in 10.

Me: K.

Sexy Sierra: Did you not like? Having doubts?

Shit, the number one rule to sexting: no regrets from either party, and I just broke my own damn rule.

Me: Hell no. I got distracted by a certain photo. H-O-T.

Sexy Sierra: Show me how hot.

"Oh shit." I look around to make sure no one is watching, unbuckle my belt, reach in, cock in hand—literally—and snap a quick pic just as a text from Clover comes across the screen.

Dammit.

Clover: B there in 15. I stopped and got us a sub.

One quick swipe to the left, Clover disappears, and the dick pic is on its way to Sierra.

Clover: Ha! It's a Google dick! <eggplant emoji>

Fuck! Of course, this would happen. Here I was trying to forget the images from this morning by sexting it up with Sexy Sierra and end up sending my rock-hard cock to Clover.

Me: Oops! Ummm…

What else can you say to that? I can't deny it.

Sexy Sierra: Hey, did you forget about me?

I'm getting too old for this.

Quickly pulling up my pics, I forward the pic to Sierra as Clover walks in.

This should be good.

CLOVER

I'm going to kill Mal for telling her brother about the Google dick incident. Isn't anything private anymore?

"Well, look what the cat dragged in," Owen Decker, Hotline Hookup's producer, hollers from inside his office.

Normally, I would stop and chit-chat, but I have places to go and people to see. Okay, maybe that's a lie, but I do have to get back to Austin's to make sure Kramer doesn't have a meltdown when the driver drops him off.

"Brought lunch." I hold up the bags and keep walking.

Reaching the studio, the On-Air light is off, and I walk right in.

"Think you're funny, don't you?" I laugh off the pic and set the subs down. "I can't believe Mal. What did they do, call as soon as I left?"

Austin holds up his finger and continues texting and I carry on, babbling about our morning coffee talk shenanigans ignoring his request.

Austin Montgomery saw me naked. No matter how hard I try to forget, I can't. It's not like modesty is my middle name. But, him catching me in my birthday suit, has me seeing him in a whole new light. I can practically feel the heat rising as his eyes raked over me. He's my best friend, I struggle to remind myself and begin the senseless chatter, talking about anything and everything and hope my best friend doesn't notice my nervous behavior. So, I do what I do best and continue talking about anything and everything. "Like, who knew Google dick was even a thing?"

"A thing?" Austin glances up with a puzzled look.

Jeez, palm to the forehead.

"What does Mal have to do with my dick?" Austin winces. "Ew." He shivers. "Pretend I didn't just say that." His phone beeps, and he's back at it. Whoever he's messaging apparently ranks higher than the station, food, and me.

"I know what a penis looks like, thank you very much." I stand there, hands on hips, giving Austin my best *go to hell* look. "I also know what a Google dick looks like, and this," I flip my phone around, flashing him the pic of one of the biggest penises I've ever seen, "is exactly that. I'm willing to bet it's a porn peen." I chuckle.

"Porn peen?" A laugh comes from Austin, like he sprung a leak—slow at first, stopping, then starting all over again. He wasn't done yet either. I could tell from the way his hands let his cell drop to the floor and he rolled his emerald eyes to the ceiling.

"It's not that funny." I cross my arms.

"I-I-I'm so sorry, but…" Austin tries to catch his breath as he bites his lip, holding his amusement hostage.

"It's not that funny," I huff out.

From somewhere deep inside his chest comes a rumble, a shaking motion as his muscles grow tight. This man is about to explode.

"Whatever," I mumble. "You are worse than a fourteen-year-old boy." I lean back on the sound board, patiently waiting for him to finish.

"Sorry, Clo, but you said that dick looked like a porn star's cock."

"Well, what normal-sized penis looks like that? It's all, like, huge…" I hold my hands out so he can get an idea that what he showed me isn't normal, "and super veiny. It's about to bust out at the seams or something." I examine the pic one last time before I finally delete it.

"What if I were to tell you that porn peen was mine?" Austin smirks as he bends down, reaching for his cell, quickly swiping it to life.

"You wish." I can't help but dip my eyes to the front of his pants.

"Eyes up here, sweetheart." Austin's lips curve up, teasing me.

"Don't flatter yourself." I roll my eyes, and then my shoulders, uncomfortable in the situation I somehow got myself into.

"Oh, trust me, I don't need to do that when—"

"Just stop!" I shout.

"Calm down." He raises his hands to shush me. "Before Owen comes in here."

"So?" I look at Austin like he's crazy. "I brought enough food." I reach in the bag and throw Austin his sub. "I'll never eat all of mine."

"It's not that. Apparently, our show has dropped from number one to the number two spot and corporate is a little pissy about it. They want him to come up with something new and trendy no one else is doing."

I'm really not sure what the station expects from a sex-talk radio show. There's nothing Austin can really do except continue giving advice. He's Dr. Feelgood. It's what he does. It's what makes Live Wire Radio their money.

"Hmm, I'm sure you guys will think of something." I tear off a piece of my turkey club and pop it into my mouth.

"Yeah, but in the meantime, Owen is moody as fuck."

Austin's phones chimes again, and he smiles.

"Who has you looking like that?"

"Like what?" Austin raises an eyebrow.

"You know what I'm talking about. That is the same look you had when you found your father's Playboy stash." I set my sub down and brush the crumbs off my hands.

"Same look, huh?" He glances at his phone and clicks his tongue. "Well, let's just say, it never gets old."

"Oh my God! What is it with you people?"

"You people? Are you being serious right now?"

"Yeah! You, your sister, CJ…even Jeffery. It's like everyone is in heat."

"You act like it's a bad thing." Austin stands, wiping off his slacks. "Sex is an instinct. When two people find each other attractive, a chemical is produced—"

"Spare me the details. I'm not one of your listeners needing advice from Dr. Feelgood. My life is going—"

"Yes?" Austin raises his eyebrows.

"It's going…"

Hell, I don't even know how it's going? Here CJ is having sex with Mr. Do It All Night Long, Mal is chatting with God knows who, Austin is sleeping his way through the alphabet, and then there's me—twenty-seven, single, sexless.

"I'll finish that for you. It's not going." He plops back down in his chair, elbows resting on the arms, fingers making a steeple, swiveling back and forth about to Dr. Feelgood me, I'm sure.

Feeling defeated, I let out a deep breath. "Austin, I'm more confused than ever. I thought I had it all worked out, but maybe everything I thought I knew was wrong. I mean, look at you." I wave my hand in his direction. "You're a—I mean, you—it's just that you sleep around so much, I'm surprised your thingy hasn't fallen off."

"My number one rule: don't be a joker, wrap your poker. It hasn't failed me yet."

"See…you don't think. You just do." I purse my lips and angle my head to the side. "And do. And do."

"Okay, I get it. You think I'm a manwhore," Austin says as he stands up, walks over to me, and places his hands on my shoulders. "But this isn't about me. This is about you and how you're feeling." Austin bends at the knees, making us eye level. "It doesn't matter who I sleep with. The problem is your relationship failed and you're trying to blame your plan, but in all reality, you guys didn't have a sexual connection and you ignored it."

"How dare you." I shift back, and his hands drop.

"Careful there." He nods toward the board.

"Whatever, Austin. I'm not bad in bed. Actually, I—"

"Clover, you haven't been listening to me," Austin cuts in. "It's not something you did, or even something Dalton did. Sometimes two people look good on paper, but when it comes to what matters, they don't fit—literally."

I giggle.

"Tell me I'm wrong."

I let out the longest sigh. "Fine. You're not wrong."

"So, what exactly are you going to do about it?" Austin asks the million-dollar question as he takes a sip of his soda.

What am I going to do?

I can't keep living my life how I have been, because plot twist—it doesn't work. The one thing I lacked in my relationship with Jeffery was passion.

I want that. I want to know what it feels like to feel the zing, the butterflies, to want to want more—to need it.

Maybe I should take Ceej's advice and try the eggs. I mean, what could it hurt? I've only had one kind, and I know there's more out there. Hell, my calls with CJ and my Google history is enough to prove that.

"This isn't something you have to decide right now." Austin glances down at his watch while he takes a big swig.

"I've got it!" I shout as I slam my hand down. "I'm going to become a whore!"

Austin spits his drink out, soaking me and the board.

"Jesus." I reach for some napkins and begin cleaning up. "What's your problem?"

"That's not what I was meaning." Austin tosses his cup in the trash. "Not at all." He rests his hands on his head.

"But it's genius, really." I continue to clean up. "How could I have had a relationship with someone for so long who couldn't provide me with multiple O's?"

Austin shrugs. "It's true."

"I know!" I hop off the board, and Austin's eyes go wide. "Calm down, Montgomery. I know this is new for you, but I promise you, everything will be A-OK."

"Clover…" Austin warns.

"Calm down, big boy." I pat him on the shoulder. "This plan is perfect. I'm going on a man-hunt to find the perfect O."

"Clover, stop talking." He pushes me to the side, but I don't stop.

"Yes!" I shout, then begin to pace the room, the ideas flowing as Austin fiddles with his board. "It's about time I trade this halo in for a pair of horns. This good girl is about to be bad. Very, very bad. I'm talking so naughty—"

"Clover!"

"Austin—" I swing around, hands on my hips, "don't you dare. This is not some kind of double-standard situation. If I want to have sex with all of New York, I can."

"Clover, it sounds like you're suffering from a brutal breakup. I'm sure after things settle down…" Austin starts, using his Dr. Feelgood therapy voice on me.

He's so dramatic.

"The dust has settled, *Dr. Feelgood*." I slowly drag out his name. "I'm about to orgasm my way to my very own happy ever after."

"Although I'm not encouraging this promiscuous activity, I am applauding you for realizing a change has to be made." Austin's voice is now clear and deep.

"A huge change," I agree. "I'm going from unlucky in love to getting lucky. You can't get any better than that."

"Well, Clover—it sounds like you're a woman who knows what she wants," Austin turns his body toward me as he continues to talk into the mic, "but how about we see what the *listeners* think? If you have gone through a similar situation or have some advice to give Ms. Unlucky in Love, pull out your phones and call in, email, text, or tweet—use whatever means you have to—the Hotline Hookup wants to hear from you."

Listeners?

Callers?

Hotline Hookup?

Thoughts accelerate inside my head. I try to slow them down so I can understand what happened, but I can't hear them over the hammering inside my chest.

I can't stay here.

I need out.

I rush to the door and fumble with the knob, but something keeps me from leaving.

Breathe.

One, two, three, four…

I can hear Austin saying something, but he sounds distant and muffled.

Breathe.

...five, six, seven, eight...

"Let me explain."

Breathe.

...nine, ten.

Taking one last deep breath, I spin around and come face-to-face with Austin Montgomery, aka Dr. Feelgood, and poke him in the chest. "What in the hell were you thinking?"

His hands fly in the air. "I swear to God, I didn't..."

"Nice try!" I walk us backward, my finger jabbing into his chest. "You needed a boost..."

"Oh, come on, Clover—" Austin grabs my hand and holds it up between us. "This accidentally hit the On-Air button, turning on the mic and overriding our taped segment."

"Ohhh." I twist around and begin to replay the events in my mind. "And when you...?"

"Yep! I wasn't trying to interrupt you because I didn't agree. I was trying to get your attention." Austin sighs, letting go of my hand. "I didn't know what to do except run with it."

"This is so embarrassing." I fall into the extra seat. "Did I say my name?" I try to wrack my brain.

"First name, yes, but I don't think you revealed your last." Austin runs a hand over his face. "I'm so sorry..."

The door suddenly swings open and Owen barges in. "Holy shit! I don't know what in the hell just happened, but emails are pouring in, calls are filling up the lines, and tweets..." Owen pulls out his phone. "They are tweeting the station inquiring how they can get ahold of UnLucky in Love."

"We need to shut this down." Austin rushes over to his computer.

"What does this mean?" I groan. "I'm so embarrassed."

"You!" Owen rushes over to my side, "have nothing to be embarrassed about." He pats my knee and continues. "You are what we need!"

"Decker…" Austin warns. "I know *exactly* what you're thinking, and she's off-limits."

"If she agrees, why does it matter?" Owen disputes.

I raise my hand. "She is right here and can hear *everything* you're saying."

"This bastard," Austin jerks his thumb in Owen's direction, "wants to use you for a ratings boost."

"Did you not hear her? She's tired of settling and wants more." Owen begins to scroll through his phone. "Listen to what these callers had to say."

"Hook me up with Unlucky in Love."

"I will pluck her four-leaf clover."

"I will give her the world."

"Unlucky in Love, where have you been all my life?"

"I wish more women were like Clover."

"No, Owen. She just went through a breakup. She isn't ready." Austin tries to defend me, but I'm not sure if I want him to.

"How will five emails boost your ratings?" I chime in.

"Oh, Clover, it's more like…" Owen scrolls through his phone, "five hundred and counting. New York is in love with you."

"Why?" Austin and I both ask at the same time.

"What do you mean *why*?" I glare at him. "Am I not lovable?"

"Who cares what he thinks." Owen offers his hand, and I take it. Pulling me up, he continues. "You are just what Hotline Hookup needs, and from what I heard, you need us too. Let us help."

"No! Dammit!" Austin steps between us, putting himself in Owen's face. "Clover is vulnerable right now. She doesn't know what she wants and I'm not going to let you push her into a decision she isn't ready to make."

"Austin," I hold up my hand, "let Owen talk."

I have lived my whole life according to a plan designed to give me my perfect forever, the problem—it's what I thought I had to do to get there. I never actually allowed myself to make a mistake, and right now, I want to make all the mistakes.

Owen waggles his eyebrows at Austin. "Let Hotline Hookup filter through all these emails, texts, calls, and what not, and find your perfect match."

"How will you do that?"

"Yeah, how will we do that?" Austin speaks up and stands beside me, not behind me.

"Austin will interview you. Find out your likes and dislikes, what you look for in a perfect date, and clear up the whole sex thing."

"Sex thing?" I question.

"Clover, the things is…" Owen tries to tiptoe around the question.

"Decker…" Austin warns, "you're treading on thin ice, man."

Owen nods once, acknowledging Austin's concerns. "Well, during your revelation, it came across like you want to find multiple partners to see who you're sexually compatible with. During your interview with Austin, we will address those comments and clear them up. Lose the wham-bam-thank-you-ma'am assholes."

"But I do want that." I turn and point to Austin. "I want what he has."

Austin coughs.

Owen practically dies laughing.

And I stand there irritated that these jerks aren't taking me seriously. "Really, guys?"

"Sorry, Clo." Austin hangs his head, covering his mouth with his fist.

"We will make sure you get what you want." Owen checks the time. "Do you have a couple hours to spare?"

"This is really happening?" Austin stands there shaking his head.

"Brother, this is going to get me and you a big raise and our number one spot back."

"Clover, if this *ever* becomes too much and you want to pull the plug—just say the words and I'll end it. No questions asked. You got it?" Austin tries to reassure me.

"Got it." I smile, then look up at Owen. "Where do I sign?"

"Clover, you won't regret this." Owen shakes his phone in the air as he walks backward to the door.

"I'm counting on it."

Hmm…maybe today isn't so bad after all.

CHAPTER SEVEN

CLOVER

What—a—day! I went from being almost engaged to single and ready to mingle. Like, who does that? Someone who was never ready to settle down in the first place—that's who. That's right! I'm admitting *almost* all my plans were bogus. Especially the sex doesn't matter rule. Obviously, it does—*a lot.*

Now, thanks to a little mishap on-air, I'll have a chance to test out my new theory—that a great relationship is not only based on how well you get along on the surface, but the tingle you get between the sheets—literally.

At first, when Owen barged into the studio and presented us with his idea, I was a little taken aback. Basically, I admitted to over thirty million listeners, that I, Clover Kelley, wanted to become a whore.

Be careful for what you wish for because it may come true.

It's not that I want to become a whore or be known as one, I just want to know what it feels like to have an orgasm that isn't self-induced. Is that so wrong?

"Hold the elevator!" CJ comes running through the parking garage with a pizza box in one hand and a bag in the other. Mal is right behind her holding a couple bottles of wine.

"Um, did I forget we had plans?" I try to recall everything we discussed at lunch and I'm pretty sure dinner at Austin's was not a topic brought up.

"Hello?" Mal pipes up. "We heard you! Hence why we brought this." She holds up the bottles. "Pinot, your fave."

"WTF, Clo? We told you to try the eggs, not broadcast it for all the United States to hear." CJ leans back against the mirrored wall.

"Okay." I clap my hands together. "This totally wasn't necessary."

"Damn if it wasn't." CJ pushes off the wall. "I know you. Don't pretend this is all okay when, deep down inside, you're shitting bricks right about now."

"Actually, all is good. I was just heading up to see Kramer and unpack." The elevator dings, the steel wall slides open, and I rush out.

"Running away from the truth!" CJ hollers after me.

"What? No!" I turn. Both Mal and CJ are looking at me like I've lost my marbles. So, I do the only thing I know how to do: distract them from the obvious and tempt them with the possibility. "I thought we could finish this inside. You know, so we can discuss the details of my new online dating show over pizza and pinot."

"Dating show?" Mal and CJ blurt out at the same time.

I shrug my shoulders and open the door. "Come in and I'll tell you all about how this girl is going to get lucky in lust."

Or love…

A girl can dream, can't she?

"Oh-em-gee! This pizza is so good!" CJ moans. "I swear, I've had it every week since you brought the leftovers home from the office." She takes another bite and continues not caring that her mouth is stuffed full. "Like, who even thought of this? Potato and bacon on a pizza?" CJ picks up a couple slices. "Is it a baked potato or is it a pizza?" She smacks them together to make one thick slice. "It's both! Genius!"

"You know that new real estate agent I hired, Antonette? Well, it's her father's place." I pick up one more slice, fold it over, and stuff it in my mouth.

"No way." Mal sticks her head up over the chair. "Her father owns Grand Avenue Pizzeria?" Mal quickly falls down as she sees Kramer in the corner, ruffling his feathers, squawking, "I see you."

Ever since she walked through the door, Kramer has been all over her and giving me the cold shoulder—which is why she's busy playing hide-and-seek while her pizza gets cold.

"Yeah, I was a Sorbillo's girl until she brought one of these bad boys into the office." I pick a potato slice off and pop it into my mouth. "There was no going back."

"Speaking of…" Mal stands and grabs her plate before plopping down into Austin's oversized recliner. "When are you going back to work?"

"Antonette assures me she has it under control." I reach for my phone and send her a quick text to check-in.

Me: How's it going?

Ant: It's good. A couple offers were accepted today.

Me: Great! Hey, has anything been delivered for me?

Ant: You mean this? <pic>

Antonette sends me a pic of a very thick legal envelope marked confidential. In the background is a weird-shaped pizza. *Is that?*

Me: Thx. What kind of pizza is that?

I quickly snap a pic of the box and hit send.

Ant: I told you the potato bacon slice was addicting.

Ant: My bro hand-delivered me a pie since I was working late. <pic>

Ant: Yes, it's exactly what you think it is.

A pic comes through, and sure enough, there it is, a Grand Avenue special in the shape of a penis.

Ant: Yeah, he told me to "eat a dick."

Me: That is a dick worth devouring.

Ant: Gross! My bro made that with his hands.

Me: #dead

I can't help it. So much has been bubbling beneath the service, I'm not sure if I want to laugh or cry. So, I do nothing. Then all it takes is getting a picture of a pizza penis and it sets me off and this isn't just a normal laugh out loud chuckle…it's a full on cross your legs and try not to pee your pants outburst.

"What in the hell?" CJ jumps up and takes my phone. "Pizza penis. Sweet!"

"I want to see." Mal grabs the cell. "Someone has a sense of humor."

"Her—br-brother," I finally choke out, "told her to eat a dick."

CJ joins in. "Ha! I would like to meet him. Sounds like a guy I would like to—"

"No!" I shout. "Brothers are off-limits."

"Are they, though?" Mal chimes in. "Because I wouldn't care if either of you wanted my brother."

I scrunch my face. "Ew."

"You hear that, Clo? I got Rainbow Brite's okay." CJ grins at Mal.

"Don't start," I warn.

"Holy shit! I told you I meant to look like this." Mal waves her hands near her brightly colored feet. "You wear statement socks all the time. I was going for the comfort look."

"Let's get one thing clear." CJ turns around. "This is a look. A style that no other could pull off. Every day is a statement. A daily warning label if you will."

"A T-shirt that says 'Shhh! No one cares." Mal tugs on the hem of Ceej's cotton tee. "And socks that say "fuck" and "off" is not a daily statement it's downright scary."

"Like I said, a warning label."

"You guys are unbelievable. How about you pick up the dinner mess, open the other bottle of wine while I wrap up this convo with Antonette, and I'll fill you in on everything that's going on."

"Fine," Mal huffs.

CJ points at her shirt, giving me a *go to hell* glare.

Me: I have a few personal things I have to take care of, but I'll pop in next week and check in.

Ant: I've got this! I'm making us some moo-lah!

Me: Good, because I need to start looking for a place of my own.

Ant: I'll keep a lookout.

Me: Thx.

Ant: No problem-o

Me: Call if you need me.

Ant: K, boss!

That went better than expected.

"Poop. Poop. Poop," Kramer squawks from the living room.

"Oh shit!" I run and open his cage. "Here buddy. There are no accidents on Uncle Austin's floor."

"Poop. Poop. Poop." He sits beside Mal, gently pecking at her arm.

"Seriously, Kramer?" I walk over to him, holding out my arm for him to climb on, but he doesn't.

"He's a little upset." Kramer climbs up her arm until he's perched on her shoulder.

"Poop. Poop. Poop," Kramer continues.

"Buddy, I didn't want to leave you," I coo.

"He's just a bird." CJ rolls her eyes.

"Well, that 'just a bird' has to poop." I point to his cage. "Mal, you better get him in his cage."

"Ew! Don't let him poop on me!" She begins to wiggle.

"Don't! You're scaring him." I reach out, and Kramer hops on. "Come on, buddy. Momma loves you." I shoot Mal a dirty look as he hops off into his cage.

"What? I thought he was going to shit on me." Mal heads to the bathroom to wash her hands.

"I swear." I shake my head, grab my glass, and take her seat…well, Austin's recliner, the most coveted seat in the house. I'm not sure whether it's because he broke it in or it's that comfortable. Either way, I'm settling in for the evening.

"Wheee…" Mal slides into the room. "Okay! I'm ready!" She skids to a stop.

"Story time with Clover!" CJ pipes up. "This should be good." She falls back onto her feet on the white fur rug.

"So, after I left Cuppa Joe's, I was going to go back to Austin's and come up with a new plan, but I remembered I forgot to grab the key so I had to swing by the studio and figured since I was dropping by I would grab us lunch as well." I clap my hands together. "Which, Ceej, that sub place was amazing."

"I told you." CJ glances over at Mal. "Let's go there tomorrow."

"I'm game." Mal gives her a thumbs-up.

"No can do, guys. You are going to have plans with me, but let me finish this story before we discuss." I look between the two. "Are we good?"

"Carry on." CJ waves her hand, and Mal leans back into the cushion and gets comfy.

"So, I was on my way up to the studio when I receive a Google dick from Austin. Actually, it was more of a porn peen, but I guess go big or go home, right?" I shoot them both a dirty look. My way of getting a little dig in for telling our secrets.

"Wait, rewind." Ceej shakes her head. "Austin sent you, Clover Kelley, his BFF, a dick pic?"

"Don't play dumb. You guys are the only ones who knew." I watch them silently point at each other and deny it. "Anyway, we were joking around about the Google dick when he kept smiling and talking to some skank."

"Oh God! I do not want to hear what my brother does in his spare time."

"I thought you didn't care about who your brother fucked." CJ smirks.

"I don't care who he dates. Big difference. Huge!"

"Back to me, guys." I point to myself. "Basically, I had a series of ah-ha moments during the time he was texting whore number who knows what when I realized Austin seems happy being a manwhore, and you, CJ…" I wince, "let's just say you know what you like."

"Damn skippy I do!" She winks.

"And, Mal, you were doing something to get that dick pic. Even if it was just putting yourself out there," I admit.

"It was stupid. All those dating sites are dumb." Mal turns her phone around and points at a few of them. "This one—dumb. That one—overrated. Oh, and this one—liars!"

"You're not hearing what I'm saying. Basically, the egg talk during coffee worked. I want to try the eggs!"

"She means dicks," CJ translates for me.

"Yup! This time, I mean dicks!" I shout.

"Whoa there, Clover! Getting a little too excited there, don't you think?" Mal tries to calm me down, but when you're as sexually deprived as I've been, excitement is an understatement.

"Guys! I have never had an orgasm. I think this calls for a party." I purse my lips for a moment, trying to decide how I want to deliver the news.

"Well, you did tell over thirty million listeners you wanted to become a whore…so, that's one way to kick the party off," CJ says, downing her glass of Pinot. "Do you need to be topped off?"

"I'm good." Mal covers her glass. "Plus, I have to wake up early tomorrow."

"Not yet!" I take a sip. "I just want to finish this story."

"Okay, tell us how you went from whore to your very own dating show." Ceej flips around and is now lying on the floor making herself comfortable.

"I'm going to skip over how pissed I was at Austin and right to where Owen walked in."

"Owen Decker, the producer?" Mal sits up a little straighter. "He's kind of hot, but also extremely annoying."

"She's just salty because she asked him out and he said no," CJ says, spilling the beans.

"I didn't ask him out," Mal huffs. "I asked him if he wanted to try this new coffee place."

"Which is a date with your big brother's friend and coworker," CJ defends.

"We were all in the studio talking about coffee. I thought…" Mal's cheeks burn red with embarrassment. "I was being nice, and he was a dick about it."

"So, let me get this straight, you don't like Owen? Because he is pretty hot." I turn to Ceej, and ask, "What is he? Six foot three, maybe four, and has the most incredible brown eyes with flecks of gold?"

"So dreamy." CJ falls back, holding her chest, then shoots right back up. "But let's talk about his body!"

"Enough!" Mal stands.

"What, Mal? Getting a little jealous?" CJ teases as I watch on.

"No! I was just refilling my glass." She quickly refills her wine and sits back down. "But let's get back to the story."

"So, Owen…" I glance over at Mal, who's casually sitting there sipping her wine. "He came storming into the office raving about my outburst. Said this was the perfect scenario for a rantings boost."

"Porn?" CJ crinkles her forehead.

"Nooo, but apparently during that short segment, there were over five hundred people who either called in, emailed, tweeted, or whatever about me. They wanted to meet Unlucky in Love."

"You do realize it's because you basically said your lady bits were open for business." CJ cackles, while Mal whispers, "You whore."

"You a whore. A whore. A whore. You a whore." Kramer clacks while bouncing up and down on his perch.

CJ dies laughing.

"Shit!" Mal spits out her wine and quickly wipes it up.

"Kramer!" I stand and rush over to his cage. "I'm not a whore!"

"You a whore. A whore."

"Shhh! You're hurting momma's feelings."

"Your bird just called you a whore!" CJ cries.

"Stop being a bitch," I snap back.

"You bitches. You all bitches. You bitches," Kramer repeats.

"Look what you did." I pull the cover out from under his cage and slide it over the frame. "Time for bed, Kramer. See you tomorrow."

Maybe this was a bad idea. I just wanted to come home, play with my bird, and unpack—not sit here and get made fun of by my friends and ridiculed by Kramer. Geesh.

"Holy cow that worked." CJ stands, then lets out a big yawn before she sits down by Mal.

"Guys, basically the whole point to all of this," I begin pacing the floor, "minus the bird, is I'm going to have my very own Hotline Hookup dating show."

"How will they make sure to keep the creepers away, because if they so much as—" CJ cracks her knuckles.

"We worked it out," I cut in. "No need to be worried."

"Austin would never let anything happen to you. Honestly, I'm surprised he let this happen. Are you sure he's okay with it?" Mal questions.

"He didn't have a choice. This was my decision and one I'm happy I made." I smile, proud I'm taking a leap for once. I'm just hoping it's in the right direction.

"Okay—" CJ scoots over and pats the seat between them. "Come over here and explain to us how this is going to work and what roles we will have to play."

"I thought you would never ask." I work my way through the living room and plop down between my two friends. "I stayed late to record an interview with Austin, and after they shuffle through the mess and find the serious inquiries, they will background check fifty men for a speed-dating round."

"I've always wanted to do that," Mal speaks up, shocking both CJ and myself. "I mean, it seems cool. Plus, you can tell a lot about a guy in a couple minutes. Everything you need to know."

"How about you both come with me? Obviously, I'm not the best judge of character."

"Okay, then what?" CJ pats me on the leg. "Keep going."

"Then I'll pick four guys to go on one-on-one dates with."

"Alone?" Mal seems concerned while CJ waves her off.

"Sort of. Austin insisted I get picked up and dropped off from the studio, and since I wouldn't let a chaperone come along, I take the company driver. That way if I need to leave, I can."

"That's my brother. Always over protective." The corner of Mal's lips turn up.

"Whatever. It protects the company's ass," CJ interjects. "Let's skip all the nonsense and tell me when you're going to get laid."

"It's my choice. I don't have to do anything I don't want to do, but if I do decide to go back to their place, I have to phone in to the studio and let them know."

"And this is where we come in." CJ stands and pulls Mal up. "Clover Kelley, we hereby declare us to be your sextistants."

"My what?"

"Your sex-tist-ants! Think of us like your tour guide to the perfect O. We will make sure this body," CJ pulls me up and twirls me around, "is waxed, plucked, and polished to perfection."

"Yeah, what she said." Mal gets a wicked grin. "Oh, and I have the perfect place to get you sexified."

"I'm thinking leather." CJ pretends to crack a whip.

"I was thinking lace. Ooh-la-la." Mal twirls a piece of my hair.

"Um—" I stand there, unsure of what to say or do and totally out of my element.

I just hope sexing me doesn't screw things up.

CHAPTER EIGHT

AUSTIN

"You heard her rant, you listened to her interview, now we are looking for the most eligible bachelors in New York City. Guys, Unlucky in Love is looking for her very own four-leaf clover! If this is you or someone you know, head on over to our website **www.hotlinehookup.com** and fill out the application and maybe you'll find yourself *getting lucky*." I repeat the words that Owen and I agreed on—for the most part—then continue with my very own little PSA. After all, it's my show, my rules. "All individuals who enter agree Clover will only be treated with the utmost respect, like the lady she is." I continue to ramble like I'm one of the voice-overs in a new drug commercial. "If anyone so much as lays a hand or even thinks about laying a hand on her, Uncle Tony will take you down to the butcher shop and serve you as their daily special. Have fun and good luck."

"What the fuck, man?" Owen bursts through the door as soon as the light goes off. "Are you trying to end this promo before it even starts?"

"You're setting her up to fucking fail. You know that, right? These men—no, vultures—don't care what that interview said. They are predators preying upon the girl who blurted out she wanted to be a whore on the fucking number one talk show in America."

"Number two," Owen correct. "Remember, that's why we're doing this."

"I could care less. These ratings teeter back and forth." I stand and gather my things. "Our only competition is two crazy guys who just so happen to make news funny. Come on, Owen, what's the big deal? I don't see their bald heads on buses. I see this." I circle my face. "This is our money maker, not getting Clover laid."

"Arrogant asshole," Owen mumbles.

"I heard that." I try to walk past him, but the fucker grabs my arm.

"I meant for you to. Listen, Austin, I won't let anything happen to her, but you know as well as I do we need to hold the top spot to keep your face on those buses."

He's right. We haven't had a problem holding the spot, but with everything that's going on in the world, these guys have tons of material to work with. Killing it daily. People want humor, they want to laugh. I also know with long-running dating shows like *The Bachelor* and *The Bachelorette*, viewers want the perfect fairy tale. Who cares if it's the network controlling their every move? They want the illusion.

"I know." I pull away and walk out the door. "It's why I agreed to this."

"You know!" Owen calls after me. "It doesn't matter how closely you orchestrate this, Clover is a big girl who will make her own decisions in the end."

"Goodbye, Owen." I raise my hand in a one-finger salute, not bothering to look back.

I'm not sure why I'm bothered by all of this. Maybe it's because I feel responsible for her misery in the first place. She asked me what I thought of Jeffery, and I told her I thought he was a cool dude. Why? Because I'm a fucking asshole who was more worried about banging the student teacher than telling my friend her new boyfriend sucked ass. In my defense, I thought I had time. How was I supposed to know that night was *the* night? After that happened, it was damned if I do, damned if I don't. So, I chose the don't and made sure she was protected from afar. Well, for the most part. I had no way of knowing he was sleeping with Angel.

"Good evening, sir." Thomas startles me, freeing me from my guilt trip.

"It will be." I wink, clap my driver on the shoulder, and climb in.

"Are plans still a go?"

"They are, Thomas. Thank you." I pull out my phone to see if Sexy Sierra has sent any more pics.

None.

"Very well." Thomas closes the door, rounds the vehicle, and gets in. "We shall arrive at your destination in twenty minutes."

I just nod. It's all I have in me. I'm going to need every single one of those minutes to switch gears. Everything that's happened in the last thirty-six hours was totally unexpected. From Clover walking off the elevator, to seeing her naked, to her deciding to be a whore, to prostituting her out to gain ratings. It's been a lot to take in.

"Fuck." I run my hands over my face.

"Everything okay, sir?" Thomas eyes me from the rearview mirror.

"Yeah, long day."

Just as I'm about to text Sierra to let her know I'll be there soon, my phone buzzes with a text from Clover.

Clover: Black or red?

Me: Are you taking one of those magazine quizzes again?

Clover: Jeez, Austin. I'm not in high school anymore.

Me: Fine. Black.

Clover: Thanks.

Clover: Short or long?

Me: Liar! It's a Buzzfeed quiz.

Clover: LOL Nope. Just answer the question.

Me: This one is difficult. Are we talking hair or dress?

Clover: Does it matter?

Hell yes, it matters. I love long hair and short dresses, but she doesn't give me time to answer.

Clover: Fine. Dress.

Me: Short.

Me: What is this for?

Clover doesn't answer me for what seems like forever, but in reality, it's probably only been a minute.

Clover: Just a couple more questions. I'll make it quick. I promise.

Clover: Pinky promise.

I chuckle at the text. If Clover Kelley pinky promises, she means every word she's saying.

Me: You still didn't answer me.

Clover: Hold your horses.

Clover: Okay, leather or lace?

What the hell?

I quickly dial Clover's number, but she sends me to voicemail.

Me: Did you just VM me?

Clover: Answer the question.

Clover: This one is tricky. Thong? Boy shorts? Commando?

No! Just no!

I dial her number, and she finally answers, "Hey, Austin?"

"What the fuck, Clover? Care to tell me what this quiz is really about?" I bite back.

"Seriously? You're getting mad at me for asking you a few questions?" Clover lowers her voice.

"Is someone there? Do you have a guy in the apartment?" I find myself suddenly getting…what? Jealous? Angry? Hell, I don't know what I'm getting, but I'm pretty sure I'm irritated as fuck. "I honestly didn't think you were taking the whore role seriously." I say the words, instantly regretting them. "Listen, I'm—"

"Fuck you, Austin. CJ and your sister are here giving me advice on what I should and shouldn't wear. One is saying leather, the other lace, and honestly, I thought why not get your advice since you are a gorgeous guy who sleeps with a lot of women. I thought maybe you could tell me what men find attractive so maybe I won't feel like a total reject on my dates." Clover's voice falters toward the end which means only one thing: I made her cry.

"Clover, I'm sorry. This whole Hotline Hookup thing you're doing is fucking with my head," I admit.

"It is?" She sniffles.

"Yeah, Clo, it is. You're like a sister to me and my gut instinct says to protect."

"Oh." She sighs.

"I know this is going to sound totally lame, but it's not about what you're wearing, it's how you project yourself while wearing it. So, find something that makes you comfortable and confident. If that's a thong, so be it, but I'm pegging you for a soft pink shelf bra and matching sheer boy shorts kind of girl."

Why me, God? Why?

Not only have I seen her naked, I just described what lingerie I thought she should wear, but I'm a guy, who's horny, and now I've pictured that lingerie on the naked body I've been trying to get out of mind.

Like a sister? Yeah, right!

"Thanks, Austin!"

"Gettin' kinky wit it," CJ and Mal sing in the background, and Clover gasps. "Na-na-na-na-na-na-nana. *Clover's* gettin' kinky wit it."

"What's that noise?" I hear a buzzing in the background. "Is that?"

"Um…hey—I've got to go." Clover giggles, telling them to stop before she ends the call.

"Well, that was fucked up," I say out loud, throwing my phone in the seat.

"Excuse me, sir?" Thomas judges me from the rearview mirror. It's almost as if he already knows what I'm about it say.

"Thomas, do you have plans tonight?" I pick my cell back up and hover over Sierra's name.

"No, sir."

Even if Thomas doesn't accept my offer, I can't go see Sierra. Hopefully, I don't rack up douche points for canceling via text.

Me: Hey, beautiful, I'm going to need a raincheck.

Sexy Sierra: Is the doctor under the weather?

Me: Something like that.

Sexy Sierra: Is there anything I can do to make you feel better? <devil emoji>

Me: Not tonight. Maybe another time?

Sexy Sierra: Don't be a stranger. xoxo

Me: TTYL

I should feel bad, but I had all day to think about this. I'm not a jerk for canceling. Sierra has had my number all this time, she could have called or texted, but she chose not to. Maybe because she thinks I'm a dick, a player, or maybe because she didn't enjoy herself. Nah, she definitely enjoyed herself. Over and over and over again.

"Austin, is something wrong?" Thomas adjusts the mirror and uses my name—something he only does when it's time to get real.

"Nope. Just a change of plans. How about dinner?"

Thomas flips his blinker. "Where to, sir?"

"Anywhere but home."

Thomas sure does know how to throw down those pints. By the end of the night, I was personally calling in a favor to have the car delivered to Thomas's garage and a taxi to get us both home.

Now, here I am, barely standing straight, fiddling with the keycard, trying to get into my own home when a loud siren goes off.

When did I get an alarm system?

"Intruder! Balk! Balk! Intruder!" the alarm repeats.

"Cloooooover!" I holler for my new roommate, who apparently got us an alarm system without asking me. "Clo—"

"What in the world?" Clover comes running out of her room, cursing the bright lights. "Are you drunk?"

"Maybe?" I sway a little.

"Intruder! Balk! Balk! Intruder!" The screeching of the alarm is like needles to my eardrums. The longer it continues, the more the room spins.

"Make it stop!" I cover my ears.

"Kramer, cage!" Clover hollers.

"Kramer?"

"How much did you have to drink?" Clover is now standing in front of me, hands on her hips, her robe gaping open.

"Enough to do this." I tug at the opening. "Did you go with black or red?"

"Stop it!" Clover slaps my hand away just as something comes flying by my face.

"Damn, Clo. No need to throw things." I take a step back when that something lands on my head.

"Poop! Poop! Poop!" someone chants, followed by a soft, moist sliding sound.

"Austin, don't move. Kramer is on your head." Clover takes a step forward, holding out her arm. "Kramer, down."

"Oh my God!" I screech like a fucking schoolgirl. "Did that fucker shit on my head?"

"Poop! Poop! Poop!" the fucking bird taunts.

Then there's an explosive blast, but oddly enough, I don't feel a thing.

"Get him off of me!" I scream, shooing him off.

Clover screams.

Kramer pecks my hand.

Next thing I know, I'm on the floor lying face up, Kramer is in his cage, and Clover is standing over me, still in her robe, still gaping open, and this time, I can see her panties.

"I see you stuck with your granny panties." I wink. "It's not exactly my thing, but your ass," I reach my fingers up and kiss the tips, "muah! Perfection."

Clover gasps, taking a step back, stumbling. "Why do you have to be such an asshole when you're drunk?"

"Wait?" I lean up on my elbows. "You stumbled. Are *you* drunk?" I turn it around on her to buy myself a little time to gain my composure.

"Uh…we had a couple bottles of Pinot," Clover finally admits. "And maybe a bottle of Sauvignon Blanc we found in your cabinet.

"Clover, that was a three-thousand-dollar gift from the station."

"I didn't know." She throws her hands over her mouth.

"I'm just kidding. I don't know where it came from." I belt out a laugh and finally stand up.

"Asshole."

"Speaking of which." I pat the top of my head. "Did your bird shit in my hair?"

"Kramer?"

"Do you have another bird around here?" I scan the room.

"Hardy-har. Kramer's potty trained." She walks over to the cage and covers it up. "That was his way of calling you a shithead." Clover's lips tilt up in a slow smile. "Kind of funny when you think about it."

"How in the hell do you potty train a bird? Does he use a litterbox?" I smirk, proud of my statement. Pretty hilarious if I do say so myself.

"Jesus, Austin—he's not a cat. Kramer goes in his cage. So, if you hear him scream poop, get him in there pronto."

"How was I supposed to know? He freaking barks like a dog, so why not piss like a cat?" I steady myself against the wall.

"Austin, that's so absurd." Clover walks by and slaps me on the shoulder.

"Hey!" I whine, rubbing the area. "I think you're missing the point. Kramer, who is supposedly potty trained, could have shit on me."

"Well, maybe—but he didn't." Clover shrugs as she slides the cover over the cage.

"What are you doing? Putting him in time-out? Because I happen to think that's a brilliant idea." I mentally pat myself on the back. I would make an exceptional bird parent. "I mean, running around all hours of the night, dodging humans, calling them names—he's old enough to know better."

"Go to bed, Austin." Clover comes up behind me, turns me around, and gives me a big push toward my bedroom. "Now."

"But—" I swing around and run right into Clover. "Ouch! You're like the night ninja, always lurking in corners."

"Jeez, Austin, Kramer is not a cat, nor a dog, and I'm not a ninja." She narrows her eyes and scrunches up her nose.

"Fine. No ninja cats here, but I do need to lock up." I wave my hand around the room like it's some kind of magical wand. "Hey, what's that movie with the fine as hell fairy who grants an online sex operator a night of all her desires?"

"What?" Clover locks the door as I stand here and wrack my brain.

"You know, she says, 'Bippity—Boppity—Boobs,' and then her tits grow the size of melons!"

"You're talking about Cinderella, who is basically a slave to her stepmother, and the fairy godmother grants wishes, not breasts."

"Not the cartoon. I'm talking the porn—*Cyber Ella*!"

"What does this have to do with locking up?" Clover walks over to turn off the lights.

"I don't remember." I stand there puzzled as a pair of panties hit me in the face, followed by a bra at my feet. "Clo, did I just die?"

"Oh shit!" She rushes around the room, picking things up off the floor. "I'm so sorry. CJ and Mal were going through my things, and, well, they got a little carried away throwing my undergarments over their shoulders as they were searching for something that would be suitable for my dates."

"Well…this," I pick the white cotton bikini briefs off my face and take a big whiff, "isn't lace or leather."

"Oh my God! Did you just sniff my panties?" Clover stands there, her hands full of bras, a grotesque look on her face.

"I'm a man, and this," I hold the piece of fabric from my fingertips, "fell from the sky. What was I supposed to do?"

"Not sniff them." She runs over, snagging them and the others that fell at my feet. "Let's just go to bed and forget about this. Okay?"

"Pinky promise." I hold out my little finger.

"Ugh!" She stops toward her room.

I may not remember this tomorrow, but my dick has other plans, which means getting drunk was a waste of a hangover.

Living with Clover Kelley is going to be the death of me. She may be my friend, but she is my friend with a smokin' hot bod who doesn't have a clue. My current situation is every man's fantasy and my nightmare.

CHAPTER NINE

CLOVER

I can't believe how fast this week has flown by. I closed on two houses, managed to survive a shopping trip, get a mani-pedi, and reluctantly waxed the lady bits, which hurt worse than that stupid four-leaf clover hip tattoo I got during spring break my senior year of college.

The good news? Forty-eight hours later, the pain is gone, and…well—the bits—are a bit tingly. However, this girl isn't going to complain—at least, *not anymore.*

"Can you believe tonight is the night?" Mal gushes.

"I can." CJ sits back in her seat, pulls out a bottle of champagne, and pours each of us a glass. "I think after the week we had with this chick," she hands me a flute and passes another to Mal, "we *all* deserve to enjoy this ride and have a little bubbly."

"Here, here." Mal tips her glass toward ours. "Clover Kelley, you look absolutely stunning. May tonight be the fresh start you were looking for."

"And the perfect orgasm!" CJ chimes in.

"Now *that* I will drink to." I clink their glasses. "Cheers, ladies."

"Cheers," they repeat.

Lifting the glass, I let the bubbles tickle my lips and drain every last drop.

"Whoa there." CJ reaches for the flute and fills it up again. "I'm guessing you need another one of these."

"I do." Mal smiles.

"Um, no," she mumbles. "Lightweight."

"I can hear you."

"Here you go, Clo." CJ passes me the champagne, and this time, I savor the sweetness. "Drink. This will loosen you up a little."

"I don't know what's wrong with me." I twist in my seat and watch the people we pass wondering if any of the men are walking to the studio. Are they coming to see me? Do I even want them to?

"It's nerves. It's totally normal," Mal tries to reassure me.

I stare at my two friends who have hopped on this crazy train with me. "I thought this was what I wanted."

"Clo, you know what you want, you just have to speak it to believe it." CJ pulls me in for a hug. "I think you have always known, you've just ignored it."

"Really?" I give her a squeeze back.

"Yes, really." She pats my head. "Now, get off me. That's enough emotional BS for now."

Sitting up, I raise an eyebrow. "You liked it."

"She did," Mal agrees.

CJ purses her lips while tilting her head to the side trying to decide if we're right or wrong. "Mmm…maybe."

"You know what, Ceej?" I examine her from head to toe. "You look incredible. Who knew an old vintage Run DMC shirt could be dressed up with black leather pants and red heels?"

"Don't forget the jewelry and red lips." Mal puts in her two cents.

"Yeah! What's the occasion?" I fluff up her hair that's been blown out and straightened for an edgier look. "Do you have a date after this?"

"I don't date." CJ begins to twist her hands.

That's weird. She doesn't usually get nervous about anything.

"Plus, there is going to be fifty men filling that studio, and you are only going to pick four. You may call it sloppy seconds, but is it really if you never got sloppy in the first place?" CJ bats her eyelashes over the rim of her champagne-filled glass, satisfied with her answer.

"Speaking of which…" I place my hand over my stomach, "my nerves are getting to me. Big time."

"Oh boy! Someone having anxious ass leak? Fluttering flatulence? Or maybe the shivery shits?" CJ seems concerned, rubbing my back. "It's going to be okay."

I just stare at her.

Mal snorts a laugh.

I twist around in my seat and really look at my friend. As crazy as she seems, her love for us is even crazier. I couldn't have asked for anyone better to be by my side tonight. CJ Collins says all the wrong things at the right times. "You're crazy."

"Thanks, sweets." Ceej pats me on the leg. "I love you too."

"We're here!" Mal scoots closer to the window. "Holy cow! They have a red carpet for you."

"What?" I peer out the window. "Why would they do that? We didn't discuss this."

CJ moves between us. "Look! Paparazzi." She starts to roll down the window.

"No!" I yell, jerking her hand away. "I need to call Austin."

"No need." Mal points to Austin easing his way down the red material with so much swagger.

"I'm sure he's loving this," I say to no one in particular.

Austin was made to be in the limelight. He talks the part, and now, he looks it, wearing some kind of black designer button-down shirt with his sleeves rolled up, gray tailored slacks, and black Armani leather dress shoes.

He's exactly the man you see plastered on buses and billboards. His unruly dark hair is slicked back, emerald eyes shining with flecks of yellow and blues, perfect white teeth and olive skin—these are just some of his natural accessories that make his six-foot-two frame of lean muscle stand out. Austin is oozing confidence.

I just wish I was.

The door opens. "Ladies," Austin greets us. "Clover." He offers his hand as the corner of his lips curve up. "You ready to get your whore on?"

I let out a groan. "I'm never going to live this down, am I?" I ask, placing my hand in his.

Helping me out, I make sure to keep my knees in as I stand. That's all I need is for someone to get a shot of my goods. It's not like I'm a famous celebrity or anything, but the attention I have been receiving lately sure does feel like it.

Austin whistles out.

"What?" I look around, waiting for someone to come from behind me.

"Clover, you look…" he lowers his mouth to my ear, whispering. His clean, woodsy scent invades my senses, making me weak in the knees. "So—damn—beautiful."

For a minute, I let myself get wrapped up in everything Dr. Feelgood, but the man standing next to me isn't him. He's just Austin Montgomery, my best friend, my go-to guy, my protector—not my date. No matter how good he looks or how yummy he smiles.

A shiver runs down my spine. I shake it off and manage a reply. "Why thank you."

Austin offers me his arm. "You ready to do this?"

Wrapping my arm through his, I lean in. "Can you believe I went from getting dumped to speed-dating fifty guys for a possible Hotline Hookup? How crazy is this?"

Austin growls. "You know how I feel about this, but I'm not going to ruin your night by trying to talk you out of it on the red carpet entrance." Austin turns us toward the crowd and lowers his voice. "Smile, hand on hip, leg out, arch back."

With the biggest smile on my face, teeth clenched, I managed to get out. "This sucks."

"Turn," he demands.

I follow his lead.

"Almost done," Austin whispers into my hair as he rubs circles on my lower back, calming my nerves.

Even though this entrance seems pretty big, the one where we actually walk through the doors is going to be huge and all eyes will be on Clover Kelley.

"Okay, Clo. There's no turning back once we open those doors," he warns, as if he's hoping I kick off my heels and run.

I let go of Austin and take a step forward, unsure of what will happen, but ready for a change.

A new look.

A new attitude.

A new *plan.*

"Clover?" Austin steps up behind me. "You don't have to do this…"

That's my cue.

I place my hands on the glass and push my way through double doors. "I want to."

CHAPTER TEN

AUSTIN

"Austin, my man!" Owen hollers from the station table where the contestants are still signing in.

"This turnout is crazy." I walk over and clasp his hand while Owen pulls me in for a bro-hug.

"Corporate is going to eat this shit up." Owen steps back and does a quick live stream for our social media account. "What do you think?" Owen zooms in on Clover. "Four of New York's finest will get to land a date with this hot chick right here." He turns the camera on me. "This wouldn't be possible without this guy, Hotline Hookup's very own Dr. Feelgood."

"What's up, New York." I give the camera a nod.

"If you want to follow Clover on her mission to get lucky, head on over to our website. The link is in the comments." Owen ends the live feed and tucks his phone in his back pocket. "Austin, this is going to catapult Hotline Hookup to the top!" Owen pauses, getting one of those lightbulb moment looks. "We should make this a regular segment."

"Whoa! That is where I'm going to have to step in. This is a one-time thing, and honestly, it should be a no-time thing. Clover may act like she's ready for this, but she is nowhere close."

"Her outfit says differently." Owen scans the audience to where Clover is with CJ and Mal eyeing up the contestants.

I open my mouth to defend my statement, but how can I? Damn if she doesn't look stunning in her red lace camisole and black leather miniskirt. Clover seems confident and ready to do this—a far cry from the girl trembling on my arm moments ago.

"See?" Owen pats my back. "She's even left Dr. Feelgood speechless."

"I-I'm…" I clear my throat and point in her direction. "I'm just going to see if she needs anything."

"You do that. I'm going to help get the rest of these guys signed in so we can get started." Owen grabs a seat and hollers for the next one in line.

Pushing my way through the crowd, I eavesdrop on what these douches are saying.

"Have you seen that skirt?"

"I would like to bend that ass over."

"Those tits."

"Do you think she likes Star Wars?"

Fuck! This place is filled with horny assholes. I wish I could blame it on the crowd we drew in, but honestly, they're men. If they aren't saying it, they're sure as hell thinking it. Now, this last guy seems harmless. But since he's here to compete for a date with Clover and has Star Wars on the brain, I'm willing to bet his mind is more on Yoda and Princess Leia than her—not cool.

"Austin!" Clover hollers over the crowd.

"Hey." I climb a few steps to get to the girls who are watching the guys from the balcony. "Are you ladies ready for this?"

"Hells yeah!" CJ high-fives me. "Let's do this!"

"I'm just here for moral support." Mal seems less enthused.

"Well, looks like someone is pumped." I laugh, wrapping my arm around Clover's waist and turning us around.

"What's going on?" Clover bites her bottom lip.

"I just want to make sure this is for sure what you want to do."

"Actually, I'm kind of excited." She nods. "Scared, but excited."

"You have no reason to be scared. Owen and I will be working the room, plus we have security ready to step in just in case."

"No, I'm not scared of them." Clover glances over the railing at the men sizing each other up. "I'm scared I won't be enough for them. What if they don't like me?"

"Clover…" I try to get her attention, but the swarming of dudes below has her distracted. "Clover," I reach around and cup her cheek, "look at me."

She does.

"You are more than any of those bastards deserve."

She smiles.

"Not only are you incredibly smart, kind, and one of the coolest chicks I know, but you are also the hottest chick in this room."

She smacks my chest and belts out a laugh. "It's because there are only three of us and one is your sister and the other one freaks you out."

"Don't sell yourself short. Look at you." I grab a hold of her hand and give her a quick twirl.

"Austin!" Clover tries to hide her giggle.

"Leather and lace. Your outfit alone is enough for any of these fools to get drunk off of."

Clover drops my hand and begins to tug on her way too short skirt. "I'm not sure, Austin. This isn't me."

"How does it make you feel?"

"Oh no! Don't you Dr. Feelgood me." Clover backs away, waving me off.

Throwing my head back, I let a laugh escape. "Come here." I reach out and pull her back in. "You aren't going to hide behind your insecurities."

"Fine." She crosses her arms, tapping her foot. "I kind of feel sexy. I never thought I could pull off this look."

I can't contain my feelings. She may be just a friend, but she's also my hot friend whose ass just so happens to look fucking perfect in that tight as hell leather skirt.

Biting my lip, I let out a whistle. "I still think you're a pale pink girl, but this role-playing thing suits you." I wink.

"That's a good thing?" She still questions me after I basically confess my attraction to her. Lord, this girl is clueless when it comes to her appearance.

"A very good thing, Clover." I smile.

"Thank you, Austin." She stretches on her tiptoes and kisses my cheek.

I reach up to wipe the lipstick off. "For what?"

"Don't worry. It doesn't come off." Clover puckers, then flashes me a cheesy-ass grin. "But seriously, thank you for always supporting me."

Reaching down, I grab a hold of her hand and give it a little squeeze. "Always. Hey, I have a question." I bring her hand up and clasp it between my two. "I think you should have a safe word for tonight."

"What?" Clover's eyes go wide.

"You know, something simple, like pineapple, porcupine, jalapeno."

"Austin, I know what a safe word is for." She narrows her eyes. "But why do *I* need one?"

"In case two minutes ends up being too long." I lean over the glass edge and scan the crowd. "I guarantee you one of these guys," I wave my hand around, "has some kind of toe fetish, picks their nose, or tries to get handsy. If that's the case, you should say your safe word."

"And what? Scream pineapple and security will come running?"

"What?" I whip my head around, laughing.

"I'm not shouting a safe word," Clover demands, her arms crossed over her chest.

"Of course you wouldn't." I signal to Owen coming up the stairs. "Explain the safe word," I holler out.

"Ahhh! The safe word." He chuckles. "That's this asshole's idea, but I have to say, it's a good one." Owen hands Clover a folder. "This has the profiles of every single guy in here. They are in numerical order." Owen hands me the mic pack while he explains the earpiece to Clover. "This is your ears. Austin will give you their names and three fun facts on the interest form they filled out to keep convo going."

"So, Austin will be able to eavesdrop on all my dates?" Clover eyes me.

I flash her an evil grin.

"Of course not."

"I won't?"

"No, Austin, you won't." Owen takes the mic pack.

Clover sticks out her tongue.

"This is your voice. If you need anything at all, use your safe word and someone will be there," Owen assures her. "I think the best place to hook this up is in back." Owen turns Clover around. "Just lift up your shirt a tad and I'll place this belt around you."

"Okay." Clover lifts her arms and lets Owen install the mic. "So, what should I use as a safe word?"

"Did someone say safe word?" CJ butts in.

"Here we go," Clover says, looking over her shoulder.

"This just so happens to be my area of expertise." CJ begins to count them out on her finger. "Sassafras, pumpernickel, Armageddon, and my favorite, Justin Bieber."

"Justin Bieber?" We all look at each other.

"Um, yeah! Wouldn't you stop what you were doing if someone screamed out Justin Bieber?" CJ gets a serious look on her face. "However, I don't suggest that one if you are role-playing. Hashtag just sayin'. Hashtag Bieber Fever. Hashtag TMI."

"Um, how about a favorite number, color, something you hate…?" Owen rambles on.

"Borrrrrrinnnnnng!" CJ fake yawns. "That's almost as bad as using a fruit, or hell, even the word safe word. That's equivalent to using password as your password. It's not advised."

"I can't believe I'm saying this, but I agree on this one." I throw my thumb in CJ's direction.

"You," Clover points to me, "don't get to agree with her. And you," Clover lowers her arms and turns around, "I would ask you how you know all this, but it's almost time to start and I don't have time to Google it." Clover holds out her phone. "Speaking of which, can one of you hold my phone?"

"Sure, Clo." CJ holds out her hand.

"Where are you going to put it?" Clover eyes her friend.

"In my bra!" CJ cups her right tit. "Mine's in my left. It will be like our phones are twins while hanging with the twins."

"No thank you." Clover pulls back. "Boob sweat is not covered under insurance."

Fuck, CJ has overrun this conversation. I came up here to see if Clover was doing okay and now we're discussing sex lives and boob sweat. Not my cup of whiskey.

"You guys are fucking nuts," Owen says, straightening her mic pack and pulling her shirt down into place.

"I think this train has derailed."

"Agreed, man." Owen backs me up. "We need to get this show on the road."

"Okay, Clo." I clasp her shoulders and look her in the eye. "Last chance."

"Man, we've talked about this," Owen complains.

Clover looks over my shoulder.

"Back here, Clo." I angle my head till we are eye to eye again. "You are one hundred percent sure you're all in?"

"I am." Clover's answer is quick and slightly hesitant.

"Okay. Well, if that's the case, I'll hold your phone." I reach between us and grab her cell, sticking it in my back pocket. "And you need to give us your safe word."

"How about seven?" She purses her lips. "It's my lucky number."

"Of course it is," I mumble.

"Seven it is." Owen glances down at his watch. "It's almost go time. Let's move."

"So soon?" Clover begins to fidget.

"Finally!" CJ pulls on Mal's arm. "Let's get into position."

"Wait." Mal breaks free and hands Clover a tube of lipstick or something. "Just in case you need to touch up."

"Thanks, guys." Clover hugs Mal and waves at CJ.

"Don't worry. We'll be where you can see us." My sister gives her a squeeze before Owen rushes them off.

"Austin, fill her in on the rules." Owen scans his phone. "The tweets are coming in from the contestants." He flips the screen around so I can see. "Hashtag 'unluckyinlove' is trending."

"Wait? I'm trending?" Clover pulls on Owen's arm so she can get a better look.

"Yeah, you are." I let out a deep breath. "Which is why we need to go over these rules."

"Yeah, you do that." Owen dials a number. "Showtime in five."

"Austin…" Clovers begins to bounce from foot to foot. "I feel like I'm going to be sick."

"You're not."

I want nothing more than to agree and tell Clover to run in the other direction—tell her this thing she's trying to find isn't down there. CJ and Mal have painted this picture of how great single life is, but it's not. Hell, I'm living proof of that.

Sure, I have my fun, but nothing worthwhile. Those women could care less about Austin Montgomery. They want Dr. Feelgood.

But you can't tell someone what they think they want isn't what they need because that will make them want it even more. So, you ride it out. Let them make their mistakes and be there to help them pick up the pieces. Just like I did with her ex. I knew he was a douche, but how do you tell a girl, who is stuck in her own make-believe fairy tale, it's never going to come true.

You don't.

"It's normal to feel this way. There are fifty guys vying for your attention."

"Oh my God! What am I doing?" Clover begins to panic. Her chest rises and falls as her breathing becomes rapid.

"Clover." I reach for her hands. "You are doing exactly what Clover Kelly wants to do. You are going to shake this off and go down there and flirt your sexy little ass off." I shake her arms a little, trying to ease the nerves.

She closes her eyes and smiles. "Wait!" They quickly open. "You think I'm sexy?"

"How many times do I have to tell you? You look fucking hot tonight!"

Too fucking hot!

"You're right. I look good, and those guys down there are here for me. I'm in control. I make the decisions. I decide who I want to go on the date with." Clover talks her own self down.

"Speaking of which." I notice the time. "I have exactly two minutes to explain this to you and get you in position."

"Let's do this. I'm all ears."

"Okay! You have the folder. Save it for later because I'm going to be in your ear telling you who is next and what their interests are."

"Got it," Clover agrees.

"You will see each contestant for two minutes. After you meet with all fifty, you will then choose ten you want to have more one-on-one time with. We will give you five minutes with each guy."

"It doesn't seem like much time." Clover worries her bottom lip. "What if I can't choose?"

"Trust me, two minutes is enough time for these douches to show their true colors."

"Austin!" Clover gasps.

"What?" I hold up my arms. "It's true."

"What if I need a break?"

"Five minutes every ten people. So, every twenty minutes or so." I pull out my sheet to make sure I'm right. "Yup, every ten contestants."

"Okay. That works."

"Do I have to choose the top four tonight?" Clover opens the folder and flips the pages. "Because that is a lot of pressure."

"How about you take your cell and keep notes?" I fish it out of my back pocket and hand it over. "Start a list."

"We are on a schedule. Won't this throw it off?"

I shrug. "If you think about it, this is your show. Your rules."

"Huh…I never thought of it that way." She pulls up her notes on the screen and begins to prep.

"Well, start thinking about it. You don't *ever* have to do anything you don't want to do. Make the demands you want."

"Austin, I think I'm ready," Clover speaks up, her voice stronger and more confident than before. "I'm still a little nervous, but knowing you're in my ear makes this process so much easier."

"Awww, someone getting a little sentimental?" I tease.

Clover intertwines her arm in mine. "All right then." We begin to walk. "Let's get me lucky."

"Not so fast." I pull her in closer. "First, let's just get you a date."

CHAPTER ELEVEN

CLOVER

This is *really* happening. I'm finally putting myself out there in the dating world…*again*. It's been over six years since I've cared about what another man thought, let alone fifty of them. Now, I have a hundred eyes on me. I have to say, my nerves are a little shot.

Fifty guys in a little over two hours—with breaks. That is totally doable. And me? Well, I'm hoping they think I'm doable as well. After all, that's my mission. Find the perfect orgasm, land the forever guy. Right?

I sure do hope so. The guy and the O should be a bundled package. Only makes sense. If one doesn't work, the other won't either.

Now, I'm standing in the center of the room with nowhere to hide. Only a cocktail tabletop stands between me and each date. Of course, that's my fault. They offered me a table with two chairs, but I have this thing with guys shorter than me when I'm in heels. Owen said they combed through all the men under five eleven, but people lie. It's not like I have something against shorter men, but when I fantasize about my dream guy, he's tall, dark, and extremely handsome.

Okay, I get it. It's just like every other girl out there. Same dream, wrong reality. According to CJ, we should blame Disney.

"Testing, one-two-three. Testing." Austin comes through my earpiece, interrupting my thoughts of possibly suing Disney for falsely advertising that dreams can come true if you kiss a frog.

I place my finger on the earpiece and lower my head to speak into the mic. "I hear you loud and clear."

Nothing.

"Testing, one-two-three. Testing," Austin repeats.

"I'm here."

"Clover, my little blonde friend, unmute the mic. It's on the remote on the table."

"Ohhh!" I see the little device sitting on the table. I thought it controlled one of the televisions lining the lobby. Tapping the little red button, I finally answer Austin. "I'm here."

"What's your safe word?"

"Seven."

"Good. Once Owen rings the bell, asshole number—"

"Austin," I warn.

"Fine. Contestant number one will walk over to the table and your date will begin. Then, as soon as the bell rings *again*, your date is over and the next one will begin in a matter of seconds," Austin explains once again. "Just remember you don't have to pick any of these bastards."

"I'm sure they aren't all like *you*, Austin." I turn around and search the stage area where Austin is sitting and flip him the bird. He stands and takes a bow, letting me know I won that round. Hopefully, it will be the last one, but with Austin in my ear, I'm assuming this isn't over. Not by a long shot.

As Owen takes the stage giving the guys their rules, I search for Mal and CJ in the cheering section they created for themselves. With all the clovers and hearts, it looks more like a St. Patty's Day celebration instead of Hotline Hookups version of the ~~Love~~ Lust Connection.

My friends may be a mess, but they are everything I need right now. CJ with all her crazy is the calm to my storm, and Mal is just Mal. She doesn't have to say much because her actions speak louder than her words. She's the sister I never had, and even though she's younger, she is wiser beyond her years.

Smiling at the two ladies sitting across the room, who refused to let me go through this alone, I hold up my hands and make a heart. Then quickly blow them a kiss letting them both know how thankful I am they're here.

Mal is about to do the same when CJ leans over, smacks her hand out of the way, and pretends to catch my kiss. She stands like she just won the world series, and shouts, "That's my ho!"

"Clover. You there?" Austin's in my ear.

"You see that I am." I turn back to the stage and hold out my hands. "Duh."

"Smart-ass. I didn't know if you had it muted or not because of the echo." Austin pauses. "Hold on." He covers his mic while Owen whispers something in his ear. I can't hear a thing, but Owen looks concerned and is pointing behind the stage.

"Is everything okay?" I ask as soon as Owen jumps off the stage behind them.

"Yeah, we're just down a dude. Apparently his girlfriend…"

"His *girlfriend*?" I cut in.

"Or his ex if you ask him, came barging in really upset about this whole thing."

"Oh my."

"Yeah—not cool. We decided to eliminate him from this round." Austin stands to make sure I can really see him and smiles his sexy as sin smile that has girls falling at his feet. Well, all of them but me. I'm immune to his charm. "Clo, you okay?"

I stand there looking at the man who cares more about me than his show. The same man who has been there through everything, from the time Justin Joliff pushed me down on the playground, to holding my hair back on my twenty-first birthday when I refused to listen and mixed all my drinks, to my boyfriend of six-years dumping me, to now—supporting me on my quest to find the perfect orgasm.

I really need to quit saying that or one of these guys will probably take me seriously. Luckily with the interview Austin had me do, it sounded less like me wanting to be a whore and more about a good girl looking for more adventure after six years with a boring fuddy-duddy.

Austin Montgomery might be a player, but if he ever finds the one, she will be one lucky lady. I just wish he would cut the Dr. Feelgood act and be who I know him to be—the man, on the stage, who cares more about me than anything else going on in this room.

"Yeah, I'm good." I grin. "Does that mean I get an extra break?"

Austin looks to the ceiling and belts out a laugh. "If we add in any more breaks, Owen will probably have a heart attack."

"Well, we don't want to do that. So, what do you say? You wanna get this show on the road?"

"Sure. I'm going to brief you on C-1, which is contestant one. As soon as you give me the thumbs-up, mute the mic, and Owen will send C-1 your way. Sound good?"

"Yep! Let's do this." I turn around and swipe my phone to life, bringing up the notes app. If anything stands out, I'm prepared to jot it down.

"C-1: Nick Reed—twenty-nine, fitness trainer, never been married, originally from California, loves to surf, moved to NYC after his online fitness/nutrition app took off on IG."

Okay, Nick Reed doesn't sound so bad on paper.

He's older, so he should know what he wants.

He's into fitness, which means we don't have to worry about stamina issues like Jeffery had. That's a huge plus.

He created a successful business from scratch, which means he knows how to work hard to get what he wants.

Sounds like a great start.

"Tell Owen I'm ready." I give Austin a thumbs-up and mute the mic.

CHAPTER TWELVE

CLOVER

It's go time.

Contestant #1

I can't even speak. The man walking toward me is one of the most beautiful men I've ever seen. And when I say beautiful, I mean this man is prettier than most women. He's so perfect, he has to be cut from the same cloth as Adonis.

A trim waist, thick shoulders, tan, bright eyes, and hair so perfect, I begin to wonder if he's even real.

I blink. *Nope. Still there.*

I blink again. *Nope. Almost to the table.*

Blink one last time.

"You must be Clover, Ms. Unlucky in Love." Adonis is now standing at my table, holding out his hand.

Oh Lord. He has manners.

"And you must be Nick." I place my hand in his, but instead of giving it a little squeeze or a quick handshake, he brings it up to his beautiful, thick, extremely kissable lips and lets his mouth linger on my skin as he properly greets me. "It's a pleasure to meet you."

I could get used to this.

I look over Nick's shoulder to see CJ standing there making an exploding motion with her hands over her lower frontal region—which can only mean one thing: ovary explosion.

Agreed, my friend.

"Well, Clover, now that I'm here, I can already tell two minutes isn't nearly enough time with you."

Swoon! I mentally fan myself. This man already has me falling at his feet and we haven't even gone on a date. His little comment has me agreeing that two minutes definitely won't be enough. Unless he screws up the next minute, he is for sure making it to the next round.

"I agree." I blush.

Idiot! Way to play hard to get. How about you just lie there and spread your legs on the table.

"So, Clover," Nick takes a step back and opens his arms, "I'm all yours. Ask me anything you want."

"Well," I stand there examining Nick as he settles back in at the table, hanging on my every word. "What made you apply?"

"Clover," Nick leans in, "I don't make it a habit of propositioning women I hear on the radio, but there was something about you."

"Oh, really?"

I know this is probably a line, but I wouldn't mind sending him through to find out. I mean, what if we do work out and we have great sex and we live…

Okay, I'm getting ahead of myself. Time to slow it down.

"Yeah." Nick nods. "You put yourself out there in the most vulnerable way possible and that speaks volume about your character."

I want to ask him a million questions about said character, but I don't. We are down to the wire and I have a lot more to find out.

"Well, thank you."

"You're welcome." He gives me the sexiest grin. Pearly whites and all.

"So, if you made it through to the next round, where would you take me on a date?"

This is the million-dollar question. Please be the right answer.

"There are so many adventures we could go on, but honestly, I'm going to treat you to a nice dinner and a movie. The classic date."

Interesting.

"Well, you can't go wrong there."

I can't stop smiling. This man has me crushing on him hard. Like I'm one step away from giggling and agreeing with every word he says.

"You can't. The first date is crucial. Why make it awkward by planning something you don't even know she would like? Stick with dinner—a quiet nice restaurant so you can hear each other talk."

"That sounds good, but the movie? That's a little too quiet, don't you think?"

"Not at all. If dinner goes well and you have everything to talk about, then a movie should complement it perfectly. There is nothing better than sitting next to someone for almost two hours," Nick reaches out and runs his fingertips over mine. "Brushing hands while reaching for the popcorn, snuggling close when she's a little frightened." He winks.

I giggle. Like a silly schoolgirl. So much for keeping her inside.

"Or laughing together during a funny moment." He smiles. "You have a nice one."

"What's that?"

"Laugh."

"Oh."

"You know what the best part about the movie is?" Nick pulls his hand back and straightens—a sign he knows our time is almost up. "Just sitting next to someone you connect with. No words are needed to fill the silence. You just know being there is enough."

"Wow. I've never thought of it like that."

Jeffery hated to go to the movies because of how crowded they were, and when we were at home, he would spend most of the time on his phone. That should have been a major clue right there. We didn't know how to communicate.

"I have a feeling we would be the best silent partners." Nick's lips curl into a smile.

Oh my God! That smile will be my undoing. It's absolutely scrumptious. It's all I can do not to jump over this table, into his arms, and yell, *"We have a winner!"* as I devour those perfect, yummy, lickable lips.

But I can't. So I won't.

"We will have to wait," the bell chimes before I can finish, "to find out."

"Clover, it's been a pleasure." He takes my hand in his again and brushes his thumb over the top, sprinkling goose bumps over my body. "Hopefully this won't be the end."

"Hopefully not," I agree as Nick Reed turns and walks away.

If this is what every two minutes is going to be like, then I'm in trouble. Because Nick was on my yes list the moment his lips met mine. Well…my hand—same difference. Either way, he made parts of me tingle that haven't tingled in—well…*forever.*

"I hope that fucker is on the no list." Austin crashes my Nick high. "He was way too handsy with you."

"I thought it was on mute." I check the remote.

"I didn't have to hear. I have twenty-twenty vision. That guy was all over you from the moment he walked up to that table."

"If I'm going to do this. I can't have you going all big bro on me." I twist around so Austin can see me as I give him a dose of his own medicine. "He's not doing anything you haven't done before."

"Ouch, Clo." Austin fakes a stumble while grasping his chest. "That hurt deep."

"Oh, shut it and give me the details on contestant two."

"Fine."

Austin runs down the list, giving me all the details I need to interview the next one. Is that what it is I'm doing—*interviewing* them? I guess I hadn't thought of it that way.

Needless to say, the next string of contestants couldn't even touch Nick Reed and his charming personality, landing them all on the "hell no" list.

Contestant #2 — Video game champion. Enough said.

Contestant #6 — Went in to swipe his nose, then ran his finger over his lips. Pretty sure he is a secret booger eating ninja.

Contestant #8 — Wore Crocs with his khakis. Comfy…not cool.

"Austin!" I holler, and everyone turns, even Austin.

"If you're talking to me, you need to unmute it." He smirks.

"I want to wipe that smirk right off your face. Tell me, where in the hell did you find these guys?"

"We didn't find them anywhere. They found you." Austin goes on and on, reminding me of the process.

"It's break time." I stomp off to the bathroom. "I'm telling you, if the next one is like the last seven, we can skip the dating round and I'll just proclaim Nick the winner."

"Come on, Clo. What's that sayin' you girls like?"

"There are no sayings for this fiasco," I spit back.

I'm fuming. This whole dating thing is a joke. Background checks my ass. Hotline Hookup is no different than those singing talent shows or whatever they are that have those crappy contestants on for all the world to laugh at. For what? *Ratings*!

"Yes, there is." Austin uses his singsong voice to irritate me—to prove he's right when he's finding this just as amusing as everyone else. "Sometimes you have to kiss a lot of frogs to meet your Prince Charming."

I lift the neck of my shirt up to my mouth and whisper very loudly into the mic, "Fuck Prince Charming."

"Whoa! Clover Kelly, breaking out the F-bomb."

"Austin," I warn.

"Lighten up. You're just frustrated. I get it."

"Do you?" I ask as I walk into the ladies' room and lock myself into a stall. "I feel like this is all fun and games for you."

"You know what? You have two minutes to make it back to that table. Make sure you're there." I hear a slam.

"Austin?" He doesn't answer. "Austin, are you there?"

Maybe I took it a little too far. After all, this wasn't Austin's idea. Actually, he's tried to stop it on more than one occasion. I guess it's true what they say, you take things out on the ones you care about the most, making me less of a goody-two-shoes and more of a dick.

Wonderful!

"Just in time." Austin's voice is low and back in my ear.

"I thought you were mad at me." I look over in his direction as I walk across the floor.

"I needed a minute."

"Yeah. Just taking a minute to go to the bathroom helped me. I felt like I was suffocating in here."

"Speaking of which, next time you go to the bathroom, could you please mute me? I'm pretty sure I heard you poof."

Poof?

I jerk my head in his direction as I reach my table. "I thought I did mute you, and what do you mean *poof*?"

Austin chuckles.

"This isn't funny."

"Sure it is. You don't' know what a poof is."

"Fine. Tell me what a poof is because I'm certain I didn't do it." I tap my toe, annoyed at my friend who is supposed to be prepping me for number eleven, but instead, he chooses to discuss my bathroom breaks. I knew this mic thing was a bad idea.

"It's that little pocket of air that releases right before you go to the bathroom. You know, the moment where you think you may have to go number two, but once the pressure is relieved, all is good. That's a poof."

"Goodbye, Austin." I scrunch up my nose, turn around, and mute the guy.

"You know you can mute me, but I can still talk to you."

Don't turn around. Don't cave.

"Just admit it. You poofed."

I flip him off.

"Okay, fine, I get it. It's slightly embarrassing, but I'm your best friend, you can tell me. No one else has to know. How about you hold up one hand if you did poof and two hands if you didn't." Austin laughs that annoying laugh he does when he thinks he's funny. It almost sounds identical to seventh grade when his voice began to change.

I don't say a word. Instead, I raise two arms in the air and let the birds fly. I've been doing that a lot lately. It's one statement that will never get old.

"Fine. I'll leave you alone about it, but next time, mute me." Austin gets the last word in.

For now.

Austin prepped me for date eleven, which wasn't so bad, and then date twelve, which started off great, but every time I spoke, he narrowed his eyes like he was either annoyed or wanted to kill me.

> **Contestant #11** — Definite maybe. Comes from a great family, from the Midwest, and loves baseball.
>
> **Contestant #12** — Has serial killer eyes. Note to self: don't date unless you want to end up on an episode of *Dateline.*

Now, hopefully, number thirteen is a little luckier.

"C-13: Logan Long. Hmm…sounds like a porn name."

"You would know."

"Sorry, I couldn't help myself. He's twenty-eight and originally from Utah. Came here when a modeling agency signed him. He has forty-five tattoos and two piercings."

"Ears aren't so bad," I chime in. "You see it more and more."

"Really, that's it." I can hear Austin shuffling through papers. "Oh, wait! He's allergic to cats and bananas. Time's up. Good luck."

"Thanks. I'll need it." This time, I don't forget to mute it.

Contestant #13

"Wow!" Logan grins from ear to ear, his pearly whites sparkling like a toothpaste commercial. I didn't even know you could get teeth so white. "Look at you." Logan walks up to me, takes my hand, and twirls me around.

"Oh!" I laugh out nervously, the twirl a little unexpected.

"Mmm-mmm-mmm!" He brings his hand up to his chin while he checks me out. "I bet you taste like a juicy peach."

"What?" I scrunch up my face, unsure if I should be offended or take that as a compliment and let these next couple minutes turn R-rated.

"I'm sorry. I shouldn't have said that." Logan's cheeks turn beet red, burning hot with embarrassment. "I grew up a PK—aka preacher's kid—and after keeping all the forbidden thoughts up here for so long," he taps his temple, "I can't help but blurt out what I'm feeling. It feels good to be truthful."

"That, I can respect." I smile, still unsure what to think of the guy. Once I get past his smile, I have a chance to really check out Logan Long. He's well over six foot, lean muscle, long, dirty blond hair wrapped up in one hell of a sexy man-bun, and colorful tattoos peeking out under his nicely pressed gray dress shirt. It's as if he came straight from a photo shoot because this guy is runway ready.

"So, Clover, what can I do to get you to go out on a date with me?" Logan unties his hair and lets it fall down around his shoulders before he secures it back into place.

This man has better hair than me.

"Well, how about we get to know each other better and see what happens?"

"Ask away. I'm all yours," Logan crosses one arm over the other as he leans forward on the table.

"Okay, um, so you love tattoos. Tell me about some of them."

This gets his attention. I found a subject we can talk about. Win for me.

"Well, these…" he stands up and rolls up his right sleeve, "most of these are spiritual. Verses or symbols that have been imprinted on my soul. Reminds me of home." Logan then rolls up his left sleeve. "And this one I just started. I call it my sin sleeve."

"So, this one…" I reach out and run my fingers over a couple shot glasses with a poison symbol crossing over it.

"Ah! Yep. It's there to remind me of an evening I first had when I landed my modeling contract. Let's just say it's the celebration that almost ended my career before it even had a chance to start."

"I think we've all been there a time or two."

"What's yours?" Logan inquires.

"Mine?"

"Yeah, your celebration that went too far." Logan watches me as he rolls his sleeves back down.

"Well, on my twenty-first birthday, I got a little too tipsy and when my best friend helped me home, I almost kissed him," I admit for the first time ever. I was pretty drunk, but the next day, Austin never brought it up, so neither did I. Seemed like the right thing to do.

"Almost?" he pries.

"Yeah, almost. Luckily for our friendship, as I was leaning in, my stomach began to heave, and I had no choice but to quickly turn and empty everything I'd consumed that night into the parking lot."

"Eck." Logan makes a sour face, which is kind of cute. "Brutal."

"Agree."

"So, back to you. Your form said you have two piercings."

Hmm?

He must have let them close up because his ears are free of any holes, there's nothing in his nose, and his lip and tongue are also metal free.

"I was wondering if you had the balls to ask me about those." Logan winks. "Well, I had a barbell in my tongue, but I had to take it out a day after I signed up for this thing for some secret modeling project. The hole is still there, but it already started to close. I couldn't get it back in."

"Interesting."

"Don't worry, though, I still have another one that's for her pleasure as well." Logan leans in, and whispers, "It will give you that orgasm you're looking for."

"Excuse me?" I clear my throat.

Logan lowers his voices. "My cock is pierced. I can guarantee you I will hit the G-spot every damn time." He clicks his tongue.

"Oh!"

I'm not sure if I'm disgusted or turned on. On one hand, he basically admitted he is here to give me the orgasm I claimed I wanted, and on the other, he basically admitted he's here to give me the orgasm I need. Same difference, I just have to decide if he's the one I want to give it to me.

I'm not sure what to say or do, so I pick up my phone and glance down at the timer. Twenty more seconds.

"Clover, you choose me, and I promise, no more two minutes. I will set you on here and let you ride this bronco." Logan begins to pelvic thrust with every single word.

All. *Thrust.*

Night. *Thrust.*

Long. *Thrust.*

"Logan." I gasp and look around the room. My eyes land on CJ, who is mimicking everything Logan is doing. I can't help but burst out laughing.

"There's nothing funny about this, sweetheart. Logan Long can love you long time."

I want to stay straight-faced. I try. I really do, but with a comment like that, how can I? The laugh is right there, bubbling from deep inside my chest. I try to hold it in, but my muscles ache as they grow tight. The soon-to-be outburst is about to break like a busted water main. There's no stopping it. It's like a domino effect.

Mouth twitching.

Eyes watering.

Knee slapping.

Cries of laughter soon follow along with my phone flying out of my hand.

"Clover, are you okay?" Logan seems concerned, which makes me laugh even harder.

"Um." I try to point to my phone that slid across the floor, but between the out-of-breath pants and hands flailing around, I'm not sure if he catches on.

"What?" He searches the area.

"My phone," I manage to choke out. "There was a picture," I lie, but can't stop laughing. "Funny." I try to get my breathing under control before security decides to come haul me away. "Fell."

"Oh!" Logan scans the area. "There it is." He bends over and grabs it, and I lose it all over again.

Logan Long is wearing a florescent pink thong, and if that isn't enough, he has an electric blue dolphin tramp stamp.

"Time's up!" Owen announces as he rings the bell.

Saved by Owen.

Logan, who I thought would be turned off by my crazy, just holds his hands out wide and hollers as he walks backward. "Pick me. Date me." He points his fingers down to his pierced peen. "And get this."

What can I say to that? *Nothing.*

If I would have met Logan Long under any other circumstances, maybe things would have been different, but when you are given two minutes to give your whole life story, sometimes things that would have been no big deal end up being way too overwhelming.

After the last break, Owen and Austin agreed we needed to fast track this night, so the contestant rundowns and bathroom breaks were the first things to go.

Contestant #15 — Cute smile guy.
Contestant #18 — Uses way too much hair product.
~~**Contestant #25** — Kicked out. Lied about girlfriend.~~
Contestant #27 — Picked his teeth with a straw.

"Clover, it's so nice to finally meet you." An extremely attractive, taller gentlemen dressed to impress comes walking up with his arms open wide.

I started cutting off the contestants who get a little too handsy with a handshake, but this one isn't creepy or looking at me like I'm his dinner. This one just seems like he wants to wrap me in his arms, and I'm okay with that. After all, I could use a hug right about now.

"You must be number thirty-one?" I wave before he pulls me in.

"I'm Derek Fulkerson." He squeezes me tight, and I practically melt in his arms.

"Nice to meet you." I begin to bring my hands up between us, but Derek is already breaking free. The perfect gentleman.

"So, Derek, I have to admit, I know absolutely nothing about you." I walk around to my side of the table.

"Well, I'm thirty-two, work on Wallstreet, and have one thousand four hundred and thirty-two kids." He smiles.

My jaw drops.

"Now, I know what you're thinking, and no, I wasn't careless one thousand four hundred and thirty-two times." He pulls out a wallet out of his suit jacket—or what I thought was a wallet—until he flips it open and its pages and pages of picture collages. "I donated my sperm to help pay my way through college, and thanks to those boxed DNA tests, they've found me.

"Interesting." It's all I can say. I'm speechless.

"I know! I made it possible for over a thousand women to have their little miracle baby. To be a part of that feels amazing."

"That is one way to look at it."

A part of me wants to turn on my mic and shout my safe word, but is this really that bad? I mean, men have donated or sold their sperm for years, why should this be any different?

"Clover, it's a great feeling, to be a dad, and even though I'm retired from the sperm selling business, I can't help but to still be a part of that."

"How so?"

I need to know. These two minutes aren't about me. I need to know how this story turns out. I'm invested.

"Well, funny you should ask." He reaches inside his other pocket and pulls out a plastic roll. "I came up with the Sperm Shooter."

Nope. Definitely not a plastic roll.

"Wow."

"I know." He reaches across the table and pulls up his sleeve. "Feel the muscles in my wrist."

"Okay." I wrap my finger and thumb around his wrist while Derek flexes his hand.

"Feel that?"

"I do."

"Well, that is what pumping a cock correctly for over ten years does. Luckily, I developed a technique that was easy on the wrist, but some guys had to give up the money because it was costing them more. Carpal tunnel is a bitch, and I created this device to save them from the years of pain and suffering."

He hands me over the little device. "Go ahead. Squeeze the sides."

"I'm not sure about this." I turn it around.

"Clover." Derek sighs. "We are both adults and this is a vagina. You have one, and I love them." He winks.

"Has this one been used?"

I look at the pale pink device, wondering where it's been and how many penises it's milked for reproduction.

"I have three of the best engineers on my team and five patents that prove this device has a self-sanitizing system that is world class." He flips the switch and the roll—er—vagina—makes a sucking sound. "Of course, it's been used." He winks. "When I travel, it gets lonely out there."

"Derek, you are an attractive man. I'm sure all you have to do is snap your fingers and women will fall into your bed."

"Oh, they will," he agrees. "But are they safe? The Sperm Sucker assures you will have safe sex one hundred percent of the time."

"So, let me get this straight, you'd rather have sex with this machine than—"

"Oh-em-gee!" CJ runs up to the table. "Is that the Sperm Sucker model 2593P?"

"I tried to stop her." Mal tugs on CJ's arm, giving me an apologetic look.

"Seriously, you guys, this guy was on Shark Tank. When they passed him up, some investor from Indonesia climbed aboard and then this electronic pussy went viral," CJ rambles, looking between me and Derek. "This man is a genius. This machine." She grabs it from Derek and flips the switch. "Look at the suction on this baby." CJ sticks her finger in there and moans. "This feels so good. Just imagine if this was a dick, it would be exploding right now."

"Clover? Is everything okay?" Austin comes through the headset, but instead of turning on the mic, I just twist around and give him a thumbs-up. "I'm not even going to ask." He rubs his hands over his face as Owen looks like he's giving him an earful.

"Did you hear that?" CJ snaps in front of my face. "There is a storage compartment for the sperm sleeves. Those little plastic bags is where all the magic happens."

"CJ is it?" Derek leans in a little closer.

"Short for Carly Jane." Mal's smile is tight and forced. Something has happened behind the scenes, but I'm not about to get into that now while I have over twenty more contestants to see.

"Snap it, Mallory." CJ narrows her eyes, daring her to say another word.

"CJ, would you like to see this baby in action?"

Derek, the father of all of New York's children, who is supposed to be interested in me, is now propositioning my friend. And CJ is falling for it. I never thought I would see the day.

"Thanks, D-Man." CJ turns with the travel vagina in hand. "I know just the person."

"Hey! Come back!" Derek hurries and grabs his wallet of kids and runs after CJ. "Susie is mine."

"So, I'm guessing he's a no?" Mal winces.

"You would be right."

Contestant #34 — Lives in his mom's basement…he's forty-two. (what does he do down there?)

Contestant #35 — Single dad looking for more. Am I ready for this? Maybe someday.

Contestant #38 — Plastic surgeon. Very attractive, stable, seems to appreciate the female form. (move him to the top of list.)

Contestant #40 — Silver fox guy? I could be down with that.

"Hi, Clover." A cute, older man with a hot dad bod, maybe in his late thirties, early forties, comes strolling toward me with flowers in one hand and coffee in the other. "I'm Joey Tribbianni. How you doin'?"

Please God no. Let this be some kind of a joke. Joey Tribbianni is a character from one of my favorite television shows of all time—not contestant forty-three and standing in front of me. How weird.

"I'm finnnne."

"Now, I know what you're thinking," the guy otherwise known as Joey 2.0 smiles as he hands me the flowers, "I'm not that guy. Many have said I resemble Matt LeBlanc, but…I don't see it."

I'm not even going to touch that comment.

"Thank you." That seems safe enough. After all, Joey 2.0 is the only man to come bearing gifts. "These smell great."

"You're welcome. And a little birdy told me this is your favorite drink."

I take a sip, and it is. Well, it's my favorite coffee from a week ago. I'm always switching it up depending on my mood.

"I didn't know we had friends in common." I wrack my brain, trying to figure out who in the heck he would know. I would remember a name like Joey Tribbianni.

"We don't. I looked you up on Facebook and apparently, you kept checking in at Cuppa Joes. So, I went there and told this really kind barista…"

"Oh! I love Monica! She always remembers my drinks."

"Yes, but wrong one."

"Huh?" I'm confused between Joey 2.0 recounting the story and his hands flying around having a conversation of their own. I'm afraid I'm not following or missing a key element here.

"I was telling Monica, the barista, about this girl I was hoping to impress. When Monica Marti introduced herself and said she was following the story of Unlucky in Love for *The New York Post.*

"The Monica Marti?"

When Owen wanted word to spread like a wildfire about Hotline Hookup playing matchmaker to Unlucky in Love, he called Monica Marti. That woman knows everything about everyone, sometimes before they even know it's happened. It's why she has millions of Instagram follower and just as many twits who tweet…or whatever those people call themselves. I'm not a huge social media person, but Monica Marti is, and she made sure the spark ignited and followed up a couple days later with an exclusive interview with me over a cup of coffee at Cuppa Joes. Explains everything.

"That's the one. Sweet lady…" he trails off.

"Joey?"

"Did I zone out again? I'm sorry. I was just reminiscing about our talk. Did you know *Friends* is her favorite TV show?"

"Yeah, most of America watched *Friends*, or at least the reruns. I loved Ross and Rachel and the whole will they or won't they…"

"I hate Ross," Joey 2.0 mumbles. "Anyway, Monica Marti knows the real Joey Tribbianni, Matt LeBlanc?"

I lift the paper cup up to my lips and start to blow when I suddenly realize Joey 2.0 mentioned he stalked my Facebook page. That's kind of weird. What if he did something to this coffee? What if he laced it with some date-rape drug and when we leave, he's going to throw a bag over my head and drag me into some unmarked vehicle where he—

"Clover?" It's Joey 2.0's turn to drag me back to reality.

"Hmmm?"

"What did you think of that movie the other night? I was wanting to see it, *especially* since it had Jennifer Aniston in it."

Okay, Joey 2.0 is taking this too far. I have most of my settings set to private, but I'm technically challenged so who knows if I've screwed it up. I only stay up-to-date because of my job, not because I actually like it.

"Joey? Are you stalking me?" I take a sip, the smell overpowering my fears.

"Well…" Joey 2.0 winces as his head bounces back and forth, "I wouldn't call it stalking. I refer to it as research."

"Not cool."

"Seven," I whisper, hoping Austin will hear me.

He doesn't.

"Seven," I call a little louder this time.

Joey smiles. *Crap!* Did he hear me? Does he know seven is my safe word?

"Seven," I holler, not giving two shits if I spare Joey 2.0's feelings.

"I knew it!" Joey slaps the table. "I knew you were a *Friends* fan." Joey scratches his head. "What was the name of that episode?"

"Shit!" I turn around and yell for Austin. "Seven. Seven. Seven. Seven!"

Austin finally hears the commotion and taps his earpiece. "Clover, your mic is off."

Dammit! Flipping the switch on, I sigh. "Seeeevvvvveeeennnn."

"On it!"

"I got it! It's *The One With Phoebe's Uterus*." Joey screams just as the security guard appears behind him.

"Joey, your time's up." Owen follows.

"No!" He begins to fight, but another bodyguard comes up and drags him closer to the door. "You don't understand. She's my Rachel!" He breaks free and darts for me again just as Austin comes to stand in front of me. "Damn you, Ross! She's mine."

"Am I Ross?" Austin twists around, wrapping an arm around my waist.

"I guess." I shrug my shoulders "Honestly, I'm confused by how Joey Tribbianni passed the background check."

"Well…"

"Austin! You told me you did background checks." I smack him on his arm.

"I did, and he passed as David Duvall."

Worn out and ready for this night to be over, I lean into Austin. "Can we be done?"

"There are only seven more." He brushes my hair away from my face and looks down at me with regret. "I'm sorry about this."

"It's okay. I wanted it, and even though it's been a long night, it really has been a productive one."

"Really?"

"Yeah, really." I flash Austin a grin. "But to make up for Joey 2.0, you are getting us Thai on the way home."

"It gives me heartburn."

I flash him a look.

"Fine. Thai it is."

"That's what I thought."

Contestant #43 — Lives with ex-girlfriend.

Contestant #45 — Lives with fiancée, but he doesn't think they will work out and wants to check out other options before he walks down the aisle. #cheatingdirtbag

Contestant #47 — Lives with his step-sister who he talked about...*a lot*...fondly. *Gross.*

Contestant #50 — Hot guy in tights. #signmeup. Right fielder for a local minor league baseball team. Can we say home run?

"Well, Clo?" Austin comes up and offers his arm. "It's been a night. Are you ready to go home?"

"Yeah." I loop my arm in his. My feet are sore from standing in these four inches heels all night long. "We're still stopping for takeout, right?"

"Already taken care of." He pats my hand. "Thomas has it waiting in the car."

"What would I do without you?"

"I don't know, and can honestly say I don't want to find out," Austin confesses.

"Me either."

"Looks like you're stuck with me."

"I can live with that."

CHAPTER THIRTEEN

CLOVER

Why is dating hard? Like, seriously? Why do we feel the need to make a grand appearance? We try so hard to get them to like us, and as soon as they do, let the transformation begin—yoga pants, old tees, and messy buns.

"This is crazy? Why can't I just wear this?" I hold up the tie-front, black-and-white striped, wide-legged jumpsuit.

"One word. Actually, three." CJ holds up her hand and begins to count. "Beetlejuice. Beetlejuice. Beetlejuice."

Mal rolls her eyes. "Come on, CJ, it's cute, trendy, and perfect for whatever the doctor has planned."

I plop down on the bed. Their back and forth has gone on all afternoon.

"He's not *just* a doctor. He's a plastic surgeon." CJ walks over to me and snaps my bra strap. "And Clo wearing this is not going to cut it."

"What's wrong with this?" I examine my delicate white lace bra. "It's natural and comfortable."

"What is wrong with you two?" CJ stomps over to my drawers and pulls out a black lace push up shelf bra and matching thong. "Comfortable doesn't get you laid." She tosses them to me. "Put those on and I'll find you something in that mess of yours." CJ heads to the closet and flips through everything, making sure she is loud enough to let me know how cookie-cutter my outfits are.

The mattress dips and Mal reaches for my hand. "I really thought the jumpsuit was suitable for your date."

"I thought so too." I squeeze her hand back. "Sometimes I wonder if I'm crazy for doing this."

"No, Clo." Mal shifts to face me. "Sometimes we have to do out of character things to find out what we truly want."

"Great." I let out a huff and fall back on the bed. "So, you do think this is a mistake."

Mal tugs on my arm. "Stop being so dramatic and get up." She stands and pulls me with her. "That is not what I'm saying. I read this one book about how you have to try something new to appreciate what's right in front of you."

"You and those self-help books." I chuckle. "It started with *Chicken Soup for the Teenage Soul* and hasn't stopped since."

"Hey," Mal smacks my arm, "those books have helped me through some crazy hormonal times."

"I know."

"Just like the whole dating app thing. That is something out of the ordinary for me, but I'm trying it. So far, not good, but how would I know if I hadn't gone out of my comfort zone?"

"Some could say that about drugs." I smirk.

Mal reaches for the throw pillow and tosses it at my head. I duck, and CJ catches it.

"Clover, everyone knows drugs are bad." CJ throws it to the floor. "Well…except for the occasional J."

"J?" My face twists in confusion.

CJ's eyes practically roll back in her head. "Okay, I know you're Ms. Goody-Two-Shoes, but Naïve Nelly doesn't suit you."

"What?" I turn to Mal. "You know what a J is?"

"I'm friends with that whore." Mal points to CJ. "How could I not?"

"Then please explain?" I cross the room to where CJ is standing.

"Fine," CJ huffs out. "It's a marijuana joint, better known as pot, dope, reefer, hash, herb, weed, or, as my doctor likes to call it, chronic."

I place my hand on her shoulder, look my friend in the eyes, and sniff.

"Clover? Are you sniffing me?"

"Are you high right now? Do you need help?" My eyes widen knowing maybe this situation is bigger than this room. "And who is this doctor you speak of?"

"Dr. Dre. He's from Cali. You know, the west side." CJ laughs out.

"This is not funny." I turn and look at Mal who's giggling. "What is wrong with you two?"

"Clo." Mal tries to keep a straight face. "Dr. Dre is a rapper who had an album called The Chronic."

"Oh! I know who that is! Austin used to listen to his music all the time. He had that song about gin and juice."

"Clo, I'm disappointed in you." CJ shoves a tight, white and blue spandex dress I wore for Halloween at me. "You're thinking of Snoop Dogg."

"Same difference."

CJ and Mal both gasp, looking at each other. "Mal, we either need to divorce Clo or we need to school her on the OGs."

"What are OGs?"

"How is my brother even friends with you? I mean, we are because you're a girl who likes girl things, and that is appealing to girls like us, but Austin? He should have known better." Mal raises a brow.

"OGs—aka original gangstas!" CJ pulls me by my hand and stands me in front of my full-length mirror. "We can fix you, but first…let's get you dressed."

"About that…" I toss the dress on the bed. "I'm not wearing the *Pretty Woman* prostitute costume. That's saying please pay for my dinner and leave a tip on the nightstand—and that is a vibe I don't want to give off."

"Hmmm—or do you?" CJ winks.

"I think I may have a compromise." Mal jumps up and pulls something out of the closet.

"She's not wearing a cotton candy dress!" CJ shakes her head to the point she has to sit down. "Whoa!"

"Come on, Ceej, it's a compromise. Not everyone can pull off the sexy, hip-hop, don't-fuck-with-me vibe." Mal tries to convince her. "This pink wrap dress paired with your sexy lingerie and the heels I picked out, and Clo will have Doctor Knockers ready to knock boots."

"Yes! That is the look I'm going for!"

"Hey, Clo." Austin opens the door. "Holy fuck. Don't you ever wear any clothes?"

"Don't you ever knock?" I hold the pink dress in front of me. Hopefully, this time he doesn't see anything.

"You know you're standing in front of a full-length mirror." Austin nods behind me. "I should turn around, but with that bodysuit you're wearing, there's nothing to see."

"What is wrong with this?" I hold the dress out and turn around, slightly pissed off. "It's lace, Austin. You can see right through it."

"Uh…yeah!" He turns his head. "I can see that now."

"Oh, shit!" I hurry and throw on one of my oversized shirts. "I wasn't thinking."

"Well, that was interesting," CJ blurts out.

Mal just sits there and smiles.

"Did you need something, Austin?"

"Yeah!" Austin finally looks at me. "I just wanted to let you know I'm heading to the station."

"I thought we were riding together?"

"Thomas will come back for you, but Owen and I have to set up a few props for the date night photo promo."

"How cute." CJ turns to Mal. "It's like prom all over again."

"Ignore them." Austin shakes his head. "We need to go over the rules one more time."

"No need. I've got this," I reassure him.

"This is for your protection." Austin continues to stand next to the door, one arm on the knob and the other resting on the frame, causing his shirt to creep up a little.

CJ whistles.

Mal covers her ears.

I swear, I kill her with my laser death beam stare.

"Sorry. The happy trail gets me every time," CJ somewhat apologizes.

"Again, ignore them and humor me by going over the rules."

"Fine." I begin to recall the rules we've gone over time and time again. "We arrive at the station where the doctor—"

"Jack Hunt," Austin corrects me.

I side-eye him. "Where Jack Hunt will be waiting for our pre-date photo op. Then Thomas will take us to wherever he has planned. While on the date, I have to tweet at least three times using the hashtags 'unluckyinlove' and 'hotlinehookup.'"

"And?"

"Austin, I have no clue." I wave my hand around the room. "And I have to get ready. So, please, just spit it out."

"Never mind. Thomas knows what to do. Just get ready so you won't be late."

"I'm trying." I wave a hand between us, letting Austin know the only thing stopping me is him.

"I guess that's my cue." Austin slowly shuts the door.

"Well, that was interesting," CJ pipes up.

"Hey, Clo!" Austin peeks his head back in and scans the room.

I'm a little annoyed now. "Yes?"

"I'm sure whatever you pick out will be perfect." Austin's lips begin to tilt up in what I think is a genuine smile.

I relax.

I'm not sure why I feel like I need Austin's approval, but I do.

"Thanks."

"And you," Austin points to his sister, "don't let CJ dress her like a whore."

CJ doesn't say a word. She just picks up the throw pillow from before and tosses it at the door, but not before Austin hollers, "Good talk!" and slams the door.

Austin—one.

Door—zero.

CHAPTER FOURTEEN

AUSTIN

Why the fuck am I so nervous? Is this what a dad feels like when his daughter goes on a date for the first time?

"Um, Austin? Have you seen Clover? She's definitely not your daughter." Owen bites his knuckle. "That girl is—"

"One—" I interrupt Owen. If he doesn't speak it, he's not thinking it. Or at least that's what I'm telling myself. "Don't go there, and two, I didn't even know I said that out loud."

"Well, you did." Owen shoots me a look as he fights with a box. "Can you hold that end so I can pull out this promo stand?"

"Sure thing." I grab the cardboard. "Is this another Dr. Feelgood cutout?"

"Nope." Owen smirks as he pulls the standup out of the box. "I'm not sure if you're ready for this since you're in overprotective daddy mode."

"Whatever, man. Clover is a big girl who can make her own decisions. Even if they are the wrong ones." I toss the box to the side and grab the standup as Owen opens it.

Holy shit!

Clover is standing in a hot pink dress I've never seen her wear before, holding her hand up to cover her matching pink lips, her mouth in the shape of a perfect O.

"What the fuck, man?"

"Clover said you would get upset." Owen tries to defend himself.

"I-I'm not...*upset.*" I pick up the cutout and place it over by the Hotline Hookup sign.

"If it helps, it's not her body. We took this photo the day she was in the studio and the marketing team photoshopped the rest."

I'm not sure what I'm more pissed about—Hot Wire using Clover's head on a stock photo body or Hot Wire thinking Clover's body doesn't carry the sex appeal they want to sell. I've seen it up close and *naked*, and it's more than qualified to sell Unlucky in Love.

"It's cool. I just hope Clover isn't offended by it." I play it off like it doesn't make a difference one way or another.

"She approved it," Owen says, like it's no big deal.

"She what?" I run my hands through my hair.

"What is your deal with Clover anyway? One minute she's just your friend, and the next…if looks could kill…"

"You think this is about Clover?" I spit back. "This is about Hotline Hookup—*my show* I created—mine—and you're telling me this went through marketing, Clover, and my producer, and the first time I find out about it is when it's delivered. That"—I jab my finger in the air—"is what I'm pissed about."

"Austin, I'm going to ignore that statement because for the past I don't know how many years you haven't given zero fucks about anything that has gone on behind the scenes. That's been me, buddy. So, figure this shit out. Get that," Owen waves his hand around my head, and I slap it away, "on straight."

Dragging my hands down my face, I realize he's right. Clover isn't the only one who had their world flipped upside down—I did too. The moment she moved in, I lost all privacy. And if she isn't home, her bird is.

"I'm sorry. This whole dating game crap is getting to me, but not for the reasons you think," I confess. "She's living with me. I haven't had a girl over since she moved in."

"Ahhh!" Owen nods. "It's making sense. Dr. Feelgood needs to get felt up." He busts out laughing. "I feel ya, man."

That isn't what I meant, but maybe it's for the best that I don't mean anything at all.

CLOVER

"I'm so sorry I'm late." I rush into the lobby and notice everyone, including my date, Dr. Jack Hunt, standing in front of the Hotline Hookup/Hot Wire Radio sign.

"Hey, beautiful." Jack turns around and throws his thumb over his shoulder. "We were just admiring you."

"You were?" I tilt my head to the side, confused as to how they would do that.

"Yeah, this," Austin takes a step to his left and raises his brow, "arrived today."

Uh oh!

"I was just saying," Jack walks over to greet me with a kiss on each cheek, "there's no way that body is yours."

"I know." I sigh. "The studio thought I wasn't—"

"Because," Jack interrupts, "that cutout is flawed, and you, my dear, are perfection. Completely flawless."

"Oh jeez," Austin grunts.

We both turn.

"Oh! Did I say that out loud?"

"Yeah, man." Owen smacks him on the back. "Don't make it a habit."

"Clover?" Jack offers his hand. "Will you do me the honor and take a selfie with me for our very first tweet?"

I chuckle. "Of course." I place my hand in his. "I would be hashtag honored."

After Jack insists, we move the imposter out of the way, snap a few pictures, and tweet our first tweets of the night. So far, so good.

Clover Kelly @UnLuckyInLove_13

Unlucky in love? Hmm…tonight isn't looking so bad. <pic> #unluckyinlove #hotlinehookup

Jack Hunt @dOc_knOckers

Not too shabby. <pic> #unluckyinlove #hotlinehookup #inspiration #realvsfake

"Ready?" Jack holds out his hand. "Ladies first."

"Why thank you, kind sir." I smile as I walk past a little, pleased with myself when I notice Mr. Hunt checking me out.

"Have fun and don't forget to tweet," Owen hollers.

"We won't." I wave them both off.

"I have a feeling this is going to be a great night." Jack grins as he opens the door.

"Me too." I walk out the doors into the city that never sleeps. If tonight goes well, maybe I won't either.

#upallnighttogetlucky *Tweet that, Owen.*

I may not have taken CJ's advice about the lingerie, but I still feel good. In fact, Jack can't take his eyes off me. His eyes keep traveling to my breasts. Now, most women would get creeped out by this, but not me.

Jack spends all day nipping, tucking, and stuffing, which means he gets to look at boobs all day every day because he *has* to, but tonight, he's choosing to, and that makes me lift my head a little higher. Not just because it's one hell of a confidence boost, but because it helps the girls stick out a little bit more.

Paging Dr. Hunt.

"We are almost there." Jack flashes me a toothy grin. "We could have walked there, but there is a chance of rain and I didn't want to risk it. Oh, and the fact the station wouldn't allow it."

"That's true." I giggle. "Where are we going?" I lean in as far as this seatbelt will let me and bump his shoulder.

"Let's just say I'm letting you get up close and personal in my world." Jack winks.

If CJ were here, this is where she would do her little pelvic-thrusting, air-slapping dance to let everyone know Mr. Hunt is indeed doable.

"I can't wait."

"Good." Jack reaches over and grabs my hand. "Is this okay?"

Yes, Jack. Just move that hand a little more up and to your left.

"Of course." Which isn't a lie. Holding hands is more than okay, but Jack is putting off some kind of sexual energy that has me wanting more. And why wouldn't he?

Jack Hunt is exactly the type of man I'm attracted to. Tall, dark, and knows what he wants. And it doesn't hurt that he has it made in the looks department with his salt and pepper hair, honey eyes, sun-kissed skin, and a smile I'm sure has melted a few panties.

"We're here." Jack leans forward and whispers something to Thomas, then climbs out, offering his hand.

"That was fast." I step out, careful not to expose myself. "So, where are we going?" I spin around. Hooters, Little Italy, a sub place. "I know! Are you taking me to one of those hidden restaurants I've heard about?"

"I'm not sure I follow."

"Well, there are these little trendy restaurants hidden in the back of…" I pause, realizing he has no clue what I'm talking about. "I'm sorry. I'm just rambling now."

"Please, Clover." Jack reaches down and tucks a piece of hair behind my ear, the tips of his fingers leaving a blazing trail of want and desire. "Don't be sorry. I want to hear everything you have to say."

"O-kay." My voice trembles. Not from fear, but from the truth of his words.

Jeffery never said much, and he didn't hear much either. When I spoke, he would just nod or shake his head. Actually, I'm not sure he even paid attention to anything I had to say.

"Have you ever been here before?" Jack's hand is on my lower back, guiding me down the crowded sidewalk.

"I haven't, but I heard their pizza is good." I head to the crosswalk wondering why he didn't have Thomas drop us off on the other side.

"Clover! Over here," Jack hollers after me.

"Oh my goodness." I hide my face as I quickly walk back. "I'm so sorry. My mind is wandering, and I thought you were taking me over there." I turn and throw my thumb over my shoulder to the pizza place.

"Their special is amazing, but tonight is wing night." He points up to the orange owl. "I come here so often, I have my own booth."

I purse my lips, unsure of what to say as Jack holds the door open for me.

"Come on. I can't wait for you to meet the girls."

Wait! What?

Jack Hunt seemed perfect on paper, and even more perfect when we met, but right now, something isn't adding up. Jack said he wanted me to get up close and personal in his world, then says he can't wait for me to meet *the girls*. Who are these girls? Surely, he doesn't have daughters who work here. Is that even possible? *Dammit. Where's Google when I need it?*

I'm sure I'm being ridiculous. This is me running, and…well, I need to try the eggs, or chicken, as the case may be. I put one foot in front of the other and follow Jack in.

"This is great! Isn't it?" Jack scans the restaurant, his eyes never straying to look at the girls in the short black bootie shorts. Nope. His eyes stay…at breast level.

Of course!

"So, Jack, I'm assuming from your comment earlier you have quite a few clients here."

"I was hoping you would ask." He points to a beautiful brunette chatting it up with a younger gentleman at the bar. "She went from an A to a perfect C, and then—" Jack catches himself. "Actually, the rest is doctor-patient privilege."

"Oh, of course. Silly for me to even ask." I relax and sip on the fruity drink the waitress insisted I get. I'm more of a Cosmo girl, but Cynthia insisted this was to die for and the perfect cool down to our spicy buffalo chicken salads—which I practically devoured. I didn't realize how hungry I was until she placed them in front of us

"No need to be shy now." Jack smiles as he catches a glimpse of my girls before he leans back and throws an arm over the seat next to him. "The waitresses here get a discount for recommendations. Augmentations are public knowledge, but the extras are off-limits." Jack takes a swig of his beer as I nod to the faint music in the background. "Everyone is paying big money to look…" He leans forward, giving me the come-hither motion with his finger.

"Yes?"

"Exactly like *you*."

"Really?" I'm not sure if this is a line he tells everyone or if he really finds my features that flattering. "Jack, my friend did my makeup." I wave a hand over my face. "It's a lot of contouring."

"Come on, Clover, give me some credit. I earned my Bachelor of Arts degree from Arizona State University in Chemistry, a master's degree in Public Policy from Harvard, and a Doctor of Medicine from Tufts University. Plus, a three-year general surgery residency at UCLA, and a plastic and reconstructive surgery residency in Memphis. My fellowship at the Harvard Medical School's Beth Israel Deaconess Medical Center is nothing to shy away from either."

If there was any doubt before, there isn't now. I'm pretty sure Jack just ran down his whole résumé. A simple, "I can see past that," would have worked. Maybe he really felt like he had to prove his point or maybe he was fishing for a compliment. I'm not sure, so I stick with the praise response. "Wow! Jack, that's really impressive."

"Thank you. I take my job seriously. Women and men come to me from all over the world. When I say I know perfection, I do. I've never seen anyone with your eyes, cheekbones, jawline…" Jack pauses as he reaches across the table and runs a finger down my nose. "Are you sure you've never had any work done? You have a perfect hundred-and-six-degree nasal tip rotation. Women pay thousands of dollars to have that slope."

"Nope. You can thank my mom and dad." I laugh awkwardly. Jack has me under a microscope, and even though he's dishing out compliments right and left, I feel more insecure. Crazy.

"Well…hopefully, if all goes well, I'll have the pleasure of doing so." Jack bites his bottom lip as he lets his eyes glance down at the girls once again.

"Hey there, Jack," Cynthia practically coos as she squats down at our booth, her double-Ds having a stare down with my date.

I know he's a boob man. It's what he does for a living, why wouldn't he want to admire his work? This isn't creepy at all. Who am I kidding? It's totally creepy. It's as if her boobs and Jack are playing a game of twenty questions. Okay, maybe not twenty questions, but she is talking to jack and he is talking to her boobs.

"Well, I'll make sure to give her your number." Cynthia lets her hand fall to Jack's knee.

Is this girl for real? I pretend to adjust in my seat and lean into the aisle. *The nerve!* Cynthia's hand isn't just on Jack's knee, it's rubbing up and down his thigh. What kind of discount does he offer these girls?

Do I run?

Do I stay?

Is this normal?

Is this just my insecurities?

I have no clue what to do. Jack is sweet, attentive, has manners…but something is off, and I'm not sure I can put a finger on what it is.

"Thank you, and if you ever want to further discuss that one issue," Jack turns to wink at me, "call the office and we'll work something out."

Cynthia giggles, and it's not the cute kind either. This is like nails on a chalkboard. "I would *love* that." Cynthia reaches for the table and stands. "By the way," she directs her attention to me, "I love your nose. Nice work, Doctor."

"Oh no," I shake my head, "this is mine."

Cynthia walks backward toward the bar. "Of course. Paid in full." Cynthia beams as she spins around and sticks her chest in another willing victim's face.

"Hey, Jack." A platinum blonde bimbo waves as she passes by.

"Kat." Jack nods at her boobs.

Maybe he isn't really staring at their chests. Maybe I'm just being a paranoid first date freak. That has to be it. I mean, we are in a place known for their wings and waitresses. Heck, I even linger a little longer than normal. How can you not when everything is eye level?

"I know what you're thinking." Jack smiles as his eyes light up with confidence. It's as if this man is on a game show and knows the answer to the million-dollar question. "The answer is yes. However," Jack holds up a finger, "she had a reduction and lift."

"A reduction, but she's…I mean…" How do you politely say, *"But she's huge?"*

"Kat was having major back issues due to having double-Gs."

"Oh, wow." I look down at my Cs. I can't even begin to imagine.

"Yeah…most girls want what you have, they just don't realize it. They come in determined on Ds and I try to talk them down, but when they make up their mind, there is usually no changing it." Jack's smile is kind and less creepy this time.

I'm sure I was just letting my mind wander places it shouldn't have gone. After all, Jack did somewhat inform me of where we were going. I just didn't add two and two together.

"That's interesting. This is all new to me," I confess.

"I chose this field not because I want to improve their physical appearance, but to increase their self-esteem. I'm more than just breast enlargements. I've worked on trauma cases, cleft lips, burn scars, and in this case, a breast reduction."

"I'm sorry. I really didn't know."

Now I feel like an ass. Jack isn't some perv who looks at boobs all day long. This man is only interested in how to make others feel good about themselves.

"Kat wasn't a happy girl. In fact, the first time I ever saw her smile was after surgery, and it wasn't from the drugs." He laughs. "Her frame was too small to carry that kind of weight, so we reduced and lifted."

"Dr. Hunt? Are you talking about me again?" Kat purrs as she stands there with her hip cocked out and eyebrow raised.

"Yes, sweetie. I am." Jack reaches out to rub her arm. "I was just telling my date here how it's great to see you smile."

"Well…" Kat turns to me, her smile beaming, "I owe everything to this man. He truly is amazing, and I haven't," she points to her mouth, "smiled this much in forever. Actually, I think it's permanent now."

"I'm so happy for you."

And I am. She's oozing confidence.

"Looks like you're finished." Kat takes our plates. "Should I send Cynthia over? Need more drinks? Maybe dessert?"

Jack doesn't wait for me. "I think we're good."

This disappoints me. I usually like the option of declining my own dessert. Coming from a man and plastic surgeon, I can't help but wonder…

"I have something else in mind." Jack winks, reaching across the table to take my hand in his.

Oh! Disappointment—poof, be gone!

"Oh!" Kat waggles her brows. "Well, I'll have her bring the check then. See you guys later!" Kat calls out as she vanishes around the corner.

"So?" I use my most seductive voice as I lean across the table. "What's this something else?"

"Well, it's something I've really never done before," Jack admits, almost unsure of his decision.

"Really? So I'm the first?" I bat my eyelashes.

"Yes, I can honestly say no one has made me ever want to do this." Jack stands and offers his hand, once again proving he's the perfect gentleman. "What do you say? Ready to get out of here?"

"I thought you would never ask."

CHAPTER FIFTEEN

CLOVER

First Hooters, and now Victoria's Secret? This has to be the oddest date I've ever been on.

"Clover Kelly, will you try on lingerie for me?" Jack holds the glass door open, waiting again for me to make a decision.

Is this even normal? I mean, sure, if you're in a committed relationship, but even then? Jeffery always hated these kinds of places. Even when I tried to shop online, he would get irritated, and say, *"Get whatever you want. It doesn't matter to me."*

So, is Jeffery the norm, or is this?

"Dr. Hunt…I would be honored."

What are the words coming out of my mouth? I wouldn't even wear the matching black bra and thong set CJ laid out for me, and now I'm going in here to try things on for this man?

Clover, he's a doctor. He makes boobs for a living.

I swear, my subconscious is at war with itself.

Is this right or wrong?

Sleezy or fun?

Will he expect more or nothing at all?

Gah! What did I get myself into?

"Clover!" A shrill, way-too-perky, I've-heard-that-voice-somewhere calls out my name. "Is that you?"

Oh God! This can't be happening.

I don't want to turn around. If I do, I won't be able to pretend this isn't happening. There's only one thing to do—look for bras.

"What do you think of this one?" I hold up a little lace-up bra.

"Clover, I think your friend…"

"The bra, Jack!" I practically shove it in his face, slightly irritated he isn't catching on.

"Well, it's a little pink," Jack responds. "Clover..."

"What?" I spin around, ready to take all my frustrations out on my date. You know, end it before it even begins because anything would be better than coming face to face with Angel—and when I say Angel, I don't mean Victoria's, but Jeffery's bimbo baby momma.

"It is you." Bimbo bitch scans me from head to toe. "Aw! Don't you look cute. It's soooo—*pink*."

"I happen to think pink is sexy." Jack catches on and moves in a little closer and holds the bra up in front of me. "What do you think? This really complements her skin tone and will only enhance her *natural*, oh-so-perfect breasts. Don't you think?"

Angel, the boyfriend stealing asshole, stands there with her mouth hanging open and an armful of thongs.

"I'm so sorry. I didn't introduce myself." Jack holds out his hand knowing her hands are too full to take it. "I'm Dr. Jack Hunt."

"Sorry." Angel holds up her arms. "Wait! Did you say Dr. Jack Hunt? *The* Dr. Jack Hunt? Plastic surgeon to the stars?"

"Well, I have consulted with a few celebrities, but I wouldn't go that far." Jack awards her with a cocky grin.

"Honey, I think I would like to try all these on." I grab one of every style, not caring if they're my size or not. "Want to come watch?"

"Well, Angel, it was a pleasure to meet you, but we have a dressing room to reserve."

"Yeah...same here." She seems confused as she pulls out her phone, and we take that as our cue to head to the back. "Jeffery, you won't believe who I ran into," we hear Angel whisper.

"Do you want to tell me what that was all about?" Jack raises an eyebrow. "I'm guessing she's the reason why you're here?"

"Hold that thought." I hand everything to the clerk who is checking shoppers into the dressing rooms. "I think I may have grabbed the wrong size. I actually need a thirty-two C."

"Thirty-four C," Jack corrects, and the clerk and I look at him. "What? I know my stuff." He winks.

"He thinks because he's a plastic surgeon he knows me." I laugh.

"Oh!" the clerk nods.

"No! Wait. These are real." I wave my fingers between the twins. *Twins?* Now I sound like CJ.

"Sure." She winks. "I've heard that a time or two. How about I just grab my measuring tape."

"For crying out loud, just grab me a thirty-four C."

"Trust me on this," Jack leans in and whispers.

"I'm trusting him." I throw my thumb over my shoulder at Jack. "But not because he's *my* plastic surgeon, because he happens to think my breasts are perfect in their natural form and has been staring at them all night," I blurt out, immediately regretting it. My shoulders slump and my face drains of all color. "I mean…"

Jack belts out a belly shaking—errr—ab-rippling laugh. There is nothing shaking on that solid surface.

"Can you point us to our room?"

"Sir, this isn't a hotel. I will show *her* to the room, and you can take a seat just outside on the bench." The clerk radios something over the headset she's wearing, then walks us back. "I had to say that back there," she whispers. "Most guys just sneak in. You know, to help their lady friends out." She hands Jack all the garments that should fit and runs off to exchange the ones that won't.

"Looks like it's just me and you." Jack gives me one devilish smirk.

"So it seems." I grab the lingerie from his hands, step inside the room, and let the door fall shut. "Let's see if you're right and I've been wearing the wrong size all these years?" I call out above the door as I unwrap my dress, letting it fall from my shoulders.

"Let's do," he agrees, the door flying open.

"Jack!" I screech, trying to cover myself the best I can. The fact that this man has probably seen hundreds, maybe even thousands, of women in their naked form doesn't make one bit of a difference.

"I thought this is why we're here?" He cocks his head to the side. "For a little one on one?" He reaches for my hands. "Let me see this perfection."

Crap! What to do? I proclaimed to all of New York I wanted to get lucky, and now that I have a guy showing interest in just that, I'm shying away.

Baby steps, Clo.

"Listen, I know why you think I'm here, and I guess I am, but there is a reason behind this whole dating ordeal, and it has to do with my ex and that pregnant bimbo out there."

"She's pregnant? You couldn't even tell she was showing."

"Seriously, Jack?" I throw my hands on my hips, letting my dress fall open. "You can tell these are real, but you couldn't tell she's with child."

"For one." He whistles.

"Shhh!" I peek my head out the door. "They are going to hear you."

"Well, how could I notice her when you are standing right next to me?"

Jack wins!

"Fine. How about you sit out there, and as I loosen up, maybe just maybe, we'll have our own little fashion show?"

Jack lifts my hand and feathers an ever-so-gentle kiss before he turns and walks out of the room.

As I'm about to try on the pale pink set, Austin tries to FaceTime me.

No way, buddy. I click the little red button. There is only room for two on this date.

However, Austin isn't getting the hint. He calls a couple more times before a text chimes.

Austin: What the hell?

Jeez…I wonder what crawled up his butt?

Me: ?

Austin: First Hooters, and now Victoria's Secret?

Me: OMG! Do you have Thomas reporting back to you?

If he doesn't stop trying to control this process, I'm going to skip the car service and take a cab—or even better, walk.

Austin: What? No! Twitter, Clo. It's everywhere. Hold please.

I wait as the three bubble dots appear right before the pic comes through.

Jack Hunt @dOc_knOckers

My real-life Hooters and now Clover's Secret. <pic> #shhh #unluckyinlove #hotlinehookup #bejealous #luckynight

Holy crap. It's a picture of my dressing room with some kind of four-leaf clover emoji plastered all over it.

Austin: So? Care to explain this?

No! Actually, I don't. Since when did this whole protective father thing start happening? Austin's never been this way before.

Me: Nope. Sorry, I'm busy.

I lock my phone and start to stick it in my purse as my horns make an appearance. Swiping it back to life, I decide to take a little photo.

Pushing down my bra straps, I snap a picture from the shoulders up for a little tweet of my own.

Two can play this game.

Hotline Hookup wants three tweets…well, here is number two.

Clover Kelly @UnLuckyInLove_13

The Dr. is just what this girl needed. Who's ready to play dress up? <pic> #unluckyinlove #hotlinehookup #ifoundmywings #ormaybehorns

My phone goes off with a string of chimes, which I'm sure a couple are from Mal and CJ rooting me on GIF style. The rest from Austin, the overprotective best friend who seems to think I'm in over my head.

"Miss?" The clerk raps on my door. "I have those pieces in the size you requested."

"Oh, thank you." I crack the door and grab the pile of lace and silk. "I really think the super sexy navy plunge teddy would look amazing on you."

"What? I didn't' grab…"

"I did." Jack stands and sticks his hands in his pockets. "I hope that's okay?"

Try the eggs.

I have walked the straight and narrow for so long, I'm ready for a change. Maybe modeling shows and stripteases are in my near future?

"It is." I can't help but smile. Jack is trying so hard to win me over. I guess I never really put the shoe on the other foot. Jack is first, but he won't be my last date. I'm sure that has a huge part in the way he planned our date. He wanted to stick out, to show me he was different. And it worked. "I'll try that one on first."

"I'll be right here," Jack whispers, but his voice echoes off the bare walls.

That's the thing. He is right here. So, I'm going to live in the *right now.*

Be bold.

Be beautiful.

"I hate that this date is almost over," I confess as we pull up to the studio tower.

Even though my date with Dr. Jack Hunt had several weird-ish moments, the not so weird outweighed them.

He's classy, honest, attentive, has manners, extremely good-looking, has a great job—the list goes on and on. There are so many more reasons why I should fall for a man like Jack Hunt than to not to?

"It doesn't have to end..." Jack opens the door to the lobby where we are supposed to say our goodbyes and post our final tweets.

What does that even mean? Is he going to offer me a nightcap—aka a roll in the sack—at his place? Will he ask to go back to mine? Because that will not fly with Austin—or Kramer, for that matter. Heck, he thought Austin was an intruder in his own home. Or maybe he just plans on asking me out on another date and ending this one with a memorable kiss.

Ah! A kiss.

It's been forever since I've had an exciting kiss. Jeffery hated any sort of PDA, and that included kissing. So, to say I'm a little rusty is an understatement.

"How about we take our goodbye picture by the sign and get the tweets out of the way?" Jack suggests, reaching for his phone.

"Perfect." I follow behind, my heels clicking against the marble floor.

"This will work." Jack spins around and swoops me into his arms.

My hands fly up to his firm chest. "I think so." I giggle.

Jack pulls me in closer with one arm as he holds his cell out in front of us with the other.

"Oops!" Jack swipes the phone to the left. "I may have snapped a memento, but only from the chest up and neck down," he defends. "I hope that's okay. I know I should have asked, but since your face wasn't included, I didn't think you would care."

"Um…"

How do I feel about this?

My first instinct is to grab his phone and delete the pic, but my second is excited. Out of all the boobs he's seen, he loves mine the most. Like maybe he'll try to model others after mine?

"I'll delete it." Jack swipes it back as his thumb hovers over the delete button.

"No!" I reach for his phone. "I mean, it kind of makes me feel good that you want to look at me."

"It does?" He almost sounds shocked.

"Yeah, I love it when your eyes are on me. It makes me feel special…*wanted*."

"Oh…I want you all right." Jack lets his eyes trail down to his favorite spot.

"You're insatiable." I smack his chest as I throw my head back and burst into a fit of laughter just as Jack snaps a picture.

"Perfect."

"Let me see." I lean in to sneak a peek as Jack types his tweet, but he quickly covers his phone. "You'll see it soon enough." He winks.

"Fine. I'll snap my own." I pose for a quick thumbs-up selfie, type out a little about my date, and hit send.

Clover Kelly @UnLuckyInLove_13

@dOc_knOckers was more than I could have imagined. <pic>
#unluckyinlove #hotlinehookup #willheorwonthe #gettinlucky

"There. All done." I tuck my phone away in my purse and set it on the granite top of the information desk. "Now, where were we?"

"Clover." Jack places his hands on either side of my face, his thumbs gently caressing the cheekbones he admires so much. "You are absolutely perfect." He inches closer.

Yes, Jack. Kiss me!

"Spending just one night with you isn't enough." His hands slowly work his way to my shoulders, igniting a spark that's about to explode. "I need more."

Touch me!

"Jack, maybe we can…" I lean forward, closing the distance, my lips parting, begging for his touch.

Jack lowers his head, and our eyes connect for the briefest of moments. "And these," his eyes fall to my breasts, "are the most amazing pair of breasts I've seen."

Okay, that's not what I was expecting, but he does love my boobs.

Jack glances up for only a second. "And I've seen a lot." He smirks. "Clover—" Jack breaths my name.

"Jack—" I moan.

If this isn't begging, I don't know what is.

His lips gently rub mine as his hands fall—to my…*breasts*?

Um—okay?

"I've been dying to touch you all night," he whispers the words I've desperately wanted to hear. "Clover, let me kiss you."

Yes! Yes! Yes!

"Please." I close my eyes, my lips parting.

Except his lips never touch mine. Nope! Apparently, I'm not kissable—*but my breasts are!*

Dr. Jack Hunt face plants my cleavage, his hands pushing my boobs together as he shakes his head back and forth, his lips vibrating like a motorboat.

Holy hell! He's motorboating the twins!

"Brbrbrrbrbrrbrbrr."

"Jaaack!" I scream, but he keeps going.

Is that tongue? Ew! It's slobber.

"Jack, enough!" I yell louder. Taking a step back, I push him forward.

"What?" Jack seems shocked as he wipes his mouth off with the back of his sleeve, a Cheshire grin replacing his slobber-soaked lips.

"You slobbered on my—on my—" I try to get the words out, but shock takes over. If I don't say it, does that mean it never happened?

"No, Clover." Jack takes a step forward.

"Don't touch me." I hold out my hand.

"You said I could kiss you!" Jack's face scrunches up. He really thought this was okay.

"On my lips!"

"Why would I want to kiss those," he nods to my lips, "when I can kiss those." He zooms in on my boobs like one of those old cartoons where Daffy Duck's eyes would bug out?

Unbelievable!

I gasp, grab my purse, and run off.

"Clover! I didn't mean it like that," he calls after me. "I mean, I did, but I'll kiss your lips as well…both of them!"

Gah!

"Goodbye, Jack!" I rush out the doors and into the car where Thomas is waiting on me.

Sliding onto the seat, Thomas shuts the door and rounds the vehicle as my phone chimes with a text from Austin.

I refuse to look at anything from earlier. I don't need to once I see his latest message.

Austin: Hunt is a cunt! <pic>

Jack Hunt @dOc_knOckers

This Doc is in heaven.

<pic>#unluckyinlove#hotlinehookup #nomnom

#cometodaddy

Ugh! How did I not see it? He was always gawking at my boobs. In the vehicle, at the restaurant, snapping the lingerie picture, and this. Plus, let's not forget the whole date in general—Hooters and Victoria's Secret on a first date?

Here's your sign.

"Where to, Ms. Kelley?" Thomas is a welcome interruption to my pity party of one. "Mr. Montgomery's?"

"Yes, please. I'm ready to go *home*."

CHAPTER SIXTEEN

AUSTIN

I begged Owen to let me put an end to the date, but according to him and that stupid fucking contract, if Clover is having a good time, I can't do shit.

Instead, I'm sitting at home while Kramer pretends to shit on my head, scrolling through the Twitter feed.

Fan-fucking-tastic.

"Buddy, how about we give Uncle Austin a break?" I pat the top of my head, hoping he'll fly back to his cage. "Hmm? Are you hungry?"

That got his attention. Kramer climbs down to my shoulder, and squawks, "Polly! Polly want a cracker. Polly! Polly want a cracker."

"Interesting. What else can you say?" I turn my head slightly, but not enough for Kramer to peck my eye out.

"Polly want a cracker. Polly! Polly want a cracker."

"Okay, bud, I can take a hint. Let's see what we have in here." I stand, and Kramer jumps to the couch and flaps his way over to his cage while I head to the kitchen.

"Austin?" Clover yells out, slamming the door. "You here?"

"Hey. I'm surprised to see you home. I figured you and Hunt the Cunt would be checking into the W right about now."

"Yeah, well, that didn't happen." Clover throws herself down on the couch and covers her face.

"Well, I can't say I'm sorry about that." I chuckle. "That dude is a class A douchebag for those tweets about you."

Clover grunts.

"Okay." I tap her legs. "Lift up."

One by one, Clover's legs raise enough for me to slide in and sit down. "Give them here." I lay them back down on my lap."

She grunts.

"I know that grunt."

She sighs.

"And that sigh."

"What do you want me to say?" Clover peeks over the pillow, her hair wild and eyes rimmed red. "That you were right? That I was delusional for even thinking I could find someone who didn't want *just* sex out of this whole crazy mess?"

Shit!

"Clover…" Her name slowly falls from my mouth.

"Don't, Austin." She sits up, hugging the pillow tight to her chest. "Don't sit there and feel sorry for poor, pitiful Clover."

"I don't feel *sorry* because you're pitiful." I try to pull the pillow away from her, but she just scoots closer to the arm, bringing up her legs.

"See, you think I am." She snorts.

"Okay, that was kind of gross." I laugh.

"Sorry." She chuckles as she rubs her eyes with the palm of her hand.

"As I was saying…" I scoot over a cushion, reach over, and pull her into my arms. "I'm sorry that asshole didn't see what I see."

I shouldn't have said it. I'm not sure what that even means. I opened my mouth to tell her I was more pissed than sorry. Pissed she made herself vulnerable to a man who obviously didn't appreciate her from the moment he set eyes on her.

Clover looks up at me through tear-soaked lashes and asks me exactly what I was afraid of. "What do you see?"

Here is where we fuck up as men. We say stuff we aren't sure about, then when asked about it, we have to somehow put the puzzle together before the buzzer goes off.

"A beautiful woman." I smile, brushing back the blond strands plastered to her face. "A woman who knows what she wants and isn't afraid to go after it. Even if it means risking her own happiness to get there."

"I did that with Jeffery," she confesses.

"You did." I nod. "Just know you can have exactly what you want and be happy."

"How?" She hangs on my every word as if I'm solving world peace.

"By putting you," I tap her nose, "first."

"Hm?" Clover sits there for a minute, her eyes moving back and forth. Hopefully, she's taking what I just said to heart. "I hope the other guys aren't like this."

Well, that came out of left field. I figured she was going to pop up and give some sort of girl power speech, but instead, she's thinking about her future dates.

"You still want to do this?" I'm confused. After Jeffery and the doctor, I figured Clover would be ready to pull the plug on this.

"Well, I have no choice. I signed a contract. Plus, I made a promise to myself to put myself out there more."

"Fine." I stand up and set her back down. "I think I have the perfect thing to put tonight behind you." I jog to the kitchen and grab Clover's favorites.

"Unless it's ice cream or wine, don't bother. It's *that* kind of night," she hollers out.

"Already on it." I walk out of the kitchen with a half carton of vanilla, a bottle of Cabernet, and two glasses. "Pick your damage."

"Oh!" Clover bites her bottom lip, trying to make a decision. "Fuck it!" Clover curses.

I belt out a laugh. "That bad, huh?"

"Gimme." She holds out her grabby hands. "I *need* them."

"Okay." I hand her the already open bottle and half-eaten carton of ice cream. "Crap." I race back to the kitchen, grab a spoon, run back, and come to a screeching halt. "Damn, Clo." Sitting on the couch is Clover, drinking from the bottle, chugging away.

"What?" she wipes off her mouth. "If you *only* knew."

Jumping over the couch, I take my seat beside her. "Well, this isn't going to solve your issues." I reach for the bottle.

"Fine, I'll take it easy…" Clover looks between the carton of ice cream and the wine bottle.

"Don't even think about it."

"Don't even try to stop me, Montgomery." She snags the bottle like she's Stretch Armstrong or something and pours the rest of the wine into the half-empty carton. "If you only knew what happened."

I sit there staring at my friend, her hand out, waiting for me to give her the spoon. If I hold it hostage, she will just get her own. Either way, this night is going to end with drunk Clover and wake up with her having one hell of a hangover.

Spoon it is.

"Wine and dairy?" I hand the utensil over, and she digs in, moaning. "This better not be a repeat of your twenty-first birthday."

She shovels a huge bite into her mouth and tries to talk. "You're never going to let me live that down, are you?" Another bite, wine dribbling down her chin.

I swipe the juices with my thumb and take a taste. "Hmm…not bad."

"I told you." She points at me with the spoon before she shovels in another load. This girl is throwing this down.

"Is there any chance of you sharing?" I reach for the carton.

"Nope!" She holds the carton close. "Did I tell you what he did?" She takes one more bite but doesn't give me time to answer. "Get this." She sets the carton on the coffee table. "Touch and you die."

"Okay." I hold my hands up. "All yours."

"He kissed me!" She gasps.

"How dare he!" I joke, even though I'm pissed as fuck he even laid a hand on her after the tweets he posted. I could only imagine what happened on that date.

"No! He didn't kiss me here." She jabs herself in the mouth. "Ouch!"

"Uh-uh! No!" I stand back up and begin to pace the floor. "I don't need to know where he kissed you if it wasn't here." I signal to her lips.

"I wish," she mumbles as she stands and wobbles, but not before she pulls us both back down on the couch.

"You're drunk." I lean back and examine my friend.

"Not drunk, but the wine is catching up with me." She begins to ramble on about how she's fine, then looks at me. "What were we talking about?"

"About this kiss."

"Ohhhh! Yes, he didn't kiss me."

"Thank God!" I accidentally blurt.

"Jeez, Austin. Even *you* think I'm not kissable." Clover reaches for the carton again.

"Stop putting words in my mouth." I take the carton and turn her around to face me.

"Well, apparently it's true. These lips aren't kissable." Clover hangs her head. "Jeffery thought so, and now Jack."

"What in the hell are you talking about?"

How are we going from kissing to not kissing, to Jack, to Jeffery, and now back to Jack?

Women are fucking confusing.

"He leaned in and whispered all these amazing things…" Clover trails off.

"What happened?" I reach down, not realizing what I'm doing, and dig into the wine float. If I'm going to subject myself to girl talk, I might as well do it right.

"Well…" Clover reaches down, places a hand on each side of her perfect round tits, and pushes them together to where they are basically spilling out of the top of her dress.

Wrong damn question!

"Instead of kissing these." She puckers up.

I smile and take another bite.

"He motorboated these." Clover fucking squeezes her tits.

"What the fuck?" Ice cream goes all over the table and onto the rug, staining it, I'm sure.

"Austin! You better not have gotten any on my dress."

"Fuck your dress. I want to know why in the hell he motorboated those things and why you let him."

"I didn't *let* him motorboat me, *Austin*." She drawls out my name like I'm the idiot. "Why would I? It's so disgusting."

"I don't know, *Clover*." I give it back to her. "Maybe because you took a half-naked photo and posted it on Twitter. I mean, come on."

"Screw you!" Clover's bottom lip begins to quiver and her eyes well with tears. She's either about to break down or go off. Either way, it's my fault. "I didn't say, 'Hey, Jack, since you think my boobs are so perfect, why don't you face-plant into them.'"

"I didn't mean—"

"Do you know how degrading that is?" Clover interrupts, not letting me get another word in edgewise. "He stuck his face between my boobs and pretended he was on a motorboat cruising down a river, slow and wet."

"I'm going to—"

"You aren't going to do anything. It's over and done with. The fact is, I'm not kissable, and that is something I'm going to have to live with."

"For crying out loud, now you're just being dramatic."

She gasps.

"What?"

"Stop being such a guy." She glares at me. "And give me that back." She yanks the carton out of my hand and starts to take another bite. "Great. Now it's like soup from you sitting there cradling it in your arms. What am I going to do?"

"Well, first things first." I take the carton and place it in the sink before I head back to the couch and sit back down. "And now you are going to come here." I lean back and stretch my arm along the back of the cushions, inviting her to settle in.

"Just because I cuddle up doesn't mean I'm less angry with you." Clover scoots over and rests her head on my shoulder.

"Good. Now, you are going to tell me why in the world you think you're not kissable."

"Well…" Clover reaches up and starts playing with a small hole in my tee. "Jeffery and I never kissed."

"And you think that's because of you?"

"Mm-hmm." Her words vibrate through my chest, straight to my heart. Clover hasn't ever given herself enough credit. It's why she created that stupid binder. She didn't trust in who she was, so she settled for who she imagined herself to be.

"Elaborate."

"Jeffery hated PDA, and he hated kissing more. So, when we finally did, it seemed more like a chore. He kept saying I used too much tongue, or I sucked too hard."

I chuckle.

"Stop. I know where your mind is going. Don't make this one of your dirty dreams."

"Sorry. Did you think you did?" I ask the question, already knowing the answer. We've discussed this topic a time or two on my show.

"No. Actually, I thought his kisses were too wet and sometimes…" Clover trailers off.

"Sometimes what?" I pry.

She gasps.

"What?"

"Austin! Sometimes I made excuses not to kiss him. Oh—my—God! I hated kissing him!"

"And there it is, folks." I begin to clap. "The truth shall set you free."

"Did you just Dr. Feelgood me?" Clover looks up with her bright blue eyes no longer filled with sadness, but with hope.

"Maybe."

"Well, how about you do it again?" She smiles.

"You mean, you want Dr. Feelgood's advice?" I point to myself. "Me?"

"Sort of." Clover begins to blush. "I want Dr. Feelgood to teach me how to kiss."

"Y-Y-You wh-what?" I stutter.

"Stop playing coy with me. You know exactly what I said. It's been way over six years since I've kissed anyone. What if I forgot how? What if I really do suck?"

"I'm not kissing you. You're like my—"

"Don't say it." Clover slaps her hand over my mouth. "Don't make this awkward."

"You already did," I mumble.

"No, what would be awkward is me asking Mal or CJ to teach me. That would be weird and slightly inappropriate."

"Yet hot!" I close my eyes. "I can almost—"

"Stop it!" She sits up, crossing her legs, and faces me. "I'm serious, Austin. You're a guy, and my best friend, who just so happens to know everything about the female anatomy and loves sex. Hell, you get paid to talk about sex."

"Well, this is true." I nod and readjust to face her.

"Right? You are the obvious choice." Clover is practically bouncing up and down, shaking us both.

"You're drunk."

"I'm tipsy—big difference."

"You're going to regret this," I warn.

"I promise you I won't."

I promise you I will.

When friends kiss, lines definitely cross and things become—well...*complicated.* And that is the number one reason why I don't want to partake in this smooch session.

Clover has been my go-to person since the moment our moving van pulled in next door. I jumped out, and Clover came skipping across the lawn with her cute little braided pigtails and ruffled little pink dress asking if I wanted to help at her lemonade stand. Since I didn't have any friends and my sister was annoying, I thought why not? Plus, she offered me a fifty percent cut.

"Fine. I'll do it."

"You will?" Clover's lips turn up in a slow grin. "We're going to make out?"

"W-What?" I choke. "Kiss, Clover. We are going to kiss."

"Same difference." She rolls her eyes. "Now look who's being dramatic."

"Clover, this is serious. If you are too *tipsy* to get serious, I suggest you call CJ to help you out." I begin to get up, but Clover grabs ahold of my sleeve and tugs me back down.

"I'm just nervous," she finally admits. "You're like Dr. Feelgood, and I'm just...*me*."

"That." I point to her. "You have to stop thinking like that."

"What?" Clover glances upward, her mouth pursed but slightly open before she lets out a deep breath. "What am I doing wrong *now*?"

"Look at me, Clover." I reach across and take her face in my hands. "Be confident."

"I'm trying." She tries to move my hands away, but I don't budge.

"Kissing is less about technique and more about feeling comfortable in the moment. If you're comfortable, then you're confident, and if you're confident, you won't worry—"

"Which means I get out of my own head."

"The student is paying attention." I reach up with my finger and tap her temple. "Gold star for Clover."

"Thanks, professor." She winks.

"No. Don't do that." I shake my head.

"What? A little too confident?" She begins to back away, and my hands fall to my lap.

"No, a little too professor-student porn." I laugh. "Again, this is a delicate situation between me and you. So, approach it as such."

"Got it. So, what are the rules exactly?" Clover scoots against the cushions, sitting back on her feet.

"Okay, no rules really. At least not for you…"

"Which is it? Do I have rules, or don't I?"

"Stop being so antsy. You don't have rules because I don't want you to be nervous. I just want you to go with the moment, and if that means you touch my face, chest, or arms, so be it, but don't let it get in your head if I don't touch you."

"That's weird." Clover raises a brow and twists her mouth. "But whatever. Kiss me."

I wish she knew how hard this is for me. Kissing isn't just kissing, and if anyone says it is, they are full of shit. When two people lock lips, it can lead to three things: a relationship, sex, or never seeing them again—aka they suck at it. And I can't do any of those with Clover. So, I have to figure out a way to shut myself off while I become Clover's kissing dummy.

"Okay." I lean forward, but she's still too far away.

"Should I maybe scoot closer?"

"Here." I stretch out my leg and place my other one on the floor. "Move in."

She does.

"Austin, what if I…?"

I can't help it. If I let her finish, she'll get into her own head, so I do the only logical thing and crash my mouth down to hers.

Big mistake.

She opens her mouth to me—tongues exploring, playing, getting to know each other.

Her hands fly up to my chest as she moans. It's my undoing. After all, I'm a man. My growing dick says so.

I told her I wasn't going to touch her, but damn if my self-control isn't disintegrating in…

Three…

Two…

One.

My hands fly up to cup her cheeks, but they have a mind of their own—the traitors—and decide to wrap around her petite waist instead, holding her to me. I don't want to make this any more intimate than it already is. Telling my conscience to fuck off, I work my palms up her back and cradle her face as I drink from her like a man dying of thirst.

I care about her.

Of course, this is intimate. What the hell was I thinking? I can't go here. I won't. It's Clover…I try not to focus on the fact that my best friend's lips are the sweetest things I've ever tasted.

She acts all shy and uncertain, but damn this girl can move. Her hands tighten their grip on my shirt as she leans into me.

I lose my balance, so caught up in this "practice kiss," and we tumble backward. I ignore the aching where I'm pretty sure I just cracked my skull on the armrest and focus on her body draped over mine.

Our contact never breaking.

My hands never leaving her face.

Stroking her hair.

Urging her on when I should be fighting her off.

Just when I'm about to take this past the friend-zone, Clover pulls back, her lips leaving me with a soft popping sound. I stare up at her swollen, red lips and wild eyes in awe as she asks, "How was that?"

She had to ask? Like the earth didn't just quake a little. Like the sight of her skin flushed from desire and red from my stubble isn't the hottest fucking thing I've ever seen.

I did that to her.

My face.

My lips.

My hands.

"I don't think you have anything to worry about." My smile is tight.

"Really?" She bounces. "I mean, it felt really good. Like, I could have kept going." *Kept going?* Does she really have no clue what she's saying? There was only one place to go from there. "How was it for you?"

How was it for me?

"Clover, the evidence is pretty clear." I glance down.

"Oh, wow!" Clover giggles. "That's good! I mean, not good for you." She nods to my cock. "Obviously."

"It's just a natural reaction. No need to be alarmed." I stand, tugging on my shorts. "I'm just going to clean up this mess and maybe hit the sack."

"Aw!" Clover whines. "I'm wide awake now. I was hoping we could binge-watch a little TV."

How do I tell my best friend I can't watch TV with her because I have something huge I have to take care of?

"We can binge-watch that reality show you like." She folds her hands together and silently begs.

"Whatever. I'll get the popcorn and water because you've had enough to drink."

"Goody." She jumps up and down before she heads down the hall. "I'm just going to throw on something a little comfier."

"Take your time," I holler after her.

I have something to take care of.

CHAPTER SEVENTEEN

AUSTIN

I can't stop thinking about that kiss. Her lips, her skin, the way she felt under my touch…*her.* Even after we watched episode after episode of horrible TV, I couldn't shake it. Clover Kelly left her mark on me, and I have no clue how I'm going to erase it.

Now, here I am, back hurting, leg cramping, and my arm numb from Clover falling asleep on me last night. A good guy would have woken her up. A better man would have carried her to bed. But I'm neither of those. I'm a selfish bastard who wanted to feel what I felt for a little while longer.

"Austin?" Clover moans. "Kiss me."

Hearing those words hit me like a sucker-punch to the chest.

"Please," she whispers.

I can't do this. I can't keep up whatever this is. We grew up together. She's seen me at my worst and cheered me on during my best. I will never let one kiss come between that.

"Austin…" Clover's eyes slowly flutter open. "I had the craziest dream."

Brushing her hair out of her face, I lower my voice, "The motorboating was real."

Clover smiles, her still tired eyes sparkling with amusement. "Oh, I know, but—"

"Get some rest," I cut in. "It's still really early."

"Austin?" Clover reaches up, scratching her fingers along my jaw. "It wasn't a dream, was it?"

This is my chance to convince her it didn't happen. To fool us both that these feelings aren't real. But I don't.

Nodding my head yes, I speak the words no.

Clover leans up. "You're lying, Austin Montgomery." She brushes her thumb over my lips as she closes her eyes.

"I don't want to be," I confess as I watch her dream become her reality.

Slowly opening one eye at a time, a lazy smile stretches across her lips.

"Why?" She asks the question I've asked myself a million times while lying here, sleepless, worrying about what today will bring.

Could we?

Can we?

What if?

"I don't want to lose you." My truth pumps new life into me—one I never knew I wanted.

Every beat.

Every thump.

It beats for her.

Clover doesn't react. She doesn't say a word. She just pushes off the couch and stands there in her barely-there tank and way-too-cheeky shorts. Tempting me. Taunting me.

I made a mistake. One I'll never be able to take back. One that will haunt me for the rest of my life and change our friendship forever.

"Clo, I'm sorry…" I shake my head, unsure of what to do. "I wish I could take it back."

"I don't," she says as a blush rises in her cheeks.

"What are you saying?"

"This." Clover places her hands on my shoulders as my hands instinctively wrap around her waist, balancing her as she places a knee on each side of my legs.

"Clover, we can't," I beg her not to do this no matter how much I want this, but my need for it to happen is stronger than my desire to stop it. My words…*vanish.*

Her mouth is mere inches from mine as she breathes me in. The neckline of her tank is loose and dangerously low, and with her hair tied up on top, I can't help but stare at the smooth creamy skin begging to be touched.

One lick.

One tease.

One taste.

I imagine the trail of kisses from here to there, but for now, I tease us both by dragging the backs of my fingertips from her ticklish spot behind her ear to the valley between her perfect breasts, dipping my finger low, running it along the inside of her bra.

She shivers.

"You cold?" I ask, already knowing the answer.

Clover shakes her head no as she reaches down and slowly pulls her tank above her head, exposing her sheer pink demi bra.

"Is this new?" I reach down and run my finger under the strap of the bra.

"I bought it tonight," Clover confesses, her chin dropping to hide her embarrassment.

My fingers tug beneath her chin. "Look at me," I demand, and she does. "Who did you buy it for?"

"You."

"Did you model this for him?" I suddenly feel possessive.

"Nope." She shakes her head back and forth. "I had hoped—"

"You wanted this to happen?"

"I did." Her lips curl into a sexy, seductive smile.

I can't help myself. My hands roam up her body to tangle in her hair before wrapping the long strands around my palm and pulling her head down, claiming her lips with my own.

The desire coursing through my veins clouds the part of my brain that's screaming this will change everything. The remaining doubt crumbles as her hips rock back and forth against mine.

It's not enough. It'll never be enough.

Now that we've crossed the line, there's no going back.

I need to be closer.

I need her.

Now.

"Austin!" Her cries of pleasure from grinding on my lap have me rock-hard as she begs for more.

Lifting her up, I work the thin cotton of her shorts down over her perfectly shaped hips and rest her back against me. There is no time for anything another than pure need.

"Touch me." My voice comes out a heavy whisper.

I need her hands on me as my own hold her tightly to me. Her fingertips slip under my waistband before withdrawing and running up my abs and back down, pulling my boxers away. "Tease." I lean forward and nip her lips with my own before the kiss deepens as she grinds on me one last time before easing up and positioning herself over my straining cock.

My hips buck in anticipation, and fuck me if I don't feel her for the first time as I brush against her soaking wet core. It's more than I could have ever imaged.

The heat.

The wetness.

The need.

Her hands grasp my shoulders, nails digging into my skin as the tip slides inside. "Austin." Her body quakes.

"You feel so good," I choke out as I lift my head back up and drink in the sight of Clover riding me. Slow. And. Steady.

"Austin," she cries out again, and then again, as I thrust into her wet heat, surrounded by her scent, her voice.

"Yeah, baby. I'm close too." I moan, sliding my mouth from hers and down her neck. "Austin!" Her cries get louder, my thrusts deeper, speeding up.

Just as I'm about to bring us both over the edge, she smacks me on the shoulder—hard.

Damn! I didn't know she was into kink.

"Austin!" She smacks me again. My eyes snap open and fly to meet hers. It takes me a minute to focus and realize Clover is leaning over me…fully dressed.

What the—?

"Ewww! Austin! What the heck?" she screeches. "Were you having one of those sex dreams?"

"What? No!" I defend myself, looking around the room as I struggle to get my breathing under control.

"Um—I'm pretty sure you are." She takes her finger and keeps pointing it like it's a fucking flashing neon sign at my dick. "Or at least you *were.*" Her lips fight the urge to smile.

"Well, you're wrong." I follow her gaze to my lap, and what do you know? I'm sporting some serious morning wood. Kill me now.

"Then what is that?" She tries to stifle a laugh.

"Nothing!" I grab a pillow in an attempt to cover my raging hard-on I just *thought* was being buried in her. My best friend. If this doesn't win asshole of the year award, I don't know what does.

"Yeah. It doesn't look like nothing to me." She laughs and walks to the kitchen, leaving me to my humiliation and thoughts of another cold shower.

"By the way," she peeks her head around the corner, "I had a really weird dream last night."

Trust me. Nothing can top mine.

"Oh, really? What about?"

"That I asked you to teach me to kiss." She stands there, waiting for me to say something, as if she *wants* me to confirm it, but I can't.

If there is any way to erase what's happened in the last eight to ten hours, this is it. If I want to save this friendship, I can only respond one way.

"Wow! That's crazy." I shake my head and roll my shoulders. "Why would you do that?"

"Exactly! Friends don't kiss," Clover points out.

“Nope. They sure don’t,” I agree

I wish she would have believed that last night.

CHAPTER EIGHTEEN

CLOVER

"Dating sucks."

"Seriously?" Mal eyes widen when she sees how serious I am. "That bad, huh?"

"Really bad." I slide into the booth next to Mal for our weekly catch up session at Cuppa Joe.

"That's why I skip to the good stuff." CJ's lips twist into a wicked smirk.

I throw my hands up in the air. "I thought that's what I was doing."

"Yeah." CJ shakes her head. "That isn't how this works."

"Totally random, but did you know if you balance a straw on your upper lip, not pursed, but relaxed, it can help reduce fine lines and wrinkles?" Mal then picks up her straw and begins to demonstrate as CJ and I look on.

"Clover, Google that shit. I'm not buying it." CJ slides her phone over to me.

I hold my hands in the air. "Not happening. I'm done with Google. We've officially broken up."

CJ gasps.

"I swear, it was in one of the beauty magazines I picked up the other day," Mal defends.

"Well, in my magazine, it said blow jobs do the same thing." She places her hands in the air like she's weighing her options. "Straw or…getting a guy off?"

"Straw!" Mal and I say in unison.

"And this is why you both are single." A grin tugs at CJ's lips.

How did I lose control of this conversation? One minute, we're talking about how sucky my dating life is, and now Cosmo and Hoover are trading beauty secrets. Lovely."

"Speaking of single…" CJ gives me the opening I was looking for. "Three dates and nothing?"

"Nothing," I confirm.

"Yeah, about that," Mal gives her two cents. "Why didn't we hear from you after date two? Sexy Smile Guy?"

"Yeah, Clover," CJ teases. "I followed your tweets until they basically put me to sleep."

"That's because I'm pretty sure I even fell asleep." I fake yawn. "Sexy Smile Guy is actually Really Boring Guy. Apparently, he didn't have a plan for our date."

"I really thought he was going to be a top contender." Mal lifts her mug to her lips and crinkles her nose. "I think this is yours." She slides her coffee over and takes mine. "It has Splenda."

"Thanks." I chuckle.

"Okay, I've got it!" CJ jumps in. "You got your coffee?" She points to Mal, who nods. "And you've now got yours, so on with the story."

Mal and I just stare at her.

"What?" CJ quickly gives us one of her *don't ask because I'm not telling* looks. "Got a problem?"

"Nope." I glance at Mal, telepathically telling her to do the same.

"Yep." She leans forward, daring Ceej. Apparently, my skills need a little work. "Did someone not get any last night?"

"It's none of your—"

"You know what *is* your business?" I cut CJ off, and finish, "My dates!"

"Yes!" CJ stands and points to me. "What she said!"

"Monica!" Mal hollers at our favorite barista. "We need another round."

This lightens the mood. CJ sits down, and I finally get to finish how Seth Brooks gave me my most boring date ever.

"So, let me get this straight, you drove around all night talking?" Mal questions.

"Yes! But only because he couldn't make up his mind on where we should go."

"How did you not see this on the speed-dating round?" CJ joins in.

"Think about it, I ask the questions and they answer. There was no way to know he lacks communication skills, the ability to make a decision, and is also a germaphobe."

"A germaphobe? Really?" Mal asks.

"Yes! I tried to reassure him and reached over to touch his hand and…he broke out the hand sanitizer."

"Nooo!" they both say in unison.

"Oh yes." I nod. "So, needless to say, when I finally chose for us to go for ice cream, I had to open the door."

"I really should have paid closer attention to the tweets." CJ gets out her phone and pulls them up. "Here is the one of you guys in the limo."

Clover Kelly @UnLuckyInLove_13
This smile. <pic> #unluckyinlove #hotlinehookup #hessexyandheknowsit

"Oh! Here is the ice cream shop where you are holding open the door." CJ zooms in and flips it around for Mal to see. "Look, there he is at the counter with his hands in his pockets."

Clover Kelly @UnLuckyInLove_13
Insta-scoop or Insta-love? <pic> #unluckyinlove #hotlinehookup #foodporn #yummy

"Where's the good night one?" Mal takes her phone and scrolls until she finds it. "Here it is."

Clover Kelly @UnLuckyInLove_13
Getting lucky? Not tonight. #unluckyinlove #hotlinehookup #sorrynotsorry #luckisnotthislady #sexyandsingle

"Daaammmn!" CJ snags her cell back. "Obviously, he was a dud. So, skip to baseball guy and how many bases he tapped, if you know what I mean."

"Well…Lane West, hot guy in tights, right fielder for one of our hometown minor league teams, so eager to go on a date with me, he showed up in his uniform for the speed-dating round."

"Right? It's why you chose him—blah, blah, blah—get to the good stuff." CJ lays her head on her hands and waits for the rest of the story.

"Here you ladies go." Monica takes this moment for a welcome interruption. At least for me and Mal. "And CJ." Monica glares while scooting her mug across the table.

"Monica! We were just about to find out if Clover scored a home run or not." CJ sighs.

"Follow her tweets, Ceej." Mal suggests.

"Spoiler alert. She didn't," Monica blurts before she pivots around and tucks behind the counter.

"I thought," I wave between the two, "you guys made up?"

"Oh, we did." CJ waves her hand over her coffee cup like she's Vanna White.

"That's a middle finger," I point out the obvious. "We have hearts."

"Uh…hello?" CJ tugs on her shirt sporting the same frothy symbol with the hashtag #coffeesaveslives. "She gets me."

"Okay then." I can't do anything but nod. Their friendship is strange.

"I'm going to ignore the fact that Monica spoiled the ending, so let's pretend and you start from the very beginning."

"Yes! What she said," Mal agrees, both of their eyes on me.

"Fine." I take a deep breath. This date is why I'm here. He was supposed to be the calm after the date number two storm, and instead, he brought the thunder and lightning.

"It started off with Owen calling me with a change of plans. Instead of meeting at the studio, the driver was going to take me to the stadium."

"Interesting," Mal chimes in.

CJ glares at her to shut her mouth.

"Once I got there, Lane greeted me in his practice uniform and walked us to the field where there was a picnic set up in center field—his position," I remind them. "He packed a bottle of wine for me, water for him, subs, fruit, and veggies. It was…nice."

"Sweet," CJ comments.

Now, it's Mal's turn to return the glare.

"Anyway, we ate, and what I didn't eat, he devoured."

"Hold up." Mal tosses CJ a look. "Sorry, but I have to know." She turns to me. "You mean he ate your sub?"

"Um…yes." I lean in. "I wasn't even done, but I set it down to take a sip of the Chardonnay, which was apparently a gift to the coach he snagged up, but that's another story. I took a sip, and he just snagged my sub and asked if I was done. I didn't know what to say, so I just let him have it."

"Holy cow." Mal's eyes and mouth are frozen open.

"I know, but it doesn't stop there. After the picnic, we cleaned up and had a little batting practice."

"Smooth." CJ smirks. "This is where dude is about to make his move." She nods, a devilish smile splayed on her lips. "I've fallen for this—willingly—a time or ten." She winks.

"Well, you would think, but not so much. He set up the pitching machine and hit a few balls to show me how it was done. Then he called me over, helped me put on a helmet, which totally ruined my hair, and positioned me. I missed every single one."

"Okay, so he helped, right?" Mal for waves me to continue.

"Yes, for a second, until he got frustrated and showed me how to do it again, and again, and again. I never got another turn because, apparently, his friend held the record for batting practice home runs and he just had this feeling he was going to top it—so he had me record him hitting since he was on a *roll*."

"Oh snap!" CJ's jaw drops.

"Yep. Then, after he was done, he took me on a tour of the locker and weight rooms. Which I thought was kind of cool."

"Of course." Mal tries to put a positive spin on this crazy story. "It's like letting you into his world."

"A little too much," I mumble. "When we were in the weight room, he stripped off his jersey and showed me a few of his favorite exercises."

"Hot damn." CJ whistles. "Please tell me you tweeted that shit."

"I did." My lips twitch remembering how crazy sexy he looked with beads of sweat rolling down his perfectly delicious, lickable abs.

Even though this date sucked, Lane's body is smokin' H-O-T and watching him work out for a couple minutes was probably the best part. It's the other fifty-seven minutes of lifting that was boring as hell.

"Here it is!" CJ bounces in her seat. "He's kink-a-licious!" CJ licks her lips as she flips the screen around for Mal to see.

Clover Kelly @UnLuckyInLove_13
One-on-one session. Who's complaining? Not me! <pic>
#unluckyinlove #hotlinehookup #yummy #lickable #iwin

"Holy cow! I'm more of a back guy, but I would totally sit on those…" CJ trails off. "I mean, he definitely looks like he's picked up a few heavy things…like *a lot.* So, I'm sure one hundred twenty-five pounds of this," she straightens up a little more, "would be easy peasy."

"Maybe if you can drag him away from the weight bench." I roll my eyes. "He literally showed me his complete workout. Like, he actually stopped midway and asked if I minded if he continued. Said he needed all the extra workouts he could get in."

"Well, he asked," Mal says, taking a side.

"Mal, girl power remember? Clo is *always* right," CJ reminds our friend. "Hoes before bros."

"I'm all about sticking together, but I'm also about being honest." Mal twists in her seat, tucking her leg under her while she leans back against the wall. "I'm just saying, you had the perfect opportunity to let him know it wasn't okay. Guys get a bad rap for not knowing, but they aren't mind readers."

"What? Read that in one of your self-help guy language dating books?" CJ jokes.

"It's called adulting," Mal spits back. "You guys should try it sometime."

"Whoa!" It's like watching a tennis match between these two. "CJ, Mal is right."

Mal's smile says it all. *She won.*

Not so fast, girlie. "I could have spoken up, but, Mal, CJ is right too."

CJ sticks out her tongue.

"I doubt he would have heard a word I said given the picnic and batting practice fail."

Both girls sit there in silence.

"Did something happen between you two?" My eyes search theirs, trying to figure out what's going on here.

"Nothing worth discussing," Mal admits.

"Oh really? This girl over here needs to grow some balls and admit she has feelings for a certain someone," CJ blurts out.

"Oh my God! I don't have feelings for him." Turning around, Mal leans over the table, and whispers, "And you need to admit to your friend over here," she points to me, "that you—"

"Yes, Mal?" CJ dares.

"That you—"

"You have nothing on me." CJ winks. "Nothing."

"That you—" Mal is about to spill her some tea. "That CJ—" Mal cocks her brow, and a slow devilish smile splays across her lips, "—wears granny panties on the weekends."

"Noooo!" I gasp. Now, this wouldn't normally be a big deal, but CJ swears by everything sexy and has even been known to go commando. "And you made fun of mine."

"Of course. You aren't getting laid." She points out the obvious. "And you," she waggles her finger at Mal, "be thankful I'm not spilling your secrets."

"I have none!" Mal shouts, and everyone in the booths surrounding us turn around. "What? I don't."

"Keep tellin' yourself that, sweets." Ceej smirks. "And as far as the granny panties are concerned…I have sex—lots of it. So, if I want to wear them around my apartment like shorts, then I can. Got it?"

I'm still not buying it. Something is going on here. This little argument is meant to be a distraction from the truth lying in there somewhere. I just nod, accept it, and move on.

"Good. Now, tell us what Mr. Homerun Derby did next." CJ sighs. "Because this girl needs to know."

"Well, after he spent an hour working out—by the way, it wasn't as sexy as you may both think—he made this weird face every time he lifted." I try to mimic his face where he puffed out his cheeks, then bared his teeth on each exhale. Except, when he did it, his top lip would always get stuck and he would have to run his teeth along the bottom of it to release it.

"OMG! That is so funny. Do it again!" Mal practically cries in a fit of laughter as CJ rolls around in her booth, gasping for air.

"I-I-I th-think I…" CJ fumbles over her words, "may have peed a little."

"You and me both." I join in the laughter. "Imagine me trying to hold this in every—single—time he did that. It was crazy, I tell ya."

"Fast forward past the crazy and get to the good stuff." CJ waves me on.

"Yeah," Mal agrees.

"There's nothing good. He showed me where he kept his lucky jockstrap and where they relaxed before a game, but after that? He literally stripped down in front of me, where I saw his very firm, you-can-bounce-a-penny-off-it ass, and hopped in the shower."

"Sweet," CJ coos.

Mal nods her appreciation.

"Yeah, it's the second best part of the date," I agree. "The worst part is when he took me to a dessert bar, paid with a gift card, and then asked me to leave the tip, because, apparently, in the minor league, you don't make that much money." I pause for a minute to let it sink in. "His words—not mine."

"I can't believe he did that," Mal speaks up.

"Hold up now, why do the guys have to pay for everything?" CJ defends Lane.

"Since the station refunds the contestant for any expenses up to five hundred dollars," Mal fights back with a little bit of information I wasn't aware of.

"Oh my God! He turned in the receipt and basically exchanged a gift card for cash?" I throw myself back in my seat, shocked.

"What a loser." CJ lifts her mug to her lips and downs the rest of her coffee. "I hope he loses his lucky strap."

"Ha-ha." Mal reaches over and high-fives CJ. "Good one."

"I have to see these tweets." CJ tries to swipe her phone to life. "Mine's dead."

"Here." I scroll through my profile, find the ones from last night, and hand my phone over to my friends. "There's really nothing to see."

Clover Kelly @UnLuckyInLove_13
Let the thirsty tweets begin ;) <pic> #unluckyinlove #hotlinehookup #thirsty #drinkthis #takemeouttotheballgame

"Holy hell!" CJ feigns licking my screen.

"Can we see the pic without the winky face covering his backside?" Mal begs, wanting more of his pre-shower strip down.

"No. I deleted it. This pic was his idea," I say, spoiling it for them.

"So, this is what Monica was talking about?" CJ pulls up the other tweet.

Clover Kelly @UnLuckyInLove_13
Lane West strikes out, but we still have another inning to go. <pic> #unluckyinlove #hotlinehookup #betterlucknexttime

"Okay, so we have Motorboat Guy, Boring Guy, and Cheap as Hell Guy. When does date four happen?" Mal leans in, nudging my shoulder. "What's his name? Nick?"

"Yes!" I shake my fists in the air. "Contestant number one—Nick Reed. They saved the best for last." I clasp my hands together. "I'm so excited I can't stand it."

"Gurrrl, *everyone* in that room could feel the sizzle you were cooking up at that table." CJ shakes her hand like it's on fire. "So, when is this big date happening so we can be on Twitter watch?"

"Oh, right! I got so excited, I totally forgot to answer you guys. It's tomorrow."

"Do you need help picking out an outfit?" CJ scoots closer to the table. "Or shopping?" She waggles her eyebrows. "I'm thinking something black, sheer, sexy?"

"I have it covered."

CJ lets out an exasperated sigh, and Mal whines.

"I grabbed a couple outfits when I was out yesterday. I'll just get Austin's opinion on which one to wear."

"You really think my brother will help you pick out something sexy for Nick?" Mal pleads. "Just let us come over and we can get this knocked out in a matter of minutes."

"I can't, girls. Antonette is off today and I have a few houses to show this evening. Plus, whatever one he picks, I'll just wear the opposite." I wink.

"Aw, you're not just a pretty face." CJ reaches over the table and pinches my cheek. "Are you?"

"Real funny, Ceej." I slap her hand away.

"Well, speaking of work. I have an interview." Mal hands me my purse, then grabs hers. "And if I don't leave here in the next five minutes, I'll be late."

"I thought you loved your job?" CJ questions.

"I love clothes, but being an online stylist isn't everything it's cracked up to be. Plus, when Austin mentioned an opening at the station, I thought, why not?"

"Oh, then you are a shoo-in." I wave it off and stand, letting Mal out. "There is no way Austin won't hire his little sis."

"The interview is with Owen." Mal stands and squeezes out of the booth. "And we don't actually see eye to eye on things."

"He's actually really nice, Mal. I'm sure it will go great."

"What's the position?" CJ stands and lays a twenty on the table. "I've got this…unless you want to leave the tip." The corner of her mouth twitches back a smile.

"Very funny." I roll my eyes and turn my attention back to Mal as we all walk out together. "As you were saying?"

"Austin said Owen needs someone to filter through Hotline Hookup's calls, interview guests, and maybe come up with new topics for future shows."

"Mal!" I reach for her hand and give it a little squeeze. "You would be perfect for this job."

"Well, she's read enough books to be." CJ cackles as she pushes through the double doors.

"True," Mal and I both agree.

"I wish I could keep chatting, but I've got to get going." Mal leans over and wraps me in an embrace. "Good luck tomorrow—and make sure to have fun!"

"I will."

"And you." Mal waggles her finger at CJ.

"I know. I know." CJ holds up her hands.

"What the hell, guys?" I throw up my arms. "I feel like you guys are leaving me out of some secret inside joke."

"You!" CJ wraps her arm around me as she hollers for Mal to run. "Don't worry your pretty little head about that. You just focus on Nick Reed, date number four."

"But—"

"No buts. Go to work, make some money, and get some beauty sleep. Tomorrow will be here before you know it!"

"Fine, but only if you promise to fill me in later when this is all over." I glance over at my friend, daring her to say no.

"I'll think about it." CJ slaps me on the butt. "Want to know something?" She doesn't give me time to answer. "I got a modeling job. Actually, I'm on my way there now."

"Ceej!" I screech. "Really? I thought you said you would never—"

"It's just a hand job." CJ slaps a palm to her forehead. "A hand *modeling* job." She flips me the bird. "Apparently, I have the perfect finger for what they need."

"That you do." We both laugh as we walk down the streets of New York.

"I have a secret too." I contemplate telling my friend about the dream I had a few nights ago.

"Like a real secret meant for *my* ears only?" CJ digs.

"Yes. Like I do not want Mal to know this."

"You fucked Austin!" CJ gasps. "I knew it!"

"No! Oh God no!" I make a face. "How could you even say that?"

"Because you guys live together, *and* you're both attractive, *and* pretty people are supposed to procreate," CJ says, as if this is no big deal. Like me having sex with Austin would be totally normal.

Wrong.

"I had a *dream* I kissed Austin." I side-eye my friend, who's walking beside me, not saying a word, nodding her head. "Well, I had a dream I asked Austin to kiss me because I was afraid I wasn't kissable."

"That's your subconscious talkin' right there."

"I do not want to kiss Austin."

"Okay, do you mind if I kiss him?" CJ teases, and I shoot her a look. "Only kidding."

"CJ!" I turn to face my friend, grab her by the shoulders, and shake. "Focus here. Why on earth did I dream this?"

"Were you drinking?"

"Yes, I had a lot of drinks," I confess. "I was a little upset after the motorboat date. I consumed a whole bottle of Cab, then fell asleep watching bad TV with Austin."

"Well, it's either one of two things: alcohol and Austin don't mix, or you really do want to kiss him."

"I don't want to kiss Austin!" I shout.

"Then why ask me?"

"I don't know." I shrug.

"If you don't want to *really* kiss Austin, then this is an open-and-closed matter. A non-issue," CJ reaffirms.

"You're absolutely right," I agree.

"I hate to cut this day short, but this is as far as I go." CJ signals a taxi. "I don't want to be late."

"Well, break a leg, or in this case, a finger!" I shout as she opens the door and flips me off.

"Hey! I do have a question," she hollers as she climbs in.

"Yeah?"

"How did *dream* Austin kiss?" Her lips curl into a small smile as she closes the door and the taxi pulls off.

It was absolutely the best kiss ever.

CHAPTER NINETEEN

AUSTIN

I can't believe I'm sitting here, on the sofa, waiting for Clover to get ready so we can ride together for the final installment of this Unlucky in Love dating round shit. I'm actually flipping through the channels as if I'm interested in this shit when I can't stop thinking about that stupid fucking kiss…and the dream that followed.

This is why friends shouldn't kiss.

This is exactly why I shouldn't have let her move in.

This is why…fuck if I know, but whatever it is, I shouldn't have done it, because I'm sure it contributed in some way or form.

If this wasn't the fourth and final date, I wouldn't go. But fuck if it's not that first contestant from the speed-dating round Clover can't stop talking about. Nick Reed—model, trainer, entrepreneur, a fucking thorn in my side.

I don't know what it is, but something about the bastard sets me off. Maybe it's the way he looked at her, or the way he kissed her hand. Hell, maybe it's because he's been texting back and forth with Owen, trying to get inside information on Clover to make sure their date is perfect.

I tossed the fucking yellow flag, but Owen overrode the call and said this is perfectly normal in this business. His call to detail will only enhance our ratings and guarantee Clover the perfect date. What could go wrong?

I'll tell you—*everything*!

"Hey, Austin?" Clover calls out from her bedroom.

"Yeah?"

"Can you come here for a moment?"

"Sure thing."

You got this.

I shake the stress out, squeeze my eyes shut, plaster a smile on my face, and casually take my time walking to her room. Maybe she'll forget what she even wanted by the time I get there.

"Hey, Austin, are you com—?" Clover shouts as she swings open the door, not realizing I'm standing right in front of it. "Oh!" she shrieks and jumps back. "You startled me." Clover takes a minute to catch her breath before her eyes go wide and grabs ahold of my shirt. "Get in here now."

"What's the nine-one-one?" I cross my arms as Clover stands in front of the mirror in her little pale pink robe holding two dresses.

"Which one?" She holds up a tiny navy-blue dress that looks like it will barely cover her ass, and then a soft pink one that resembles the dress from date one, but this one has long sleeves and is shorter.

"Do either of them cover your ass?" I walk over to her and hold them both up.

"Of course they do." She snags the pink one from my hands. "I just don't know which one screams, '*I want to get lucky, but date me too*,' you know?"

Blowing out a deep breath, I try to gather my thoughts—something I've been doing a lot of lately.

"Listen, Clo. I'm not sure if those two things ever really go together," I admit, as if I'm breaking some kind of top-secret bro-code rule. "If you have sex on the first date, nine times out of ten, the guy isn't going to call, let alone date you. And if he does, it's just to hook up again."

"And why is that, huh?" Clover pops out her hip.

"Hey." I hold up my hands and the little blue dress hanging from my finger. "I don't make the rules. I just follow them."

She gasps and turns back around. "Get out. I don't need your help."

"Come on. Don't be this way," I beg.

I honestly wasn't trying to be a dick. The facts are the facts, and the truth of it is men are assholes. Plain and fucking simple.

"Austin, I know you're trying to be helpful, but you have been acting really weird lately, and tonight, I just needed you not to be." She raises her eyes, meeting mine through the reflection standing in front of us both and I can see the hurt that I put there and damn if I don't want to make that look go away.

"You're right." Taking a step closer, I wrap my arm around her and hold up the dress. "This one will be perfect."

"Really?" She angles her head, watching me.

"Really." I nod. "The color will make your eyes pop. It's short so your legs will constantly be on display, and the dip…well, how about we ignore that."

"Perfect. Pink it is." Her lips curl into a small smile. "Thanks, Austin. I'll be ready soon."

I narrow my eyes, running a hand through my hair. "Am I missing something? I thought I just said blue?"

"You did, and I decided on pink." Clover begins messing with her hair, ignoring I'm still here, waiting for her to change her mind.

"You can't." I find myself saying the words for all the wrong reasons.

"Why not?" She spins around while slicking a pink gloss over her lips.

Because pink…is mine.

The dress.

The lingerie.

Her lips.

But it's not—it will *never* be.

I have no words, no excuses…none that will matter.

"Well?" Clover stands in front of me, arms crossed, toe tapping. "I'm waiting."

"You know what? It's absolutely perfect." I give her a weak smile. "I'm sure your date will be very pleased."

"Aw! Thanks, Austin."

"No problem." I nod and head out the door.

I can't do this. I can't stand on the sideline and let this happen.

"Oh, hey." I pop my head back in.

"What's up?" Clover doesn't even bother to look up as she continues fussing with her hair.

"Owen just texted," I lie. "He needs me come to the station early."

"Oh?"

"Yeah. I'll send Thomas back for you in," I glance down at my watch, "about an hour. Will that work?"

"Sure. I'll be ready." Clover twists around, flashing me one hell of a smile.

The problem? It's not for me. It's for the man she's excited about seeing in an hour.

"Hey, man." I peek my head into Owen's office. "If Clover asks, you needed me to come in early."

"Uh-uh. Nope!" Owen stands and walks over to me. "You are not going to bring me in on your lying ways." He slaps me on the shoulder as he pushes by.

"Come on. It's nothing really." I spin around and follow him down the hallway.

"Sure it isn't." He keeps going.

"Living with her is impossible!" Which is kind of true. "Clothes and makeup are everywhere," I plead—a total lie. Clover is a neat freak. Even Kramer picks up his own toys.

"Think of it as a trial run for when you are ready to settle down." He turns around and walks backward for a second. "Your future wife will thank you for that." He pivots back around and keeps going. "By the way, Nick will be here early. He wants to discuss a few things."

"What in the hell does he want now?"

"I don't know." He throws his hands up in the air. "Maybe to get us both on a fitness regimen or something. That guy likes to talk shop." He holds up the bottled protein shake in his hand. "This shit isn't half bad, and I've been hitting the gym before coming to work."

"I don't like him," I blurt out.

"You," he spins around as soon as we hit the lobby, "just don't want Clover to be happy."

"Not true, man." I rub my hands over my face. "It's just these guys—"

"What are you getting at?"

I throw my finger at the Hotline Hookup/Hot Wire Radio sign. "We failed her."

"We didn't fail Clover. This is what *she* wanted. You heard her." Owen waves a hand over his head. "Hell, they all did."

"That!" I jab my finger at Owen. "Is the point I'm trying to make. She just got out of a relationship! She was confused! That outburst wasn't for the world to hear…it was for *me*."

"She could have said no."

"Come on, you really didn't give her a choice."

"That's not fair."

"No!" I shout, not giving a fuck who's standing around. "What's not fair is building her up only for these dates to tear her down."

"Buddy." Owen takes a step closer and clasps my shoulder. "I think you're too close to this situation and not giving your friend enough credit." He nods once. "You good? Because Nick should be here any moment."

I let out a deep breath. "Owen…"

Owen waves and walks off, and I'm left standing here wondering how in the hell I'm going to fix this.

I have to fix this.

"Austin, I have someone I want you to meet." Owen walks over with Nick Reed.

"Dr. Feelgood." Nick lets my name roll off his tongue and offers his hand with a slimy, up-to-no-good smirk plastered on his face. "I'm a huge fan."

I bet you are.

"Sweet. It's good to finally meet you."

No, really, it's not.

I clasp his hand, gripping it a little tighter than necessary to show Nick he doesn't want to fuck with me. It's basically a cleaner version of whose dick is bigger.

I win.

Nick was about to say something when Owen's phone starts to ring. "Well, shit." He holds up his cell. "I have to take this. Give me ten." Owen then turns and rounds the corner, leaving me here to make small talk with this chump.

"So, Nick? Owen says—"

"He's talked to you?" Nick immediately cuts in. "I mean, if it's something you're interested in, I have some ideas." Nick pulls out an envelope from his back pocket and hands it over to me. "I brought this just in case."

I glance at Nick sideways, trying to figure out his angle. Looking between him and the envelope, I decide to open it.

What is Owen up to?

"You've discussed this with Owen?" I unfold the paper.

"Yeah. He said it wasn't a good idea to approach you about it until after the final round." He nods at the proposal I'm holding.

A fucking business plan.

Blowing out a deep breath, I roll my tongue, fighting off the words I want to throw at this goon.

"What's the matter?" Nick begins to shuffle his feet. "Did I…?" His voice raises an octave, losing his cockiness from before. "I mean, we can make any adjustments you deem fit."

I hold up the paper and carefully stuff it back in the envelope buying me some time to cool off.

"I've also been working on my radio voice." Nick deepens his voice, slowly enunciating each word. "Mr. Muscles here, ready to answer all your fitness questions—"

"Just stop," I interrupt this fool before he makes an even bigger ass out of himself.

"Okay. I've got it. It needs some work, but what about the concept?" Nick slides his hands in his pockets and rocks back on his heels. "Genius, right?"

Slapping the envelope repeatedly against my palm, I examine this bastard in front of me. It's all making sense now.

"Why did you sign up for Unlucky in Love?" I ask the simple question that requires an easy answer.

Nick's head flips around as if I just asked him to recite the periodic table.

"Okay…" My lips curl up and I shake my head. "It's not that hard. Did you sign up for Clover or a little self-promotion?"

"Um…uh…"

I take a step closer to this prick who probably has a good twenty pounds of muscle on me. But I don't give a fuck. I'm one step away from shoving my fucking fist down his goddamn throat.

"I'm losing my patience, Nick." I stand in front of this asshole who probably is shitting bricks right about now.

"Come on, Austin." He gives me a tight smile. "Of course, I came here for Clover. Look at her." He waves a hand over to the cutout standing a few feet away.

"This proves otherwise." I slap the envelope in his hands.

"Okay." He exhales. "Maybe it was a little bit of both?"

And there it is.

"Is everything okay over here?" Owen walks up, and I hold up a hand.

"Not now, man."

"Go on, Nick. Explain."

"Come on," Nick argues. "This is no different than *The Bachelor*. Those guys who are artists, actors, models, or whatever—they are there to further their careers."

"Nick, this isn't the fucking *Bachelor*."

"I thought you talked to him?" Nick turns to Owen, sidestepping me.

"Oh shit!" Owen rolls his head back. "Niiick, buddy. I told you to wait. This wasn't the time." Owen sighs.

"And you…" I spin around to face Owen, "you didn't say a fucking word?"

"I didn't think it would go anywhere. I thought he was coming today to talk to you about a contest." Owen holds up his hands, but this fucker is just as guilty.

"He wrote a fucking business plan. First, a spotlight on Hotline Hookup, then his own show—Fit-Bits with Mr. Muscle." I laugh out. "Come on now."

"That's a great name. Don't you think?" Nick smirks. "Get it? Fit Bits? Fitness chat?" Owen and I both stare at this moron for a minute. "What?"

"I'll deal with you in a minute."

"Owen, you knew he was chasing his dream and you didn't boot him from the fucking show." I'm in Owen's face.

"I didn't know until *after* Clover chose him," Owen defends, as if that is some kind of excuse.

"Then why didn't you tell her?"

"Because he seemed interested." Owen drags out the sentence, trying to make his point.

"She—deserved—to—know."

"Austin," Owen slaps my shoulder, "you're too close to this, bud."

I'm not sure what happens in this moment, but everything comes crashing down at once. Nick, Owen, the show, the dates…*Clover.* It's become too much.

"I think everyone here," I whirl my finger in the air, seething at the situation surrounding me, "forgot who's in charge." I smack Owen's shoulder. "Hotline Hookup is my show. I made it." I jab my thumb to my chest. "Me! My face is on the billboards and buses. It's my voice the girls swoon over and guys trust. I'm Dr. Feelgood, and you are *just* my fucking producer. Do you understand?"

"Fuck you, Austin." Owen walks off.

"No! Fuck you, Owen!" I holler after him. "You don't get to gamble with my best friend's heart to boost ratings!"

Owen spins around. "And you don't get to hold her back because *you* are afraid of letting her go. Grow up. She has."

"Sooo…does that mean the date is off?" Nick picks the wrong fucking moment to speak up.

Closing my eyes, I try to gather my emotions, but everything from Clover moving in to the kiss to the dream is catching up with me.

I'm doing this to protect Clover. Or maybe myself…

"Nick, I'm going to give you two seconds to fucking walk away, man." I stand still, my back turned.

"Come on, I didn't mean…."

I spin around. "Get the fuck out now! You're done."

"You know what? You sure in hell are taking this a little too far for some chick who basically said she wanted to get laid."

Who the fuck does he think he is? It takes everything in me not to knock this guy's lights out, but if I do—if I lay one fucking hand on this bastard—he could be the one running Hotline Hookup and I'll get a one-way ticket to the unemployment line.

"Your two seconds are up." My voice is flat and worn out from this back and forth.

"Fine. I don't need you or your show anyway." Nick spins around and heads for the door just as Clover walks in.

Fuck my life.

CHAPTER TWENTY

CLOVER

I feel beautiful, excited, and extremely nervous. More so than the last three dates. There is something about this one, like maybe he's…the one. It felt like we had a real connection.

Nick Reed, contestant number one, and my date number four. My very own Mr. Perfect. I can't help but wonder if there is such a thing as I push through the glass door.

A feeling comes over me. It's not fear or dread, but almost panic as I see Nick and Austin talking in what seems like a heated conversation. My best friend and date are obviously butting heads.

Oh my God.

"Austin, no," I whisper as he steps closer to Nick. "Please don't." My pleas go unheard.

I could have sworn I came to a complete stop, except the click-clack of my heels against the marble floor says otherwise.

Nick spins around and heads straight for me, head down.

"Nick?" I call out. "Is everything—okay?"

The sound of my voice breaks his concentration. "Clover." Nick skids to a stop as he glances back at Austin, who now has his back turned to us. "Um—I don't know how to say this…"

I reach up and rub his arm. "It's okay. I know this whole ordeal is a little stressful with all the rules and tweets, but I promise, it's not that bad," I try to reassure him.

"It's not that." Nick rubs a thumb across his jaw before it lands against the beautiful lips I hope are on me later.

"Well, something is on your mind." I reach out to ease his worry and take his hand in mine.

He jerks away.

"Nick?"

"I can't do this." He takes a step back.

"What do you mean?"

"Clover," he shakes his head, "you seem like a nice girl," he clears his throat, "but apparently what you said you want and what *he* says you want—" Nick nods toward Austin, "—are two different things." He takes another step back.

"I-I don't..." I stumble over my words, confused as to what is going on.

"I'm sorry. It's just not worth it. Good luck." Nick turns and walks out the door, away from my perfect possibility.

I'm totally confused; being pulled in opposite directions. My brain the narrator, wanting to chase after Nick, and my feet the navigator, working their way to the man I know has all the answers and reason why I'm standing here alone.

"Austin?" I call out, but he just stands there with his head hanging low. "Austin?" I'm finally standing in front of him as I place my hand on his shoulder and spin him around.

"Clover..." he breathes out my name in a guilty breath.

"Do you care to tell me why I'm standing here all alone when I should be on my date with Nick?"

And just like that, the mention of his name is like flipping a switch. Austin, who just seconds ago seemed defeated, stands tall, ready to take the bullets I'm about to shoot his way.

"You should be thanking me." He grunts out a laugh.

"Seriously? Thanking you?" I take a step forward. "Why would I thank you when I *wanted* to go on this date—and because of something that transpired between the two of you, I'm not?"

"That's what you think, huh?" Austin shakes his head and lets out a knowing chuckle.

"Yeah." I nod. "It is."

"Well, you're wrong," he claims as his eyes roam above my head. The jerk doesn't even have the balls to look me in the eye.

"Look at me, Austin."

He does.

"Talk to me," I plead.

"Cover..." he says my name, but this time, with pity.

"Please." I close my eyes and blink back the tears. "I just need the truth."

"He wasn't right for you," he casually confesses.

What? He wasn't right for you?

That isn't a confession, this is a coward's way out. Austin would rather hide behind an excuse than face the truth.

I can't even with him right now. My blood is boiling. How can he stand there, and admit, "*He wasn't right for you.*"? I have never said one word about the women he's chosen to date. I may have made fun a time or two, but interfere? *Never.*

This isn't acceptable.

"Why, Austin?" A hand flies to my hip. "Why wasn't he right for me?"

Austin looks up to the ceiling. "Jesus, Clover, are you really going to make me say it?"

"Yes!" I smack his chest. "Tell me."

This is typical Austin. He's never lied to me, but he will avoid me at all costs.

"Fine," he huffs out. "You asked for it."

"I did," I agree.

"Nick Reed, your perfect match or whatever...*only* signed up for Unlucky in Love because he wanted to pitch his idea for *his* own radio show."

I'm not sure why Austin thinks this is even an issue. Nick was completely honest about what brought him to New York in the first place. He's already taken his mobile fitness app and turned it into something much bigger. What's wrong with him wanting more?

"And?" I stand there, waiting for Austin to give me something else, because his reason just pisses me off.

Austin narrows his eyes. "Did you *hear* what I said? Nick was using this as an opportunity to further his career."

"I heard you loud and clear, but it's not exactly what you think."

"He's. Using. You." Austin keeps up this back and forth, and honestly, I'm getting tired of it.

"God!" I groan out. "He's not using me. He's using *you* and your ridiculous sex show," I spit out. "You weren't at my table. You didn't feel what was happening between us."

"Fuck." Austin pulls at his hair.

"If there's more, just spit it out."

"How can you be so naïve right now? Not only did he use the show, but he was going to use you—just like every other guy who applied for the show," Austin seethes.

"How dare you!" I gasp.

"Clover." Austin clasps his hands together as if he's praying and lifts them to his lips. "It's true."

"No." I shake my head. "Don't say that. We did that interview…"

Austin takes a deep breath. "You declared on national airwaves you wanted to become a whore." He takes a step closer. "And agreeing to this dating thing made you seem like one."

I hold my hand to my chest, the pain of this conversation too much for me to bear. The tears begin to fall. My body begins to shake.

"Clover." Austin tries to wrap his arms around me, but I jerk away. "Please don't cry. I didn't mean—"

"I know what this seems like, but I agreed to do this, not because I actually wanted to get laid. I mean, I do," I swipe at the tears that slowly begin to fall, "but to prove to myself I am worth something. That I'm not some…" I search for the word he used. "Some naïve girl who turns a blind eye when their boyfriend of six years dumps them for some supermodel he happened to knock up."

"Listen to what you just said," Austin begs for me to hear him. "This situation is *exactly* like that."

Damn!

"Come here, sweetie." Austin stretches his arm out wide and wiggles his fingers, but his words are like a punch to the gut.

The one person I have always turned to to lift me up is tearing me down—even if it is with the truth.

Maybe Nick was using me, but isn't that for me to decide, not Austin? How can I be seen as a strong woman if I don't even have the chance to prove it? Healing takes time. It's not something a magic wand, or these dates, or even Austin, can fix.

Only me.

"I can't." I shake my head, unable to say anything else.

This is the moment where our words fail us and our actions scold us.

The problem? The guy I run to has now become the guy I want to run from.

"I have to go." I turn and do exactly that.

CHAPTER TWENTY-ONE

CLOVER

You know that moment in the movies when the heroine runs away crying? Remember how graceful she looks? Yeah, that's not me, and this is definitely not the movies.

My eyes are swollen, my face is blotchy, and my nose won't stop running. I swear, each time I sniffle, it's the snort heard around the world. Stupid echo.

And my new fun and flirty delicate pale pink dress? It's so short, when I run, you can see everything, and when I say everything, I mean *everything*. Thanks to the new sheer panties I just had to buy. So, I had to make a difficult choice: flash the world or wipe my tears? I chose the makeup, tear-streaked face.

Stupid tears.

"Whoa!" Owen rounds the corner and steps right into my path.

I skid to a stop. "Sorry."

I try to side-step him, but he has the same idea and we continue to dance.

"You okay?" Owen tilts his head, and I drop mine, causing my loose curls to fall in my face, blocking my vision—and hopefully Owen's.

"Yeah. I'm fine." I sniffle.

"Clover." Owen places a finger under my chin and lifts. "This doesn't look like fine."

"I'll be okay." I try to convince him and myself, but my trembling lip says otherwise.

"Clover." Owen's lips curve up in a slow, kind smile. "What happened?"

It's just a silly question, but the moment the words leave his mouth, I fall into his arms. Two words asked by the wrong person. Except the right person is who caused this.

"I-I ca-can't," I choke out.

"Come here." Owen places his hand behind my head and pulls me into his rock-hard chest. "Tell me what happened."

Sniffling. "You sure you want to know?" I lean back to give us both some space.

He chuckles. "Of course, I do."

"Well." I take a breath and let it all out. "Nick was supposed to be the *real* deal. Not like the others. They were okay, but Nick…I've been looking forward to his date since the moment he walked up to my table." I lift my head up to see if Owen is even paying attention. His eyes are fixed firmly on my face, and he seems concerned, which is more than I can say for Austin. "I got this new dress, a mani-pedi, waxed *everything*, and bought some new panties."

"So I saw." Owen's lips curve into a smile—a real, genuine smile.

I smack him on the chest. "Stop. It's hard to look cute. These dresses weren't made for damsels in distress."

"Definitely not." He laughs. "They're more for taking off." He clicks his tongue and smirks.

"Exactly!" I point my finger in the air. "Which is why I'm wearing it, but then I get here to see Austin and Nick going toe to toe, and next thing you know, mascara is running down my cheeks and I'm dateless."

"Wait! Hold up." Owen narrows his eyes. "Did you say dateless?"

"Yes! Are you not following along?" I circle his puzzled face. "Come on, Dr. Phil. Keep up. This hot mess is because Nick said I wasn't worth it. Then Austin basically said I was too naïve to date."

"Oh, is that what *he* said?" Owen seems surprised. "Well, let me inform you of what I think. You are beautiful, kind, funny, and have this raw innocence about you that's appealing. I wouldn't necessarily call you naïve."

I sniffle, taking everything in. "Go on." I wave him on.

He smiles.

So do I.

"You are very much datable." Owen offers his arm. "Actually, how about *we* go on this fourth date?"

"If you haven't noticed," I point to my face, "I haven't figured out how to cry pretty." I chuckle. "I can't go out like this."

"Okay." He stands up straight. "How about you go wash up, then we'll grab some takeout and go back to my place."

I know Owen is just trying to be nice and buy me some time from having to go home and deal with Austin, but it's not necessary. I'm sure CJ is home and willing to go all voodoo doll on him.

"I don't know." My eyes wander around, trying to come up with a good excuse.

"Listen, you have a contract, I need ratings, and we can sit and bash Austin all night while we tweet about how much fun we're having." He winks.

"Owen." I shake my head. "Austin's *your* friend. You don't have to do that."

I give Owen an out from dealing with my crazy. I'm sure a part of him feels responsible for this mess, considering it was his idea in the first place.

"I want to." He holds out his arm and nods toward the door. "Come on."

Maybe this isn't such a bad idea. Food, getting away from Austin, and not having to worry about whether or not the evening will lead to more. Dating is stressful.

"I see those wheels turning." He taps the side of his head.

"I'm sorry…"

"How about I make it easy for you?" He reaches out and grabs my hand.

I look down between us, unsure of what's going on here.

"Remember that contract I talked about?" Own cocks his brow, daring me to argue.

I don't.

"Yeah, this is happening."

"So it is," I agree, giving his hand a little squeeze. "Lead the way."

"When you said we were going back to your place, I thought you meant to your apartment?" I look out the window at the perfect little houses that pass us by. "Not in suburbia."

"Well, I thought with everything that's happened, it wouldn't hurt for us both to get away." Owen smiles, one hand on the steering wheel, and one on the console dividing us. "Plus, I like coming here."

"Where is here?"

Cocking his head, Owen flashes me a smile. "My mom's."

"Wait? I'm meeting your—mother?" I pull down the visor to examine the damage. "Looking like this?" I slightly panic.

"No, unfortunately not. She's in a nursing home." Owen gives me a weak smile. "Basically, this is the only thing I have left of her."

"Oh, I'm so sorry." I reach out and place my hand over his. "I didn't know."

"It's okay. I'm dealing with it." Owen's smile is weak, but his eyes light up when we pull up to a cute, brick, Cape Code style home. "Here we are."

I unbuckle the seatbelt and reach for the Chinese takeout we picked up on our way. "Owen, this is perfect. I can see why you wouldn't want to give this up." I open the door and climb out.

"It wasn't an easy decision. The taxes are outrageous and the utilities are kind of high for not even making my way over here." Owen holds out his arm for me to pass. "After you."

"Why thank you."

Owen keeps surprising me. Austin has been friends with Owen for years, but I've only hung out with him a handful of times, and that was usually when we went out as a group, not one-on-one like this.

Unlocking the door, Owen swings it open. "To your right is the family room, and over there"—he motions to the dark hallway—"is the bathroom. Make yourself at home while I heat this grub up."

"I can help."

"I've got this. Sit. Relax. Unwind…" Owen trails off as he heads to the kitchen.

Walking around, I take in all the pictures of a young Owen. Dark, curly hair, which is now slicked back, and deep brown eyes that twinkle with mischief. "You were a cute kid."

Owen's laugh echoes from the kitchen. "Were?"

"Well, you're definitely not a kid anymore." I smile at Owen fishing for a compliment. "But still cute."

"That's better." Owen chuckles.

"I feel like I should be doing something to help. I can get plates, napkins, drinks, or something?"

"Plates?" Owen laughs as he walks in with a tray of takeout cartons and a couple bottles. "We are doing this buffet style." He nods toward the coffee table. "Can you move those albums for me?"

"Sure." I stack them on top of each other and set them underneath.

"I'm going to apologize in advance. I don't make it out here enough and I didn't think about drinks." He sets the tray down and holds up two bottles of Stella. "I found these from the last time I was here." He examines the bottle. "I'm not sure if they're out of date." He pops the top and takes a swig. "Tastes fine." He shrugs. "If it's not your thing, I have tap water, but no ice. I forgot the maker was broken." Owen cringes.

"Actually, fun fact: Mal got me started on those last year." I grab a bottle and twist the cap. "Good stuff."

"Yeah, it's not my first choice, but in this case, it works." He tilts the bottle in my direction. "Cheers."

"Cheers." I gently tap the longnecks together. "You know, one time," I chuckle, "I accidently bumped Austin's beer and it exploded all over his shirt…" I trail off. "I'm sorry. When I get nervous, I ramble."

"Why are you sorry?" Owen gives me a puzzled look while handing me a carton of sweet and sour chicken. "I like hearing your stories."

My small smile grows wider. "Thank you." I take the red box and search for the plastic utensils. "Um, Owen, where's the fork?"

"You've got to be kidding me?" He holds up his chopsticks. "You do know how to use these, right?"

"Okay, don't make fun." I hold the paper-wrapped wooden utensils in my hand. "But these things and me don't get along."

"You're kidding me right now." His lips tilt up in a smirky smile.

I drop the sticks to the table. "No. So, can I get a fork?" I hold out my hand.

"Absolutely not." He picks them back up and rips open the wrapper. "You are going to learn." He sets the wooden device in the palm of my hand.

"If I close my eyes real tight and say the magic words, do you think these will turn into a fork?" I nod down to the chopsticks. These little wooden sticks are the only thing standing between me and dinner.

"It's simple." He reaches across the table. "You're right-handed, right?" I nod. "Cool. Give it here."

"I'm telling you, Austin has tried to teach me so many times and I just end up flinging my food across the restaurant or down myself."

"Well, I'm not Austin, and we aren't in a restaurant." He reaches for a napkin and tosses it my way. "And this will protect your dress." He raises a brow. "I mean, what there is of one."

"Hey!" I pick up the napkin and throw it back at him. "I thought I was going to dinner and a movie with a guy. I thought"

"I know what you thought." He waggles his brow as he stuffs another bite of General Tso in his mouth.

"Whatever." I roll my eyes. "Are you going to show me how to use these or am I going to starve to death?"

"Patience, my friend," Owen teases.

"But I'm starving." I can't help but whine as my rumbling stomach backs up my statement.

"Holy shit." Owen's eyes shoot up. "Was that you?"

"Yeah." I nod frantically. "It's screaming, '*Feed me.*'"

"Take those," he nods to the wooden sticks, "and place the first chopstick in the valley between your pointer finger and thumb. Balance it on your ring finger."

I mimic his process. "Like this?"

"Yes. Good." He holds up the other stick. "Now, do the same thing with this one, but rest it on your middle finger instead of your ring finger."

"It won't stay." I let the chopsticks fall to the table.

"That's because you're not relaxing your hand. Shake it off like this." He flips his other wrist up and down.

"All this work to eat?" I roll my eyes, feeling a little crazy sitting here flapping my wrists. "Is this how birds feel?"

Owen throws his head back and lets out a rumble of a laugh. "You're something else, Clover Kelly." He shakes his head.

"Whatever." I grab the chopsticks and hold them out in front of me. "Now, where did we leave off?"

"I wasn't kidding when I said patience. These things are easy to use, you just have to relax and chill."

"I'm chillaxin, brah." I flash him a smile.

Being with Owen is almost as easy as being with Austin, but without all the history. Instead of Austin, who knows exactly what I want, Owen has to find out for himself. It's refreshing. Almost like we are on a *real* date.

Interesting.

"Don't say 'brah' again." He nods the bottle toward me before he tilts it up to his lips.

"Feed me and I won't."

"Okay." He grabs his sticks. "Now that everything is in place, use your thumb, pointer, and middle fingers to grasp the second chopstick a bit more tightly."

"Like this?" I don't bother to look up as I try to finagle my way through his instructions.

"Yes! Exactly! Now, using your index and middle fingers, try to move the top chopstick up and down."

"Oh my God! It's moving!" I glance up and see Owen leaning back against the front of the oversized chair behind him with a huge, satisfied grin plastered across his face.

"Now, how do I get the food in between there?" I nod toward the sticks, afraid to actually move my wrist.

"Keep your hand loose, the chopstick steady, and once you've got a good grip, eat," Owen says, as if this isn't a big deal.

"This better work." I slowly lower the wooden sticks in the carton.

"Go ahead and pick it up." Owen cheers me on.

Opening and closing a few times, I fumble with a piece of chicken. "I'm going to get you in my belly," I warn all the little nuggets.

"Um, are you talking to the chicken or"

"Shhh!" I lift my eyes and shoot Owen a look. "It's do or starve time!" I announce as I manage to balance a piece of chicken and slowly raise it to my mouth.

"You've got this," Owen whispers as I finally get close enough and snag the piece of chicken with my teeth.

"I did it." I pump my fists in the air. "Go me!"

"Pretty simple, right?" Owen sits across from me and just smiles, as if this is exactly where he wants to be.

"Yep. Totally simple." I drop one of the chopsticks to the table. "But so is this." I jab a piece of pineapple with the other one and stuff it in my mouth.

"Nooooooo!" he hollers as he falls back and rests his head on the chair cushion. "All that hard work!" He slaps the top of his head and drags his hands down the sides of his face.

"A girl's gotta eat." I shrug and take another bite.

He seems equal parts shocked and amused at my tactics. I prefer to think of them as innovative. I continue eating as we fall into a comfortable conversation and I master using chopsticks. Using the term "master" very lightly. But with Owen's help, I get the hang of it. His patience is refreshing.

"You know what?" Owen wipes his mouth and tosses the napkin on the table. "This is a perfect time for a date tweet."

"Yeah. I can show off my new skills." I hold up my chopsticks and snap at the air.

Owen pushes himself up and crosses to where I'm sitting.

"Oh! Are we going to take a selfie?" I push the coffee table to where Owen was sitting to make room for him.

"We sure are." He plops down beside me and stretches out. "I'm not going to let you take all the credit for that." He swipes the chopsticks from me and pinches my nose with them.

"Hey!" I snatch them back.

"Okay, smile!" He holds out the camera in front of us.

"Wait!" I take the chopsticks and grab some noodles. "Open wide."

Owen opens his mouth as I gracefully slide the noodles in.

"Say Chiiiiiii-nese."

Snap.

Owen laughs and noodles go flying, but there I am still clasping my chopsticks smiling and having a good time.

"I think this is the perfect pic for this evening." Owen flashes me his cell.

"I need a filter," I mumble.

"I happen to think you look beautiful." Owen turns to me and slowly begins to lean as his phone rings.

Austin.

"Do you want me to get this?" he asks my permission.

What do I say to that? Austin is his friend, his coworker, and I'm just the girl who happened to get dumped at the right place, right time.

"Up to you."

"I'm still pissed." Owen presses the red button, sending Austin to voicemail. "I think I need the night to get over it."

"About that? What exactly happened between you two?"

"I'll tell you about it when we clean up. But first…" Owen swipes his phone to life and texts me our picture. "Let's tweet."

"Okay." I download the selfie and upload it to Twitter while Owen does the same.

Clover Kelly @UnLuckyInLove_13
Finally! Thx @Decker_LIVE for the personal lessons.<pic>
#unluckyinlove #hotlinehookup #datenight

Owen Decker @Decker_LIVE
Nick who? This girl's got skillz! <pic> #luckyme #doubletake
#unluckyinlove #hotlinehookup

"All done." Owen stuffs his phone in his front pocket and stands.

"I've been sitting for so long, I'm not sure I can get up gracefully without flashing you." I let out an awkward chuckle.

"Here." Owen pulls me up, and I crash face-first into his muscular chest.

"Oh my." I can't help but inhale. Owen smells so good—like clean soap, spice, and something else—Chinese? "In case I forget to tell you later, I really enjoyed tonight." I look up and get lost in his big brown eyes.

Owen clears his throat. "Me too." He tucks my hair behind my ear. "Clover?"

"Yes?" Owen leans in, his lips brushing my ear as he whispers, "Can I kiss—?" *Nooo!*

Owen's phone begins to chime, and not just once, but multiple times. He hangs his head as he pulls out his phone and flashes me the screen. "It's Austin. He saw the tweets."

"What did he say?" I stand on my tiptoes to look over the phone.

"I haven't opened it." He tucks it in his back pocket. "It's not polite to be on your phone while on a date with a pretty girl."

I just want to jump up and down, point to myself, and scream, *"That's me! I'm the pretty girl!"* Instead, I hand over my device. "In that case, can you hold on to mine. I'm kinda on a date with a pretty amazing guy."

I'm not sure what this is, but for once, I'm not going to overthink it or analyze every detail. This is me living in the moment.

I'm just thankful he was able to turn my tears into laughs.

Austin's usually the one who does that. But this time, Owen's the cause.

CHAPTER TWENTY-TWO

AUSTIN

How in the hell did I become the bad guy? Everything I have ever done is to protect Clover, and now the person who got her in this mess is on a date with her? That doesn't even make sense.

Then again, Owen isn't the bad guy—Nick is. Somehow, in my fit of rage trying to protect Clover, Owen got caught in the crossfire, and I said things I shouldn't have. Which is why I tried to call to apologize, but the asshole sent me to voicemail because *he* decided to take Clover on the fourth date.

And not just any fourth date—he took her back to his house where it would take a good thirty minutes or so with no traffic to get there. For all I know, he could have her perky little tits in his face living out my dream.

"Fucking kiss," I mumble to no one. It's only me and the annoying-ass bird who keeps making these ridiculous sucking, slobbering noises while squawking, "Kiss me," over and over again.

I've tried to escape that night. Hell, even Clover was able to forget it, but me? It felt so fucking real and so goddamn good, it's on my own personal instant replay.

"Mwah—moo-wah—smmmmmck." Kramer hops out of his cage and mocks me. "Kiss me. Kiss, kiss, kiss me. Kiss, kiss me. Kiss, kiss, kiss me." Kramer stands in front of me, bopping his head as if this is some stupid song he just made up.

"I'm not singing this one, dude. You're flying solo."

Great. Now I'm talking to a fucking bird.

My phone beeps with a Twitter notification. "Another one?" As much as I don't want to look, I can't help it. I'm following all her dates and designated hashtags—and Clover's date with Owen is now trending thanks to their series of tweets and stupid-ass pics.

Clover feeding Owen with the chopsticks—whatever.

Them watching a movie with only their feet and the screen in the picture—blah.

Owen and Clover's fingertips touching in the buttery popcorn—what is this junior high?

This date has been going on for over five hours. FIVE—FUCKING—HOURS. What do you even do on a first date for that long?

Get lucky!

"Dammit." I've never wanted to punch myself more for thinking something like that. Clover wouldn't sleep with Owen. *Would she?*

"Intruder! Balk! Balk! Intruder!" Kramer alerts.

"Thanks, buddy." I run to the door and look through the peephole. Clover isn't home, but the elevator is coming up.

"Intruder! Balk! Balk! Intruder!"

"Shhh, it's just your mom." I try to calm my new feathered friend down.

"Intruder! Balk! Balk! Intruder!"

I turn around and shout at the bird, "Kramer! Shut—up! I can't hear them."

Kramer just stares at me, opening and closing his little black beak.

"Yes!" I point to him. "Just like that." I nod, turn around, and place my ear against the door.

Voices!

I peek through the hole, but I can't see them.

The logical thing would be for me to take a seat on the couch and wait for Clover to come in so I can apologize for earlier today, then casually discuss her date, but I'm not a logical man. Nope! I'm a man who can't stop.

I grab a baseball bat out of the umbrella stand and swing open the door.

Thank you, Clover, for being a paranoid freak.

"Gotcha!" I yell, startling Owen and Clover, who are wrapped in an embrace.

"Austin!" Clover screams, jumping back. "What are you doing?"

"Austin, put the bat down." Owen holds up his hands.

"Sorry, guys. Kramer," I throw my thumb over my shoulder, "set off his alarm."

"Kramer is an alarm?" Owen seems confused.

"He's my white cockatoo who can mimic an alarm when he thinks someone is breaking in."

"Yeah. He's growing on me." I nod just as Kramer comes strolling out. That is, until he sees Owen—and freezes.

"Buddy, are you okay?" I bend down and pet the little creature who seems to be growing on me. He doesn't move.

"Kramer?" Clover steps forward and whistles. "Come here, baby."

You know how I said Kramer was growing on me. Well, my little buddy just moved up to side-kick status.

"Little dick. Little. Little. Little dick." Kramer begins to kick his feet up like he's a bull in a rodeo. He's out for blood, and this time, it's not mine.

"Kramer!" Clover shouts, dragging out his name for a straight minute, as this whole scene plays in slow motion.

Kramer flaps his wings, takes off for Owen's thigh, attaches himself at eye-level, and begins pecking Owen's cock.

"Son of a bitch!" Owen screams, doing a little dance, trying to shake the bird free.

"Owen! You're going to hurt him." Falling to her knees, Clover tries to reach for her bird and misses.

"Wrong cock," I holler out, and her head spins around.

"Not funny, Austin. A little help would be nice."

Now, I could help out, but I'm loving this. It's a huge mood killer for Owen and a little revenge for me. I call this a win-win scenario.

"Austin," Clover pleads.

Normally, this wouldn't faze me, but every time I hear Clover say my name, it's as if she's moaning it like my dream. So, of course, I'm going to do what she asks.

"Kramer, cage," I repeat the words Clover said the night I came home a tad drunk, and what do you know—it works. Kramer hops down and wobbles his way past me into our apartment.

"I guess I'll leave you two be." I slowly walk backward. "Carry on with whatever it is you were doing." I motion between the two.

"Actually, I have to get going." Owen bends down to give Clover a little peck on the cheek, and the look of disappointment kills me.

Clover just wants to be happy, and for some fucking reason, she thinks Unlucky in Love can give her that. Maybe Owen was right. Maybe it was her choice and I took that away from her. How was I supposed to know Owen would come and sweep her off her feet?

This whole thing went from a disaster to a state of emergency.

I don't like this. I mean, it's literally only been a minute and I can hear them talking so I know they aren't sucking face, but still. She needs to get her ass inside. It's almost midnight.

"Hey, Austin." Clover tiptoes in.

"You don't have to be quiet. I put the cover on already." I point to the cage.

"Oh." She lets her heels, which she must have taken off earlier, slide to the ground, and plops back onto the couch.

"So, Owen?" I ask the question I already know the answer to.

"We're just friends." She gives the standard excuse when two people are attracted to each other but don't know what to call it.

Just friends.

Or maybe best friends?

"Well, thanks to your date with Owen, our website is getting a shit ton of hits and Unlucky in Love is all over Twitter. Hell, they are even shipping you two." I pull up my phone and read off a few.

Monica Marti @kNOw_It_All_6
Is Clover finally going to #getlucky? I think so Clover+Owen=Cloven #cloven #pagesix #unluckyinlove #hotlinehookup

"No way." Clover giggles. "That's crazy."

Cary Hart @authorcaryhart
Hello, Owen Decker! #cloven #nomnom #cometomama #unluckyinlove #hotlinehookup

"Oh! I love her books." Clover grins, loving all the attention. "Maybe she will write a romance novel based on my dating story?"

"Oh jeez." I shake my head and lean back in my chair. "I can't believe you're buying into this shit."

"What? Apparently, they think Owen and I should be an item." Clover glares at me while she twists her hair into a pile on top of her head and searches the room. "Hey, throw me that pin over there." She nods to the end table beside me. Tossing it her way, she shoves it in her hair "Thanks."

"You're welcome."

"So…" Clover stretches out on the sofa and settles in. "You don't like Cloven?" She rolls over to her side so she can get a better look at me and winces. "Can you turn that light off over there?"

"Then you will fall asleep," I try to argue, but I know this will be a losing battle, so I reach over and flip the switch.

"Thanks." She yawns. "You never answered me about Cloven."

"Because Cloven sounds like an STD."

"It does now!" Clover gasps.

"Yeah, it's like one step away from the clap."

And to make it more dramatic, I actually clap.

"Whatever, Austin," she defends the mash-up of their names.

"Fine. Maybe an STD is a little harsh. I mean, after all, it's two of my favorite people." I wink. "It's more like an antibiotic for an STD."

"Oh my God!" Clover sits up, resting her back against the armrest. "What is your problem?"

"Nothing. Well," I lower myself to my middle school ways. "this was supposed to be my radio show, and now we are shipping my producer and best friend, and have an after-hours on the website and a Twitter following," I state the facts. How can anyone argue those?

"Speaking of *your* radio show." Clover sits up and pats the seat beside her. "Owen told me what happened."

I hang my head and puff out my cheeks. "I called him to apologize." I stand and cross the room, falling onto the seat next to her.

"Owen figured as much, but he admitted he was wrong."

"Good."

"But," she rests her hand on my leg, "you were wrong too."

I'm pretty sure she said I was wrong, but with her hand on my thigh, I'm kind of distracted. Wrong, right—it all sounds the same.

"Listen." I turn to face Clover and take her hands in mine. One, I really want her to pay attention, and two, I need her as far away from my cock as I can get her. "It was no secret I *never* approved of this, but what I also didn't approve of is the way it was handled. Owen knew Nick wanted to run a proposal by me and told him not to, but he did it anyway." I give her hands a little squeeze. "That tells me the man was desperate for an 'in.'"

"Maybe," she somewhat agrees.

"It also was disrespectful to you because he could have waited. To me, that shows he didn't give a flying fuck about your feelings."

"I get that now, but what upset me the most is when you said I'm naïve." Her eyes begin to water. "I know it may seem that way, but I'm not."

"Shhh." I reach up and swipe away the tear that escaped—the one I caused to fall. "I know, Clover. You had a life you thought you were happy in. You worked hard to make it that way by not letting all the messy stuff dirty it up. There is nothing wrong with that." I lean in a little, and whisper, "That actually makes you wiser than most."

"You really think so?" her lips curl into a small smile.

"Yeah. Because when you really do find the one and get married, that all-for-love mentality will be what makes you last forever. It's like you hold the secret recipe."

"Thanks, Austin."

"You know I love you, right?" I say the words I've said a few times, but this time, I want them to mean *more.*

"Yeah, Austin, I love you too." She leans up and lets her lips linger on the side of my cheek.

"Hmm?" I purse my lips. "I just had one of those déjà vu moments."

Why must I tempt fate? If she's supposed to remember that kiss, she would have remembered it. Now, here I am, being a dick because even if she does remember…then what?

She laughs?

Turns me down?

We stop being friends? *That's not going to happen.*

"Yeah…" Clover side-eyes me as she yawns, "I've had that happen a time or two." She stands and stretches, her little pink dress riding up almost enough for me to…

Cool it, Austin.

"I've missed this." I wave between the two of us. "What do you think about Friday night—pizza and Netflix?"

Clover's lips curve into a sleepy smile. "I would like that. It's a date." She freezes, and her eyes widen. "I mean…" She yawns once more.

"I think we're both exhausted." I wink. "You have the right idea." I stand and stretch. "Morning will be here before you know it." I begin to lock up and turn everything off as Clo nods and shuffles to her room. "Clo?"

"Yes, Austin?" She turns around, and the hallway light hits her just right to where her long golden hair hangs around her shoulders like a halo, her innocent face a contrast to the sexy-as-sin dress she's wearing.

I groan.

"Are you okay?" She takes a step closer.

"Yeah, I'm just checking to see if we're good? You know, after today."

"For sure. Friends forever, right?"

Always.

CHAPTER TWENTY-THREE

CLOVER

It's been a few days since my first non-date with Owen, but given the Twitter response and that we enjoyed hanging out together, Owen decided to ask me on another date as soon as he dropped me off from the first one. The Twitterverse went wild since he asked me via Tweet.

Owen Decker @Decker_LIVE
@UnLuckyInLove_13 Date 2? Check Y or N #cloven #unluckyinlove #hotlinehookup #instaconnection #werkurflirt

I didn't need time to think about it. I instantly responded.

Replying to @Decker_LIVE
Clover Kelly @UnLuckyInLove_13
I thought you were never going to ask…Y #unluckyinlove #cloven #hotlinehookup #whattowear

Owen Decker @Decker_LIVE
@UnLuckyInLove_13 SHE SAID YES! #whew #closecall #unluckyinlove #hotlinehookup #luckyguy #cloven

I did say yes!

Owen was a complete and total surprise. I never thought when Owen barged into Austin's studio and propositioned me he would actually be the one on the final date, but he is, and I couldn't be more excited…and *nervous.*

Replying to @Decker_LIVE
Clover Kelly @UnLuckyInLove_13
Twitterverse…what should I wear? #polltime #unluckyinlove #cloven #hotlinehookup #fashionista

We've been going back and forth for the past two days, tweeting, replying, posting pics. And if we weren't doing that, we were on the phone or texting if he was at work.

Now, it's date night, and I have no clue what to wear, so I call up my friends for a little group chat.

"Hey, whore!" CJ shouts into the phone.

"Well, not yet," I tease.

"Yeah! That's my girl." She hits the video feature. "Now, about this date you're going on—"

"That's why I'm calling," I interrupt. "I haven't been this nervous since—"

"You dyed your hair blond?" CJ snickers. "I get it. I would be too. Those chemicals can fry your hair from the inside out."

I gasp. "CJ! I'm a natural!"

"Interesting. There goes the theory blondes have more fun." CJ taps her lips as if she's actually contemplating this statement.

"I think you have single-handedly proven that wrong."

"True dat." She twists her lips and nods.

"I tried to call Mal to get her input on a few outfits, but every time I call, she sends me to voicemail."

CJ looks around what looks like her bedroom. "She called me yesterday."

"What!" I shout. "I tried to call her yesterday."

"Um, I think I just got her at the right time." CJ tries to cover whatever is going on.

"What aren't you telling me? Is there something going on with Mal I need to know about?"

"No!" CJ blurts out. "I mean, there is, but this is something she has to work through." CJ gives me a sympathetic look. "I know you feel like you're out of the loop, but Mal doesn't want to burden you."

"Me?" I throw up my hands. "She's like my sister. I'll always have time for her."

"I can tell you she did get that job, but only because Austin fought for her. *Owen* refused to hire her, even though she was more than qualified."

"Do you think that's why she's not talking to me? Because I'm sort of sleeping with the enemy?" I try to get something from CJ that will help me understand why this is going on.

"Wait—are you saying?" CJ gets a wicked gleam in her eye.

"Oh God no! I mean, I wouldn't mind it, but no, we aren't." I wave my hands in the air. "It's just a figure of speech."

"Too bad. Anywho, I don't think that's exactly this issue, but when she finally decides to grow some balls, she'll deal with it and we'll get our Mal back."

"Okay. I guess I just have to be good with that."

"Hey, speaking of the enemy, how's Austin?"

"He's not the enemy…anymore. That didn't even last half the night," I remind her.

"Have you seen him naked yet?" CJ waggles her brows.

"Wait! What?" I crinkle my face in confusion. "How did we get from worrying about Mal to fantasizing about Austin?"

"So, you admit it." CJ smirks.

"I should hang up on you." I hold my finger over the button.

"Nooo!" She waves her hand in front of the phone. "I promise, I'll be good."

"Fine. Now help me with what to wear." I prop the phone up on my nightstand and hold the navy-blue plunging neckline dress in front of the camera.

"I love that one. That is what you should have worn for your non-date with Not Nick."

"That's what Austin said. So, how about…?"

"Homie, say what?" CJ jumps in. "Austin agreed?"

"Yeah, but who cares?" I hold up the sexy little black number that dips low in the back. "How about this one?"

"The blue. Always showcase the twins."

"But does it seem too slutty?" I hold it up and look between my phone and the dress. "Owen's really nice. I don't want to seem too eager if you know what I mean."

I swear, talking to Ceej is like riding on a roller coaster with lots of twists and turns. You never know which direction you're going to go. The only thing you can do is hold on and enjoy the ride.

"Speaking of eager, I *need* to know—how does he kiss?" CJ sits there holding her phone in one hand while she pretends to make out with her pillow in the other.

"You have issues." I roll my eyes.

"Well?" CJ tosses the pillow to the side and lies down. "A girl needs to know. Did he use tongue? Is he into biting? Did he go old-school and leave a hickey? Or is he like Jeffery—aka the slobber king?"

"No. No. No! And why in the hell would you compare Owen to Jeffery. That's ew. Ugh!" I fall back onto my bed. "We haven't even kissed."

"Gasp!"

"You do realize when you actually say 'gasp,' it's not the same effect as gasping," I point out.

"And you realize by nit-picking all my little quirks you are avoiding the question. So, spit it out. Why haven't you kissed Owen yet?"

"There has only been one date."

One very fabulous date.

"So?"

"Okay, we almost kissed like three times."

"Almost kissing is like it was just the tip, so I don't count it as sex. It's the tip! It's sex!" CJ makes a valid point.

"We almost kissed after our first tweet, but Austin called. Then every time we started to get close, Austin texted. When he dropped me off, I thought it would finally happen but Austin came popping out and Kramer attacked Owen."

"What?" CJ's eyes go wide, and her mouth falls open.

"Yeah, Kramer kind of told Owen he had a little dick and then preceding to peck at said dick."

"The cockblockers!" She holds up her fist and shakes it. "Damn them."

I can't help but shake my head.

"Well, I guess I better get going. I have to reply to a few emails since it's just me and my secretary at the office this week. Antonette won a trip to Bora Bora."

"Lucky bitch."

"Yeah, she wasn't going to go because it was short notice, but I told her if she didn't, she was fired."

"Sweet. I never get lucky."

"Neither do I," I mumble.

"Now, that's on you." CJ gives me one of her *I told you what you got to do, but you don't listen to me* looks.

"Anyway," I snort a laugh, "I have to get going."

"This time, call me with all the deets!" CJ warns.

"All right. All right," I agree.

CHAPTER TWENTY-FOUR

AUSTIN

"Hey, Clo…" I holler out. "I'm home." I throw my keys on the table and head to the kitchen to pour myself a drink.

"Hey!" She peeks her head out. "I'll be out in a minute."

"Okay," I call back and head to the kitchen.

After the day I had, I need something to turn down the volume on my thoughts, and this bottle of whiskey I've been nursing all week better do the fucking trick.

Each day since I woke up with a raging hard-on thanks to Clover, I've had this voice inside my head that grows louder. And today, it's fucking screaming.

"So, what do you think?"

"Holy shit!" I spin around.

One minute, she's in her room, and the next, she's standing in front of me looking absolutely gorgeous.

"That bad, huh?" Clover tucks her chin.

One single comment is all it took to replace her confidence with lingering doubt.

I toss down the warm honey liquid, unsure if the burn is from the whiskey or the heat of her being mere inches away.

Clover has this kind of understated beauty. Maybe it's because she is completely unaware of how beautiful she really is. But that's Clover. She's never thought she's good enough. I'm sure that's part of the reason she created that stupid binder.

Clover wasn't the girl she thought she needed to be, so she created this perfect path, this plan to become that person—to become who she needed to be, to get what she thought she wanted.

"I mean, I guess I could try on something else." Clover picks up the short hem of her navy-blue dress, and just as quickly, lets it fall from her fingertips.

Dammit.

I'm the reason her doubt is there. *Me.*

"Why?" I pour myself another double and tilt the glass to my lips, letting the amber liquid spill down my throat.

"I-I don't know? I guess I was expecting a little more of a reaction." There is a shyness to her voice and hesitation in her movements. "I mean, was 'holy shit' short for 'damn, she's fine' or 'that dress needs to go'?"

Clover is gorgeous enough to grace any magazine cover, but the girl has no clue. Hell, she's better than those two-dimensional photoshopped models. Her imperfections are what make her perfect.

Snap out of it.

I can't keep this up. I'm standing here fighting with the voices screaming in my head instead of easing my *friend's* mind.

"You know what I think." I take a step forward and drain the rest of the liquid from the glass before I set it down. "I'd do you." I test the waters, letting my lips curl up in a devilish smirk.

Her head snaps up, and we stand there face-to-face until her laugh breaks the awkward silence. Of course, Clover Kelly didn't take me seriously.

"You're crazy, Austin Montgomery." This time, her smile reaches her eyes. "For a second, I thought you were serious." She waggles her finger at me. "Can you imagine? A*wkward*!" She says the last work in a singsong voice.

"Yeah, awkward."

Not really.

"So, do you think Owen will like this?" She twirls, and the bottom of her dress flies up just enough for me to get a glimpse of the matching cheeky panties.

Kill me now.

"Oh? Seeing Owen tonight?" I play dumb.

"I thought I told you?" She stands there, wracking her brain.

I'm sure she did, but if she didn't, Twitter did. I was front and center watching the shit-storm go down as I watched our numbers climb.

I'm sure Owen is loving this.

"Owen is a guy, so I'm sure this," I wave my hand in front of her, "will work just fine."

"Thank God!" She reaches for her cell. "Because I'm hoping tonight I'll get a little...*you know.*"

Of course, she is. This is why she agreed to this dating shit in the first place.

"So, where are you going?" I ask the question I already know the answer to. Owen asked which restaurants Clover liked, and I told him her absolute favorite where I know she won't be able to help but gorge herself and be too miserable to do anything but talk or go home—hopefully, the latter.

"Well, he offered to take me to STK, and you know how I love that place." Clover rubs her stomach and makes a perfect O face that would nicely wrap around my di— "But we aren't going there," Clover thankfully continues, and my very naughty thought does not.

"Really?"

This is news to me.

"Yeah. Even though I *really* want to go there, because you know how I can't help myself, I love everything, I suggested maybe the Sugar Factory."

"That's our place," I mumble, and she shoots me a look. "I mean, we've been there a few times."

"I know. It's perfect. The atmosphere, the food—we can share dinner and dessert and still have room in case..."

"In case what?" I cock my head, waiting for her to say it.

"You know..." She waggles her brows.

"If you can't say it, you shouldn't do it." I wink and move past her. Suddenly, my kitchen seems way too small for us both.

"Fine. In case we *kiss.*" She smiles, and I stop in place and spin around.

"Kiss?"

"Yeah."

"Like, your lips?" I stand there, not understanding. I figured they had already…

Thank God.

"Jeez, Austin." Clover walks past me and pats my shoulder. "When's the last time you got laid?"

Before you moved in.

She chuckles. "Don't worry, I hear it's like riding a bike."

They haven't kissed?

I'm not sure what comes over me, but the need to tie her to a chair and hang a sign that says *mine* is strong.

"Don't wait up!" she hollers.

Her hand is on the knob.

Door open.

One foot out the door.

"Son of a bitch." I fall to the floor, grabbing my ankle. "Fuck me."

"Austin, what's wrong?" Clover comes rushing to my side and falls to her knees. "Are you okay?"

"My ankle." I roll around dramatically on the floor. A little too much, I know, but I haven't faked an injury since freshman year when I was trying to get out of football practice to feel up Christina Manis in the janitor's closet. Best. Decision. Ever.

So is this, I think.

"Come on. Let's get you to the couch and get some ice on it." Clover tugs on my arm and manages to get me up.

I feel bad. I know moving me is no easy feat—especially since I have a good seventy pounds on her.

"Sit down," she demands.

"Son of a bitch." I wince.

I'm getting good at this.

"Lie down." She tucks a pillow behind my head and grabs a couple more to prop under my ankle. "We probably should keep it elevated."

"Thanks, Clo." I nod toward the clock on the wall. "You need to go."

"No way." She rushes to the kitchen. "First, we get you settled, then we can worry about my date."

Not happening, Clo.

I'm all in and pretty sure I'll win the best actor award after this performance.

"You're out of baggies." Clover comes back with a bag of frozen corn and a bottle of ibuprofen. "But this should work." She rolls down my sock and examines it before she puts the ice on.

"Thank you." I give her my best *I appreciate this, but I'm in a shit ton of pain* smile.

I'm so good.

"It doesn't look swollen, but it's already bruising." Clover lays a small towel over my ankle, then the corn over that. "How many?" She opens the pill bottle and shakes out a couple.

"That will work." I swallow the pills and chase them with water.

"Clover, your date," I remind her. After all, what kind of friend would I be if I didn't?

"I texted him when I was in the kitchen and told him I couldn't make it." Her smile is gone, but is it because of not going on the date or because I broke my ankle? *Allegedly.*

"No." I reach for her hand. "I'll be fine. I have everything I need here."

"Are you sure?"

What? No!

This is where I should tell her I'm not fine, but I gamble. It's like inviting your boss over for dinner knowing he's always going to say no, but each time you ask, there's that slight chance he will say *yes*.

Please let this work.

"Of course." I wince. You know—for the role.

"Thanks, Austin." She reaches for her cell and punches out a quick text. "I'll go, but only if you promise not to get up unless you have to use the restroom."

"Deal."

"Get some rest." She brushes my hair back and places a kiss on my forehead.

A kiss.

With her lips.

My lips.

"I promise I won't be too late." She waves.

And just like that, she's gone.

I could sit here and drink thoughts of her away, fight, or throw every stupid little fucking insecurity out the window and take a chance.

Or better yet, I can do this…

Me: SOS! I've fallen and I can't get up.

Clover: Funny, Austin.

Yeah, it kind of is. I chuckle. I always loved that stupid commercial growing up.

Me: This is not a joke. I repeat. This is not a joke.

All lies.

Clover: I'm calling an ambulance.

Shit.

Me: No. The press.

Clover: I'm coming. Stay put, I'm in the lobby.

Me: Sorry…

Fuck. I obviously didn't think this through. Clover will be up here any minute and if I don't figure out something soon, I'm going to be caught red-handed.

Jumping up, I rush to make a mess of the area.

Knock over the water.

Push out the coffee table.

Sprinkle some water on my face.

Fall to the floor and hold my ankle.

"Austin!" Clover shouts as she runs through the front door. "Let's get you to the hospital."

"I hate hospitals!" I shout.

"Fine. Then how about the clinic?" She bends down and tries to help me up.

"Yes, the clinic," I agree

"Oh, Austin, I'm so sorry."

"Clover. It hurts so bad," I confess. The problem? I don't mean my ankle, but my *heart.*

CHAPTER TWENTY-FIVE

AUSTIN

I never thought I would go as far as I did last night, but it sure as hell seemed a lot better than the alternative. So, I did what any fucking crazy lunatic would do and spent six hours in the closest clinic having my perfectly healthy ankle checked out. *The diagnoses: a bruised ankle.*

"Hey, man." Owen raps on my door. "You got a minute?" Owen walks in, not giving a damn if I did or didn't, and leans against the board.

"By all means," I wave my hand, "make yourself at home.

Owen narrows his eyes. "How's the foot?" He nods to my foot, which just so happens to be crossed over the other as I lean back in my chair, taking it all in.

"It's the ankle."

"Okaaay…" he draws out the word.

"Good, man. It's like new." I stand and do a few jumping jacks.

"Good. Good." He tightens his lips.

"You know—Flintstones work wonders. Especially those green ones."

"They don't make green," Owen calls me out, a slow smirk making an appearance.

"I meant red." I point to my eyes. "Color blind."

"Hmm."

"It's a miracle it wasn't broken. The doctor said I was a lucky guy to just walk away with a bruise," I tell another lie. I wasn't about to be charged with insurance fraud, so I denied the x-ray and I told them I was paying cash.

"Well, glad you're better."

"It was touch and go there for a minute."

"Sure, Austin." Owen shakes his head. "Let me ask you a question."

Here we go.

It's time to play whose dick is bigger. According to Clover, my dick is so huge and veiny, it could be mistaken for a porn peen. *I win again.*

"Is there something between you and Clover?" He crosses his arms and waits for the answer.

I should say yes and end this right now because the bro-code is legit. No good friend would fuck with it. But something holds me back.

"Austin? If you like her, let me know, man. Because Clover is pretty damn amazing." *Yes, she is.* "So, if there isn't anything going on, let me see where this goes."

"Is it hot in here?" I fan myself.

"No." He sighs. "Austin? Are you going to—?"

"I think it may be that breakfast casserole Liza brought in." I stand up and gather my things.

"I ate it and I'm good," Owen defends Liza's award-winning casserole.

"Did you eat it from the right side or left?" I know it's not the food, but damn I need to get out of here.

"The left." He raises a brow.

"That must be it." I stop and stand in front of him. "I ate the right. That casserole was so big, I bet she had to use two things of sausage. I bet mine was undercooked."

"Austin…"

"I've got to go." I slap him on the shoulder and head to the door. "I'm talking explosion, and I'm not sure which end it's going to detonate from."

"Austin," he calls after me.

"See you later, man!" I holler, not bothering to look back.

"We need to talk about this!" Owen shouts.

Not today.

Owen keeps going. "It's not going to go away."

It will!

Clover and I made plans to order pizza and binge watch Netflix tonight, but since she hasn't said anything else about it, I'm beginning to wonder if it's still happening. So, being the extremely creative guy I am, I came up with a Plan B to assure it will. We'll call it EBTKS—aka everything but the kitchen sink. Trust me, this will work, and it all starts with a little housework.

Time to clean out the fridge.

Cottage cheese.

Moldy hamburger.

Hot sauce.

Expired yogurt.

"This is going to be so good." I give myself a fucking pat on the back.

Opening the cabinet, I reach for a pitcher and begin to dump all the ingredients into it. "Still too thick. Hmm…think, Montgomery." I open up all the cabinets until I find it. "Ah-ha!" I grab the vinegar from the bottom shelf and pour a little into the mixture. *Fuck it.* I dump the rest.

"Phew." This shit stinks. I give it a little stir and carry it to the bathroom where I place it next to the toilet.

Stopping in front of the mirror, I stand there and gaze at my reflection. "Who are you?"

What kind of pansy have I become that instead of going out and getting laid Dr. Feelgood style, I'm home alone, mixing up fake puke to trick my best friend into canceling her date? Just a little insurance policy.

Because I'm jealous?

No. I'm just looking out for her. Owen doesn't know her like I do.

Fuck it. I've come too far to turn back now. I'm all in, and that means I have to get rid of the evidence. Taking all the empty containers, I stuff them under the pizza box from two nights ago.

"Intruder! Balk! Balk! Intruder!" Kramer lets me know Clover's here. Running to the bathroom, I lock the door and get into position.

"Austin! Are you here?" Clover's heels click across the wooden floor.

Lowering my voice and feigning like I'm weak, I shout out, "In the bathroom."

"I'm so excited!" She stands on the other side of the bathroom door. "Owen got us tickets to see some band at this new club, Spotlight."

"Clover," I whine as I pick up the pitcher and slowly pour my concoction in the toilet. Now, I know this seems like an easy task, but it's not. I need to pour enough in so it sounds like I'm vomiting, but not too fast to where it will fly up everywhere.

"Austin? Are you okay in there?" Clover sounds worried.

"I think I have food poisoning," I tell another lie, but this time, I have a witness. Owen can't question me now.

Clover twists the handle.

Fuck.

"Are you dressed?" I can hear her fumbling for the key I hide above the frame.

Damn it. I hurry and rinse out the pitcher and stuff it under the sink. "Yeah." I pretend to gargle with water just as she opens the door.

Now, when you're *really* sick, the first thing you do is flush the toilet before you rinse your mouth or even brush your teeth, but not in my case. This is evidence, and I need her to see it.

"Oh no!" She rushes over and feels my forehead right before she gags. "Flush that," she chokes out.

"I'm sorry." I slowly lean down and flush it.

"Owen said you left early, but he didn't say anything about you being sick." Clover pulls a washcloth out of the drawer and runs it under the water. "If I would have known, I would have come home sooner." She begins to run the damp cloth over my face, cleaning the small chucks that managed to splatter when I was testing out the pour factor. "Can you make it to your bed?" She runs her hand up and down my back.

I wince and nod toward the family room. "The couch."

"You need to get comfortable." She tries to direct me to my bed, which would be nice if she'd join me, but I'll settle for the couch.

"But I don't want to miss our movie night." I throw in the little reminder that she apparently forgot.

"Oh no. I completely forgot." She crinkles her nose. "I mean, I didn't forget, but when Owen called, I kind of forgot." She winces. "Rain check?"

Oh hell! She's fucking rain checking me. Even when Jeffery was in the picture, if I called, she came running. I know that sounds like a douche thing to say, but it's true, and it wasn't just her, I would do the same. It's always been us. Until now. Until Owen.

"You really like him, don't you?"

There! I asked it.

"First, let's get you to bed." She runs ahead of me and pulls down my covers. "Then we'll talk." She pats the bed. "In you go."

Climbing in, I let Clover tuck me in, enjoying every single minute of it. The way her fingers brush my skin as she pulls up the covers. The softness of her lips when she presses them against my skin to check for a fever. The smell of her hair when she reaches over me to fluff up the pillows in case I want to sprawl out. Clover is everything. Not only will she make someone a great wife, but she will also make a phenomenal mom.

"Stay with me," I plead.

The words mean so much more than taking care of her friend who is feigning sick. I want her to choose me. *Again.*

"I don't think…I mean, I guess I can…" she teeter-totters back and forth.

"Please, Clover. Maybe until I fall asleep." I raise my hands and act like I'm praying. "Please."

"Of course, Austin." She nods to the hall. "I'm just going to text Owen and get you something to drink."

"You're the best." I force a smile.

Clover *is* the best, and I'm the fucking asshole taking advantage of it. Not those other dicks, not Nick, not Owen, but me—*her best fucking friend.*

I turn on the TV and quickly mute it when I hear Clover's phone ring.

"I'm so sorry, Owen, but he's sick. I know. I know. I was looking forward to it too." She pauses while Owen probably tries his best to convince her to come. "As much as I wish it did, chicken soup doesn't cure food poisoning." She gets quiet for a moment. "Really? The same thing? Then maybe it's the summer flu?" I have to give Owen props, he sure is trying hard. "I'm sorry, but Austin needs me right now. I'll call you later." Then, as quickly as she hangs up, she's in my room, in my doorway, looking like someone just stole her favorite Holiday Barbie.

Oh! That was me too. I was eleven and Barbie had boobs. *Sue me.*

"Looks like I'm free for the evening." She walks around to the other side of the bed and climbs in next to me.

"You better not get too close. I may have the summer flu," I accidentally repeat the words I just heard her say.

She cringes. "You heard me?"

"Yeah." I roll to my side to face Clover. "You never answered me earlier."

"If I really like Owen?"

I nod.

"Well—he's fun, our conversations are easy." She counts off what she likes. "Honestly, he's a lot like you. It's probably why I enjoy being around him." She flashes me a smile.

"I can see that." I nod.

Owen is a good guy. It's why he's my producer, my friend, and it's also why I'm scared of him right now. He is going after the one thing I never thought I could have.

"He was a little disappointed I canceled but supported my decision." She reaches over and tugs up my blankets a little more.

Dammit, Owen.

He's making it harder and harder for me to hold on. Maybe he was right. Maybe I'm holding her back because I'm afraid of letting her go.

Those words are ringing true right now. Hell, my antics over the last couple days should be proof of it.

I'm a desperate man, holding onto a dream, but Owen is her reality.

"You know what? I'm feeling really tired." I feign a yawn. "Is it too late to make it to that concert?"

"Really?" Her eyes light up. "I mean, if you're just going to sleep." She sits up and begins counting off her list. "I can get you a cup of soup, some crackers, a Sprite, and maybe a bowl just in case you get sick again and can't make it to the bathroom." She hops out of bed.

"Honesty, I'm good." I hold up my hand to stop her.

"You sure?" She stands there fiddling with her phone, her fingers inching to call Owen.

"Have fun. Don't do anything I wouldn't do." I wink.

"If all goes right, maybe I'll do *exactly* everything you would do." She winks back.

That's what I'm afraid of.

CHAPTER TWENTY-SIX

CLOVER

"That concert was ah-mazing!" I can't help but bounce up and down as Thomas drives us back to Owen's apartment. "I mean, I'm not usually into country music, but Ellie Thorne *killed* it."

"I have to agree." Owen smiles. "I'm not usually a club guy, but Spotlight was pretty laid back." He gives me a little side-glance. "I enjoyed it."

"I can't wait to tell the girls about it." I reach for my phone and point to the screen. "Just a quick text. I promise."

"Uh-huh." He gives me one of his knowing smirks. "I know how that goes."

"I promise." I hurry and tap out a group message to the girls.

Me: One word. Spotlight.

"I bet CJ will reply first. Mal's been busy." I shoot Owen a look to see if he'll chime in.

"Hmm." Owen doesn't say much of anything.

Mal: We have to go there!

"Oh my God. Mal responded." I flip the phone for him to see.

Me: We do!

I really want to ask Mal all the questions since it seems like forever since we've last talked. How's the new job? Why haven't you answered your phone? What's this secret you're keeping? However, I opt for the quick sentimental text to let her know I've been thinking about her.

Me: I've missed you.

Mal: I've missed you too.

Me: Where's CJ?

Mal: I don't know. I haven't talked to her today.

CJ: Here, bitches! Cleaning house.

Me: It's the weekend.

Mal: It's the weekend.

Me: Jinx.

Mal: LOL.

CJ: I heard Spotlight has great food.

Mal: Me too.

Me: Lunch this week?

CJ: Perf.

CJ: I got 2 go. Have fun on your date…

CJ With OWEN! TTYL

Me: What's that about?

Mal: Who knows.

Me: Is lunch good with you?

Mal: Yes! I can't wait to catch up.

Mal: Hopefully, my new boss will give me a break.

I glare at Owen. "Do you not give Mal a lunch break?" I tease.

"What? She gets breaks. Is she saying she doesn't?" He tries to reach for my phone, but I yank it back.

"Well, we have lunch plans next week, so you"—I tap his leg—"better let her go."

"She's a big girl, Clover." He glares.

"Okay, this convo is turning into a huge mood killer."

"I'm sorry." Owen frowns.

I smile, tapping his nose. "Well, how about you turn that frown upside down?"

Owen belts out a laugh.

"See! Perfect." I give him my best cheese-worthy grin.

"Mal will be able to go to lunch…*if* you get off that phone and slide over here."

"Deal!" I hold out my hand to shake on it, and he does.

Me: Owen said you can go. #girltalk

Mal: <middle finger> That's for your date.

Mal: <3 That's for you.

Me: Should I ask?

Mal: <pic> current situation.

Mal sends me a picture of her swamped behind tons of paperwork.

Mal: Courtesy of Owen Decker.

Me: Gasp!

"I thought we had a deal," Owen reminds me.

Me: Hey, I have to go. TTYL.

Mal: Love ya.

I hold up my phone. "See? Done." Then slide it into my purse and scoot over to Owen. "Now what?"

"How about another date tweet?" Owen holds up his phone.

"Ohhh! I'm going to post the one where I'm right by the stage."

Clover Kelly @UnLuckyInLove_13

@Real_Ellie_Thorne #EPIC Best date ever! @Decker_Live <pic> #unluckyinlove #hotlinehookup #spotlight #cloven

"Come here." Owen holds out his arm. "Get close." He snaps a pic of us in the limo and posts it.

Owen Decker @Decker_LIVE

Now for the after-party with @UnLuckyInLove_13 <pic> #cloven #spotlight #unluckyinlove #hotlinehookup

"After-party, huh?" I nudge his shoulder. "Who's all going to be there?" I tease.

"Well, me and you, for starters."

"Yeah?"

"Uh-huh." He smirks. "Plus, maybe my couch."

"I like couches." I nod slowly as I move in a little closer.

"That's good," Owen breathes.

"I thought so."

"What would you like to do on this couch?" I dare him to say more.

"I could think of a few things."

"As in?"

"Getting lucky?" He waggles his brows.

"Hmm…" I tap my chin. "How about we settle—for a *kiss*?"

"Sounds perfect." Owen wraps a hand around the back of my head and pulls me in for a kiss just as his phone begins to vibrate.

"I swear to God, if this is Austin…" He swipes his phone to life and just stares at it.

"Owen? Is everything okay?"

"Yeah. Your friend just quit." He tosses the phone on the seat next to him.

"Mal? Why?" I reach for my phone to see if she's okay.

"Something about paperwork and I'm an asshole." He hands me his phone. "Want to put these up?"

A part of me wants to call Mal to see how's she doing. But given the previous middle finger text and her messaging Owen, I'm going to assume she's mad right now.

"Yeah. If we don't," I reach over and grab his hand, "we'll never get past this."

"Silence those bitches." Owen winks.

"Done and done." I lean in. "Where were we?"

AUSTIN

"Intruder! Balk! Balk! Intruder!" Kramer squawks as he struts in my room. He's been doing this since the moment Clover walked out that door trying to get me out of bed.

The little shit may have fooled me once, maybe even twice, but the fifth—or maybe it's the sixth?—not happening, buddy.

"Intruder! Balk! Balk! Intruder!" He bounces over to my bed and uses his little beak to climb up the sheets until he's sitting on my chest.

"Why?" I throw my hands up. "Why must you do this?"

"Intruder! Balk! Balk! Intruder!"

"Kramer, come here." I pat the pillow next to me, and he wobbles over to it.

I roll over and face him.

"Buddy, we need to talk."

Kramer falls to the pillow, mimicking me. I can't help but smile. This bird has hit every single nerve since he's been delivered, just like his mom, but having him here has been kind of nice.

"We have to talk about your mama." I reach over and pet his little Mohawk. "I know this is going to be hard to hear—"

Wait—is Kramer even breathing? I lay still, trying to see if I can see his chest rise and fall.

Nothing.

"Oh shit!" I raise up on my elbow. "Kramer?" I poke his little head. "You alive?"

His eyes fly open. "Booooo. Boo. Boo-boo-boo. Booooo," he squawks.

"Dammit." I roll to my back, my hands resting on my chest, trying to catch my breath. "That wasn't funny." I turn my head to look at the little asshole. "You scared the fuck out of me."

I swear the bastard smiles. Can a bird even do that?

"As I was saying…" I raise my brow, daring the little shit to interrupt me again. "I don't think this is going to work. Your mom and I." I pause, trying to find the right words. "She likes another—"

What in the hell am I doing? Am I seriously going to have the whole break up talk with Kramer? Clover and I aren't even together.

But you wish you were.

"Mwah—moo-wah—smmmmmck." Kramer hops up. "Kiss me. Kiss, kiss, kiss me. Kiss, kiss me. Kiss, kiss, kiss me." Kramer climbs his way on top of my head and looks at me upside down. Or maybe I'm upside down. Either way, we are face-to-face and my little buddy is repeating what he heard when Clover and I shared our tender moment.

Tender fucking moment.

Jeez, I've turned into a pussy. That's what she's doing to me. Long, lonely, sexless nights.

"I'm not kissing you, buddy." I reach up and pat his little head.

Kramer's head shoots up. "Intruder! Balk! Balk! Intruder!" he warns as he lifts his wings and flutters his way to the ground.

"I heard it too." I throw my legs over the side of the bed and follow Kramer to the front room.

"Rrrr-rrrrruff. Rrrrrruff. Rrrr-rrrrruff," Kramer barks, pecking at the door.

"Huh?" I stand there in amazement. Clover always said he could bark, but I've never witnessed it.

"Austin!" Mal hollers from the other side as she beats on the door. "I know you're in there." She pounds harder.

"Rrrr-rrrrruff. Rrrrrruff. Rrrr-rrrrruff," Kramer echoes.

"Calm down, Fido. It's just Mal." I open the door, Kramer flies to his cage, and Mal pushes her way in.

"Where have you been?" She passes by me and heads straight to the kitchen, opening and closing cabinet doors.

"I was in bed." I close the door.

"Seriously?" Mal peeks her head around the corner. "Are you sick?"

"Um…yes?" I stick with the lie, just in case she talks to Clover later.

"You don't look sick." She narrows her eyes. "Want a drink?"

"I'm good."

"Suit yourself." She ducks back in to grab her glass and comes casually strolling out, downing a glass of amber liquid.

"Shit, Mal." I nod toward her glass. "That bad, huh?"

Mal shrugs. "I quit."

"You've got to be kidding me." I throw up my hands. "I fought like hell to get you that gig."

"Well, Owen is an asshat." She tips the glass to her lips and takes a long pull, wincing as she drains every last drop.

"No arguments there."

Mal's eyes go wide before they quickly narrow. "Really? You aren't going to defend him?"

"Not today."

"Tomorrow?"

"I don't know. Maybe." I lean back into the cushions and prop my feet onto the coffee table.

"Well, I don't think I'll ever like him—*ever*." She turns toward me and tucks her leg underneath her on the sofa.

I clasp her knee. "Tell me what's going on."

"Fine." She closes her eyes and takes a deep breath. "I love this job, Austin. Like I really, *really* love it, but Owen keeps giving me these shit projects that keep me so busy, I barely have time to leave my office."

"Owen isn't my favorite person right now, but…"

"No buts, Austin. He had me sorting papers for no reason."

"I'm sure there was a reason. He wouldn't just give you—"

I try to finish another sentence, but when Mal gets going, there's no stopping her.

"Yes. He. Would," she spits out. "And he did. I had a question, and I didn't want to bother Owen on his *date*." Mal shoots me a look. "Which is a *whole* other convo." She purses her lips. "Anyway, I called Elizabeth, and she informed me the papers I was sorting were converted into an electronic filing system—*Two. Years. Ago.*"

"That doesn't make sense."

Mal stretches forward and sets her glass on the table. "Tell me about it." She falls back on an exhale. "That's why I quit."

"Mal, I'm not going to let you quit." I reach over and squeeze her knee. "There is no one better for this job than you."

"I know, but I can't—"

"Take a few days off, and when you're ready, come back. I'll talk to Owen."

Mal lets out a sigh. "I honestly don't have a choice. I left my styling job for this."

"It will all work out," I promise her.

I hate that Owen has her this worked up. Honestly, since this Unlucky in Love shit started, he's been extremely moody and totally unpredictable. Like, where did this whole #cloven thing come from anyway? He's never talked about her before, so why now?

"Speaking of working out…" She leans over and pokes me in the side. "How are things with Clover?"

Not good.

I moan and let my head fall back.

"That bad?"

I can either keep lying to myself and pretend nothing happened, or I can confess my sins so everything can go back to the way it was.

Rolling my head to the side, I look at my sister, who is also one of Clover's best friends, and admit the truth. "I kissed her."

"I knew it." She jumps up. "Wait? Why didn't she tell me?" She points to me. "You! You told her not to, didn't you?"

"Sit down." I reach up, grab onto the hem of her shirt, and tug. "Stop being dramatic."

"I'm not, but keeping something like this from your *sister* is not acceptable," she scolds.

"She doesn't remember," I whisper.

"What do you mean?" She doesn't wait for me to answer. "Never mind that." She waves me off. "Was she drinking? I bet she was. You know what they say about things people confess when they've been drinking—it's things they are thinking but are too afraid to say when they are sober."

"It wasn't like that." I stand and cross the room, sitting in the chair across from Mal.

"Stop running from the truth." Mal crosses her arms.

"What are you talking about? I just crossed the room."

"Clover is into you. She always has been." A huge smile breaks across her face.

"She told you that?"

"Well, no, but..."

"Just stop." I lean forward and rest my elbows on my knees. "Clover was worried she wasn't kissable."

"That's stupid," Mal cuts in.

"I know...Mal, she begged me to kiss her, and I tried to convince her it was a bad idea, but she kept pressing and pressing."

"You gave in."

"I did."

"Now what?" She asks the question I've been thinking about since then.

I stand and run a hand through my hair, my nerves on high alert. The truth is on the tip of my tongue waiting to be freed. "I can't stop thinking about her."

"Hmm..."

"That's all you have to say?" I walk over to where she's sitting. "What kind of response is that?" I plop down next to my sister. "You've read like a million self-help books and this is the best you've got?" I lie down. "I need you to self-help me," I plead. "I'm going crazy here."

"I haven't read that many." She pats my leg. "However, it's called self-help for a reason."

The truth is exhausting, and now she wants me to figure this shit out on my own?

"What the hell, Mal? I'm a guy. Spell it out, draw me a picture, translate that shit. I have no clue what language you're speaking over there."

"Fine." She stands and walks down the hall.

"Where're you going?" I lean my head back, trying to see what she's up to.

"You ready for this?" Mal comes in with Clover's huge ass binder.

"Clover is going to kick your ass if she finds out you have that." I nod toward the book.

"Well, she's a little busy right now, isn't she?" Mal's smile fades.

"Don't remind me." I sit up as she sits down. "What is this, story time with Mallory Montgomery?" I try to joke, but it falls flat.

"Something like that." She flips it open to the first page. "Clover created this binder in middle school. It was her fail-proof plan to find her very own Prince Charming."

"Look how well that turned out." I roll my eyes.

"Or did it?" She continues to flip through the pages. "Austin, this binder is filled with memories of you and Clover."

"What? Why?" My face twists in confusion. "Let me see."

Mal hands over the book.

Flipping through the pages is like thumbing through an old photo album—dances, ball games, bad hair, good music. Photo after photo of the best times of my life, Clover was always there, and if her book, her perfect future, was built around a past with me, that has to mean something. Could I be a part of her future?

"Clover was never going to find her happily ever after because it was always supposed to be with you." Mal points to the binder. "It's all in there."

"I don't understand."

"You idiot." Mal flicks my arm.

"Ow." I flinch. "What did you do that for?"

"Do I have to spell it out for you? Clover loves you, and after that kiss, I'm supposing you *finally* figured out you feel the same way."

I shake my head. "Mal, this isn't some fairy tale."

"Sure it is." She reaches for the binder.

"She's with Owen," I point out the obvious.

"Because you never gave her reason not to be." She stands. "I better put this up." Mal takes off for Clover's room, leaving me more confused than I was before she came over.

"Mal!" I holler.

"What?" She comes strolling out with a satisfied smirk on her face.

"What are you still doing here?" Mal points to the door. "Go."

"Go where?" I throw my hands up in the air. "I don't know what I'm supposed to do?"

Mal lets out an exasperated sigh. "Austin, go be the knight in shining amour and rescue your princess."

The more I think about it, the more it makes sense. I can't let her not be a part of my future. Our lives are too intertwined, and I'm not ever letting her go.

"Okay. Okay." I nod. "I've got this." I jump up and run to my bedroom.

"Make sure you brush your teeth!" Mal hollers out. "Every happy ever after is sealed with a kiss."

"Good call!"

I can't believe I'm doing this. Clover Kelly is the girl who walked into my life all those years ago, and now, I'm running back into hers.

Sliding on my shoes, I rush back into the family room and grab my keys.

"Good luck!" Mal waves. "I'll lock up."

"Mal?" I stand there with one hand on the knob, a lump forming in my throat. "What if she doesn't want to be saved?"

"Austin, it's her fairy tale, of course, she wants to be saved."

Let's hope she's right.

CHAPTER TWENTY-SEVEN

CLOVER

We've been sitting here for the last twenty minutes trying to figure out what to watch. If this were Austin, we would have agreed by now. If not, he would have let me win. It's just how we work.

Why am I even thinking about him?

I've texted Austin a few times to see how he's feeling, but he hasn't responded. Maybe he's still sleeping? Or maybe he thinks I've abandoned him when he needed me the most? Is he mad? Upset? Or maybe he's praying to the porcelain god?

"Looks like a Julia Roberts marathon is on," Owen interrupts my wandering thoughts.

"Sounds great. Which one's next?"

"*My Best Friend's Wedding* is almost over. Then," he flips through the guide, "looks like *Runaway Bride*."

"Sounds great." I smile.

You've got to be kidding me.

It's like the universe is trying to tell me something. I hate *My Best Friend's Wedding*. It's actually funny because Austin got so tired of me complaining, he finally created me a "do not watch" list—at the top of it? This movie.

Who wants to spend ninety minutes totally invested in a movie, where—spoiler alert—they don't end up together? That's not how fairy tales work.

Lucky for me, it's almost over. I'm willing to bet CJ's whole cleaning house thing is code for vegging out in front of the TV binging Julia's greatest flicks.

"Want some more popcorn?" Owen stands and stretches, causing his shirt to rise up a little. I can't help but stare. "Like what you see?" Owen stops mid-stretch, flashing me a teasing smile. "Because that's just the sample." He winks.

I got caught red-handed with my hand in the cookie jar—or, in this case, the popcorn bowl.

"Sure it is." My lips curl in a wicked smile as I grab a handful of what's left of the popcorn and toss it his way.

"Hey now!" He nods to the mess I made. "You're going to clean that up."

Knock! Knock!

We both freeze.

Owen's eyes go wide and bounce between me and the door.

He throws his thumb up. "Are you expecting someone?"

I hold my hands up. "Hey, it's not my place."

"Hmm?" Owen's eyes narrow, and his lips twist. "Let's see who it is, shall we?" He peers through the peephole.

"Shit." Owen sighs, letting his head fall.

"Who is it?"

Owen doesn't say a word. He just opens and steps out of the way as Austin comes barging in.

"Clover, we need to talk."

"You know what?" Owen nods, as if he's trying to convince himself. "You guys talk. Um…I'm going to run downstairs and deal with a little matter."

"Owen, wait!" I call after him, but it's too late. He was halfway out the door the moment Austin stepped through.

"Great!" I throw my hands up. "First Nick, and now Owen." I begin to gather my things.

"Clover." Austin tries to get my attention, but I'm too pissed.

"Don't Clover me. You aren't even supposed to be here." I walk over and stand in front of him. "You!" I poke at his chest. "Are supposed to be in bed—*sick*."

"I faked it," Austin blurts out.

You've got to be kidding me.

"I can't even believe this right now." I shake my fists. "Why? Why would you do that?"

Austin doesn't move. He stands there, his hands in his pockets, and takes everything I throw his way.

"What? A cat got your tongue?" I seethe.

I can't even begin to explain the betrayal I'm feeling right now. Austin took advantage of me, of our friendship. What kind of person does that?

"I was jealous," he admits.

"No." I shake my head back and forth, not wanting to believe this. *I can't believe this.*

"It's true." His hand encircles mine.

I jerk my hand away. "Don't."

"Jesus, Clover." Austin tugs at his hair. "I thought I was losing you."

I lift my head to the ceiling and let out a frustrated groan. "What does that even mean?"

Austin shrugs. "God, I wish I knew."

My head flies forward. "No." The tears begin to well up in my eyes. My vision becomes blurry. "You don't get to involve yourself in my dating life, fake sick, and then barge in here and not *know*."

"Clo—" Austin takes a step forward, closing the distance between us. "This isn't you."

"What do you mean this isn't me?" I hold out my arms. "I'm still the same girl next door. I haven't changed."

"But you have." He tries to rationalize with me. "Since Jeffery broke up with you, you've been on this mission when—"

"Oh, please." I barrel toward him until we're face-to-face. "It's okay for *Dr. Feelgood* to have his cake and eat it too, but I can't. You pick up, use, and dispose of women right and left." I jab my finger at his chest. "That's disgusting."

"I have never treated any woman I have been with like that," he bites back. "You act like I'm some whore, but I have never disrespected them. If anything, they were the ones using me." He takes his fist and pounds on his chest. "*Me.*"

"I'm supposed to believe that?"

Austin takes a deep breath and shakes his head. "Yes, you are. Because you *know* me."

"I thought I did."

"I'm still the same boy who fucking carried you two miles home when you scraped your knee riding your bike. The same guy who helped you egg the house of the girl who stole your first boyfriend. And the man who held you when you thought you lost the love of your life." Austin's eyes begin to water. "That's who I am." Austin refuses to look away, even as his lips tremble and his shoulders heave with emotion. He isn't backing down. "Clover, I haven't changed."

Everything he's saying is true. There hasn't been a day since we've met that we haven't talked. It didn't matter who his girlfriend was or the flavor of the month. He always made time for me. Even when Jeffery and I moved in together, we made time. He has been my constant. That is why this hurts so much more than I ever thought it would.

"I know." I collapse in his arms. Salty drops fall from my chin, drenching his shirt.

"Shh," he whispers in my ear as he wraps his arms around me. "We'll get through this. We always do."

"I'm not sure we can." My voice is barely audible.

Tipping my head back, I look to gauge his reaction. It nearly ripped my heart out to speak those words.

I stare through my tears at the man who came barging through those doors, desperate to save me from a situation that didn't need saving. That man—had a purpose. I just need him to admit it. Maybe if he could, things would end up different.

But he can't, and I'm not sure if he ever will. So, I do the only thing I know how to do and set him free. "Austin, I need you to go."

He doesn't say a word. He doesn't blink. He just turns and walks away.

What have I done?

"Hey." Owen comes strolling in. "I just passed Austin in the hall."

I'm not sure what comes over me, maybe it's everything that happened with Austin…or what didn't. But seeing Owen standing there looking at me all concerned sends me into emotional overload.

I can cry or I can react. Before I have time to think, I'm moving toward Owen.

I don't say a word. I just rush forward and fall into Owen's arms. I need to know.

Is it me? I push the doubt from my mind and press my lips to his.

And instantly, I know. I feel…nothing.

"Clover." Owen sighs my name like it's foreign to him. "I think we both know what this is about." He releases me.

"Austin, it's not like that. I promise." I try to convince him of something I'm not even sure of, because kissing him was like kissing my best friend. Only not. Because my dream kiss with Austin was everything. And this…was a mistake.

"Owen."

"Huh?" I look up in confusion.

"You called me Austin," Owen points out, taking a step back.

"What are you saying?" I ask, even though I already know.

"I think we both jumped into this for the wrong reasons. Under any other circumstances, maybe we could have worked, because Lord knows you are absolutely amazing." He smiles shyly at me. "Any guy would be lucky to have you. But I think someone already does. Even if neither of you wants to admit it."

"Owen, I don't know what to say." I begin gathering my things, hoping I don't make this goodbye awkward.

"I think goodbye is a good place to start." He smiles and hands me my purse.

"Thanks for understanding." I lean in, and we share a brief hug. "Thanks for everything."

"Should I call Thomas?"

"I will when I get downstairs. It'll give me time to think while I wait."

"Okay." He smiles as I turn to walk away. "Clover?"

"Yeah?" I look over my shoulder.

"Good luck." He winks.

"Thanks." I smile, glad things aren't awkward between us.

CHAPTER TWENTY-EIGHT

CLOVER

One night, one moment, can change *everything.*

I choose my words wisely as I try to figure out what's going on. All he has to do is tell me why, but this silence between us makes my blood boil. There's more happening here than he wants to admit—more than either one of us wants to admit.

"So, now all of a sudden you have nothing to say?" The hurt balances out the anger as I walk toward where he sits on the couch.

"I don't know what you want me to say." He won't meet my eyes.

Tell me why.

I know Austin. Maybe better than I know myself. And something isn't adding up. "Is this about the show? About Owen?"

"Yes, for starters." He stares up at me, hurt in his own eyes. "Owen isn't right for you."

"I know that now." I give him a small smile.

"You do?" His eyes widen as he continues starting at me.

"For starters, I called him by the wrong name. Apparently, the number one rule to dating is remembering who you're with." I try to make light of the situation.

Austin just nods. It's not exactly what I thought he'd do, but it's something—and something is better than nothing.

"And when I kissed him, I realized something." I pause. "Okay, maybe I realized one thing then, and the other on the ride here," I ramble, unsure of where I'm going with this. All I know is whatever I'm about to say needs to be said.

"I wanted that dream. I wanted that kiss and how it made me feel. The problem? It wasn't him in my dream." I turn away and sigh. "Austin, it was *you*."

I hear him standing and feel him behind me. His wide palms rest on my shoulder and turn me toward him.

"Clo…" his voice is heavy with emotion, "it wasn't a dream." He looks into my eyes.

I'm not sure I heard him right. "What are you talking about?"

"This..." He growls before his mouth slams over mine, robbing me of breath in one hell of a demanding kiss.

It all comes crashing to the surface as his lips move over mine. I'm lost in moment—in him. *His familiar lips.* His tongue skims my bottom lip, seeking entry and I don't deny him. *I can't.*

I've kissed these lips before. They've already claimed me. Just as I realize, I remember *everything.* He pulls back, and we stare at each other, breathless.

"It was real?" I whisper.

"It was." He wraps his arms tighter around me as his forehead falls against mine.

"Why didn't you tell me?" I snuggle into his grasp. "I was afraid it would ruin things…if you didn't feel the same. I couldn't chance losing you. Not just you as my friend, but you, us...this—the way I feel about you."

"And how do you feel about me?" I risk the rejection that could come, but I have to know.

He leans back and gazes at me. "I feel everything. Things I didn't know were possible. Things I didn't think I should feel for my friend."

"Austin..." My hands frame his face.

He leans into my touch. "I need to get this out."

I don't say anything. I just stand there and let him explain what he couldn't admit earlier.

"It killed me after our kiss to watch you go on another date. To think someone else might be kissing this gorgeous, perfect mouth." His finger traces my lips, and they open in response. "I only wanted to give you the space to find what you were looking for. Your perfect man, your happy ending."

"It wasn't about that," I try to argue.

"Come on, Clo—it's me you're talking to." He takes my face in his hands, and his lips brush over mine as he speaks. "The short dresses, the talk about getting lucky, it wasn't you—I know *you.* You might have thought you were looking for a good time, but I know you were hoping to find forever. You're *that* kind of girl."

"Maybe with you, I can have it all." I surprise us both, flinging my arms over his shoulders to pull him in closer.

We walk backwards until I feel the brush of the cool wall against my back.

"Austin." His name falls from my lips in a moan.

He breathes it in, deepening the kiss. Our tongues tangle. He devours my mouth, until the urgency slows, and our foreheads fall against each other.

My heart hammering out of my chest while his eyes fixate on mine. Austin Montgomery wipes any fear, doubt, and reason for not doing this away. He has cleaned my slate and decided to write his own plan, and I'm going to let him.

Take me.

He's as close as he can be without physically touching me, but electricity crackles between us, filling the air with a charge. It runs from the top of my head to the soles of my feet. It's like everything has been leading toward this moment, and in just a few seconds, it all shifts into place.

He reaches for me once more, and goosebumps cover my skin at the anticipation of his touch.

This is really happening.

He presses his entire front against my back, his mouth dropping to my ear. "Can I remove this?" Leaning back, he runs a finger along the nape of my neck and down my spine, dragging the zipper of my dress as he goes. Cool air kisses my skin as he pauses, his wide palms resting at my waist. I nudge my hips against his as he nips my neck, encouraging him, trying to show him what my mouth won't say.

Pressure builds from the friction of our bodies. I'm desperate for more, needing satisfaction only he can give.

"Clo, you've never looked more beautiful than you do right now." He skims his lips across my ear, whispering words of adoration. I never realized how much I needed to hear those words, but him saying them while feeling his warm breath tickle my skin causes my emotions to turn inside out.

Nipping. "Stunning."

Licking. "Innocent."

Biting. "Mine."

"Oh, God." I melt into him.

"Not God, Clo," Austin mumbles, smiling against my skin as he feathers tender kisses down my back. "Just a man who has never needed anything more in his entire life. Let me have you."

"Austin," I plead. His confession causes a relentless sensation in my already throbbing core.

Grasping the zipper, he breathes into my ear. "Is this what you want?"

I nod.

Slowly, he pulls it down. Inch by inch, he teases me. I'm at serious risk of falling apart if he keeps this up. I want to scream for him to rip it off—anything so I can be under him.

Austin groans his appreciation as he lets it fall to the floor. His hands slide around my hips, and he spins me toward him.

I've never felt more exposed, standing in front of the man I have loved all my life as he looks at me with hungry eyes.

His lips curl up in a satisfied smile. "My fucking wet dream." He reaches out and runs a finger under my bra strap. "Later, this will be gone, but for now, it stays—for me." He continues his trail as he lowers himself in front of me.

I never thought I would be a part of any man's fantasy, let alone a wet one. I close my eyes as my body hums with satisfaction. But I need more.

His hands.

His mouth.

His love.

"Please, Clo, tell me this is okay." He looks up from under his hooded eyes, begging. "Tell me I can kiss every single inch of you."

I can't speak, I can't scream, I can't do anything but admire the man kneeling in front of me. My prince, my fairytale.

He runs his palms up my front. "From here…." he trails his finger over the lace and drags it down, circling my navel, "to here…." down to the top of my soft pink sheer panties, "to here."

I gulp.

Yes, right there.

"Tell me."

He waits for me, asking if he can have me, taste me, pleading for me to let him lose control.

Words disappear, but I nod frantically.

Austin rises to his feet as stares at me with complete intent, drinking me in. There is nothing friendly about this. He's starving, and I'm about to be his next meal.

Austin stands as he crashes his mouth to mine, accepting me for everything I am and taking everything he knows we can be. This isn't just a kiss, this is one that will forever be imprinted on my soul.

Our tongues dance together wildly as his hand lifts my breast, circling my nipple through my bra with his thumb. The sheer and lace is like sandpaper scratching the surface.

He rolls his hips, pushing his erection into me.

I fist my hands in his hair, moaning an invitation.

He's claiming my body, but there's no need. It's already his. Always has been.

His mouth flutters gentle kisses as he hooks his thumbs into the waistband of my panties. Looking up one last time, his eyes ask permission.

"Yes," I whisper, threading my fingers in his hair and guiding him down to where I need him to be, my body aching for *more.*

"Jesus," he groans, nipping above my sensitive bud.

He places a hand on my hip as he slowly pulls my sheer barrier down, and I step out. His hot breath chills me to the core, sending a shiver up my spine.

His fingertips trace up the insides of my thighs, and my legs shift open to give him better access. I should feel embarrassed, but I'm too overcome with need and desire to care that my best friend is eye level with my lady bits.

"Austin, please," I moan as I feel Austin's finger run up the center of my core and I slump forward, resting my forehead on his. "I need you."

One side of his mouth lifts into a semblance of a smile as his thumb brushes the tip of my clit.

"Please." I roll my body waiting for him to do something. Anything to make this ache go away.

"So needy," he rumbles low in my ear as he plunges a finger inside me, working me into a frenzy. "Is this what you want?"

"Yes," I cry, digging my nails into his strained muscles.

I hear a groan of satisfaction as he adds another finger.

Pumping.

Grinding.

Teasing.

I barely have time to think before his mouth replaces his hand. His tongue darts out, teasing me before taking his sweet time tasting me. The gentle rhythm of my hips has me riding him, desperate for *more*. It's a torturous pleasure I could endure forever.

Gah! My legs turn to jelly, and I reach out to steady myself as he throws one leg over his shoulder, helping me to balance while gaining better access to devour me.

Every flick.

Every suck.

Every cell in my body is on fire. A freaking inferno.

I'm consumed.

The pleasure is too much.

My body convulses, and I explode around his tongue, clenching my eyes closed. I'm thrown off a cliff and freefalling into nothing.

Panting.

Shaking.

Boneless.

I'm delirious with pleasure as he continues to lick and suck, spreading a fire through my veins. Falling apart in an explosion of stars, I toss my head back and cry out, holding onto his shoulders for dear life as he continues his attack, building me back up before I even have a chance to come down.

"Austin!" I gasp.

"You want more?" He smiles against my slick skin.

"I want you." It's the only words I can form. My confession, my truth.

Austin lowers lowers my leg and peppers kisses across my abdomen. His tongue peeks out, and he traces his way around my navel and up between my breast as he rises to his feet after worshipping me with his mouth.

"Kiss me." He smiles lightly.

Our eyes lock for the briefest of moments before we lean forward, undeniably drawn together. My eyes fall closed on a sigh as our lips seal every emotion I can think of, and even the ones I can't.

Austin's mouth, his hands, his touch...mark me inside and out. This time, it's not about claiming or teasing. This time is about sharing. This kiss and every one to come. This moment is different.

This is us.

AUSTIN

I never knew how thirsty I was until I tasted her. Once would never be enough. I drank her in like a man in the desert, desperate to quench his thirst.

Clover falls into my arms, and I lift, carrying her to the bedroom to continue claiming her. I lean over to lay her on the bed—*my bed*—and lose my footing.

She's so spent, she lands with a bounce and almost rolls off.

"Clover!" I reach out, pulling her back up. As she sits up, our heads bump with a loud crack.

"Shit!" we say at the same time, rubbing our heads.

A giggle erupts from her throat, and I steady her, easing her back onto the mattress. Her hair is wild, not just from her little bounce, but from me, from earlier.

"Are you okay?" I brush a stray tendril of hair from her face, meeting her dark, satisfied stare.

"I am." She smiles lightly, turning her face to kiss my palm. "I'm more than fine."

Clover confirms what they had just done was good. It was more than good it was fucking perfect. The kiss, how she felt, the way she tasted...one night would never be enough. Clover Kelly is my drug, and I'm addicted.

Stepping back, my hand falls from her face as I take a moment to appreciate the sight of her, still unable to believe this is really happening.

Her.

Here.

In my bed.

"Is everything okay?" Clover worries her bottom lip.

"More than okay." I take my sweet ass time appreciating how fucking perfect she is. Golden blonde hair frames her gorgeous face. Ocean blue eyes hold me captive. Those perfect pink kissable lips are all mine.

"I was hoping you were going to say that." Clover arches her brow, a wicked gleam in her eye as she reaches up and unclasps her bra—the same fucking one from my dream.

Pink. Mine.

"And I was hoping you were going to do that." I moan as she pulls the straps down, giving me my own little peep show.

"Really?" Clover covers her breasts as she tosses her bra to the floor.

I nod. Seeing clover splayed out on my bed—naked—offering herself to me is an agony I'm willing to endure. This moment is everything I never knew I wanted. Clover Kelly is my end game.

Clover bites her bottom lip as she runs her eyes down my jean-clad thighs. Her eyes widen noticing the bulge straining against the fabric.

"There is nothing more than I want in this moment."

"Mmm." She nods her appreciation as she shifts on the bed, the friction giving her a temporary relief I will satisfy.

"Fuck," I mumble. I tasted her, now it's time to feel her hands on me.

Exploring.

Teasing.

Clawing.

I pull my shirt over my head and toss it across the room before stopping at the foot of the bed, and just like the in the dream, I ask her for what I want. "Touch me."

Fuck the dream. Real life is so much better.

She leans forward, and her hands glide over my lower stomach, my muscles clenching in response. A hiss leaves my mouth as she continues to explore my body. Her hands stop on my jeans, and she looks up at me. I nod.

I've never wanted anything more.

She unbuckles my belt and sets me free.

"It wasn't a Google Dick!" she screams. Her eyes pop wide and her jaw drops. "Oh. My. Gawd! Austin, it was really you?"

"I prefer the other name you called it..." I play dumb, running my thumb along my chin. "What was it? Porn peen?"

She slaps my chest. "Stop being so weird."

"I'm not...this is me," I remind her, pulling her to me. The amusement in her eyes is replaced with desire. "This is *us*."

Her lips are like fire as she kisses her way up my chest until she's up on her knees, standing in front of me. She places one gentle kiss to my lips before climbing off the bed and walking around me—*naked*.

She's like a fucking tigress on the prowl. Her fingertips never leave my body as she stalks around me. She's curious, but not hesitant. And for that, I'm grateful.

That fucker Jeffrey never let her take the lead, and it made her doubt herself. I'm glad I get to be the one to show her how it's supposed to be. And not just in the bedroom.

Her hands reach around from behind and caress my chest. Her breathing is heavy, tickling my back. She moves lower, and lower, holding her breath as she takes me into her hand and strokes me.

Once.

Twice.

I can't take it.

I turn toward her and lift her into my arms as my mouth crashes against hers once more. I lay her back on the mattress, gently this time, and prepare to give her everything I am.

She's thinks she's about to lucky, but I'm the lucky one.

Settling between her legs, I massage my hands up her thighs, then drag my finger through her slick folds. Touching her doesn't compare to tasting to her. But I need to get her ready—I need to conquer her like I'm making up for lost time.

"Austin," she breathes my name, and I almost collapse.

I can't wait another second to be inside her. Just the sight of her in my bed coming undone with a single touch will have me blowing my load like a teenage boy on prom night.

Adding another finger, I circle her opening as she reaches her arms around and claws at my back.

"Austin! Oh—" she cries out. I continue teasing her, and myself, until she's dripping for me.

Now comes the part that matters most: her safety. I know she's on the pill, but I want her to *feel* safe. To trust me.

She looks up as I hesitate. "Austin?"

"I've never been with anyone without protection..."

She smiles up at me, her eyes hooded with lust.

"I want to feel you. All of you."

"I'm on the pill," she whispers.

"I just want to make sure you're comfortable."

"Austin," her hands frame my face, "I trust you. With my body...and my heart."

The combination of her words and the way she licks her lips is all I need. "You ready?"

"More than. I want this. I want *you*." She snakes her arms around my neck and pulls me down. "Kiss me, " she breathes.

I crash my mouth to hers. Our tongues tangle, our moans silenced, she consumes me.

"Clover," I hiss.

She whimpers as her legs fall open, inviting me in. I tease us both, sliding my throbbing cock through her folds. Back and forth, again and again, until her eyes close and her hands wrap around my ass, trying to get closer.

Just the tip is too much. But I need more. *I need her.*

"Clo, look at me, baby," I whisper.

She opens her eyes just as I drive all the way in, my eyes locked on hers as I thrust. A gasp leaves her throat, and a moan rumbles in my chest.

"Are you okay?"

"Yes." It's a simple satisfying reply.

Slow, steady pumps allow me to learn her body. To claim it.

Pump—You.

Pump—Are.

Pump—Mine.

Our lips fuse, and we breathe moans back and forth. The pressure is building in the base of my spine and no words can describe what I'm feeling.

"More!" she cries out, and I pick up the pace. "So close..." Her lustful voice fills the air.

"God, Clover!" I grunt, sweat building on my brow.

Faster!

Harder!

Deeper!

More!

Demands she cries out in the throes of passion—and I fulfill every one as she fulfills every fantasy I never knew I had.

"Austin! Now!" her voice calls out.

"Me too, babe. Me too!" I silence her cries and drink in her moans as I lose myself in her. My best friend. We both come together—just like it should be.

After a couple moments of dizzying aftershocks, I fall to the mattress and flip us, taking her with me.

"Wow."

"Yeah." I catch my breath before adding, "I should have known you would be a screamer."

She smacks my chest and bursts out laughing, then starts laughing so hard, she's crying.

"What the fuck?"

She rolls over to her side and looks up at me with her sexy smile and wild hair falling. "That is so much better than my super-duper handy friend, Bob."

"It better be!" I warn her. "Because you're mine now. This wasn't a one-time thing."

"You don't own me," she huffs out, but she's still smiling.

"Wanna bet?" I lean forward, dropping my hand farther south to tease her.

"Okay," she moans as I massage her, her hips bucking in response.

"Thought so." I laugh, pulling back my hand, and she groans in frustration.

"How'd I get so lucky?" She smiles and reaches for me.

"You're about to—if you keep touching me like that. Again and again and again."

"I hope that's a promise."

"It is."

Now that I know what it's like, what we are like, I can't believe this didn't happen sooner. How could I have known I wouldn't have to choose between sex and my best friend?

I can have both.

CHAPTER TWENTY-NINE

CLOVER

Getting lucky was a phrase I could barely say without blushing, but after last night, I feel like I could shout it from Austin Montgomery's forty-ninth story apartment balcony.

That's right. This good girl didn't finish first, but she did get laid! Again, and again, and again. Did I mention it happened to be with my best friend, who happens to be a guy—and really freakin' hot? Because he is and—*He's. All. Mine.*

"Hey you." Austin stirs beside me, interrupting my internal high-five moment. "Did you sleep good?" A lazy smile stretches across his lips, and my pulse thrums.

"Mm-hmm." I pull the white cotton sheets up over my mouth to cover the huge grin that has been there since the moment I woke up feeling completely happy and one hundred percent satisfied.

And why wouldn't I? I just had the best sex of my life with someone who has a penis the size of an eggplant. Okay, maybe not exactly, but it's still ginormous and extremely satisfying. Austin is so blessed, he should be the mold for all dildos out there. Wait—that would mean I would technically be sharing him with the rest of the world. Nope. I can't do that. The theme to this story? Austin Montgomery is all mine and always has been. It just took us over fifteen years to get there.

"So?" Austin rolls over to face me. A sexy-as-sin smile creeps up on his face. "Last night?" He reaches over and hooks the top of the sheet with the tip of his index finger—the same finger he hooked in all the right places last night—then drags it down.

Busted.

Austin falls to his back with a deep rumble of a belly shaking laugh.

I roll over, propping myself up. "What?"

"I was going to ask if you're good." He reaches over and runs his thumb over my lips.

"Oh! I'm definitely good," I mumble.

"I can *definitely* tell." He lets his thumb fall from my lips as he drags it down, creating a path from my neck to in between my breasts. "You know what else I can tell?" He splays his hand across my chest.

"What's that?"

"That this right here only beats for me." He lets his fingers repeat the rhythm that only sings for him.

There was a moment when I thought maybe this was a mistake. That we jumped in when we should have dipped a toe. But then Austin says something that dissolves any doubt.

"It does." I reach up and hold my hand over his. "I've searched my whole life for something that was right in front of me. My plan may have sucked, but I'm glad I made it."

Austin scrunches his nose. "You are?"

"Yeah." I lower my face for Austin to take my lips in one of his slow and passionate kisses. I try to focus on what I'm feeling, but all I can think about is the way his mouth feels moving over mine. "Because it led me to you," I confess, breathless from his kisses. "I've compared everyone to you, and no one could live up to it. It's always been you, Austin. I love you."

"You know that sounds really cheesy." He taps my nose.

"Hey."

"But I like it." His lips hover over mine as he makes a confession of his own. "I love you."

There it is…

Every doubt.

Every insecurity.

Every question that whispered this was wrong…

Is washed away by three little words. Words we have said to each other before, but the meaning has completely changed.

Everything has changed.

"I love you too."

We lie like this, wrapped in each other's arms, neither of us wanting to let go. Not because of fear, but because we have waited so long, searching in all the wrong places for what was always here. But now we're one in a whole new way, we're complete.

"You know what else I like?" Austin flashes me a wicked grin that sends a surge of heat between my legs.

"Tell me." I nip at his lips. "I want to know."

"This." Austin reaches for my hand, pulling it under the covers and over his rock-hard cock. "Your hands on me."

"This is like that *one* morning." His mouth gapes open as I gently start stroking him up and down. "But this time, it's because of me."

Austin furrows his brows as he reaches below the covers and slides his hand over mine, stopping me.

"Austin?" My stomach drops as I wait for him to continue.

"That morning—this morning—and every morning after—this is for you." He slowly begins to work our hands, and together, he lets me feel what I do to him. *Me.*

Up—down.

Tugging—pulling.

Throbbing—jerking.

"That dream?" Austin sucks in his bottom lip and moans. "Clover, it was just as real to me as this right here—" His eyes are locked on mine with such an intensity. "Right now."

Seeing the fire in his eyes, the desire for only me, is my undoing.

Turned on and feeling ambitious, I take his hand and place it over my core.

"So wet." He begins to work his fingers in as I continue to pump him.

Our bodies find a steady rhythm as we climb closer to climax together. When it happens, my palm grasps him tighter as he hisses and empties himself while my own orgasm crashes through me like a tidal wave.

"Holy shit." Austin sits up, sweat dripping down his perfect chest.

"I know," I pant, trying to catch my breath.

"Clo?" Austin looks down at me with the widest, cheesiest smile.

"Mm-um-yeah?" I try to answer with real words.

"That was the best 'I'll show you mine if you show me yours' moment *ever.*"

"Whatever." I smack his leg.

"You know it's true." He nods with a satisfied grin. "Well, as much as I want to continue this, we have to get to the studio for your final interview."

I groan.

"I know. I feel the same way." Austin lifts up the covers and winces. "But first, we get cleaned up." Austin jumps out of the bed. "Last one to the bathroom has to go down."

I'm glad it's not awkward between us. Even after we professed our love and shared the best sex of my life, he's still Austin, my perverted best friend.

Rolling out of bed, I rush toward the bathroom, before I realize he's still standing there. He hasn't even moved an inch.

"Hey! I thought this was a race?" I'm practically out of breath as I stand there watching Austin watching me with no inhibitions.

"It is." Austin rubs his hands together. "And I just won."

My heart swells, and my thighs clench as he stalks toward me.

I may have to get dirty more often…

CHAPTER THIRTY

CLOVER

The sunshine feels brighter today—and I know it's not the best sex of my life that has an extra pep in my step. It's a contentment from knowing I've finally figured out what I was looking for was by my side the whole time. And now, he's been beneath me, over me—

A ding interrupts my wicked thoughts.

Pausing on the sidewalk, I reach into my back pocket and pull out my cell.

CJ: Hey, hoe! Whatcha doin?

Me: Headed to get coffee.

Me: Although, I'm more in the mood for a…SNOW CONE!

CJ: YOU GOT LAID!

How does she do that?

Me: What makes you say that?

CJ: Come on…

CJ: Clover Kelly doesn't do messy.

I do now!

Me: What if I told you I got dirty & I liked it?

CJ: I knew it!

CJ: UR killin' me smalls. Fuckin' work.

CJ: This is phone call material!

Me: I will fill you in later, but…

Looking back, my friends had to know. All the times CJ teased me? She was trying to get a confession.

CJ: I guess Austin is off limits 4 reals now?

Me: AUSTIN IS MINE. <3

Every single glorious inch of that porn peen is mine.

Me: But you already knew that, didn't you?

CJ: Yeppers!

CJ: So, how was your first orgasm?

Amazing. Earth shattering. Addicting.

Me: You mean orgasms. As in multiple.

One before bed.

Two before we slept.

One in the middle of the night.

And one this morning, give or take a few.

CJ: It's nice to give the fingers a break, right?

Fingers are nice. Especially Austin's.

CJ: Think about the batteries you will save…

Me: Batteries could be fun if…

CJ: Hold please while I Google that. JK LOL

My days of being the Google Queen are over.

Me: CJ…I love him. I really love him.

CJ: Sweets, I could have told you that.

Me: I wish someone would have told me.

CJ: Now what is the fun in that?

Me: OMG! Mal! What do you think she will say?

CJ: Dude. Mal knows. Everyone knew.

CJ: I think you knew too.

CJ: Hellooooo! You spread your legs faster than a forest fire.

Me: OMG!

CJ: Shit, looks like they are ready for me.

CJ: Call me later?

Me: YES!

CJ: Bye, sweets.

Me: XOXO

I can't help the smile plastered on my face as I float through the door to the coffee shop, the glorious smell of coffee surrounding me.

"Oh! H-H-H-Hot!" I screech as the liquid splashes on my bare legs.

"Watch where you're going next time." The familiar voice makes my stomach turn as I reach down to brush the dark drops from my skin.

"Jeffery?" I'm unsure of what to say or do.

Do you shake hands?

Pat him on the back?

Kiss on the cheek?

High-five to the face?

Swift kick in the nuts?

How do you greet a man who told you he loved you only to knock up someone else? Kind of awkward.

"Clover?" Jeffery runs a hand through his greasy hair.

He's usually so put together, but I hardly recognize the disheveled man before me.

"So, I see you're back in the dating game." Jeffery's fake smile drips with sarcasm.

"Yeah. That was interesting, to say the least."

"I've been following your tweets."

Stalk much?

Jeffery didn't follow my tweets because he cared. He followed to see if I was going to say anything about him. I mean, I did call the guy out for being a sucky lover.

Selfish bastard.

"So? How's everything going? The baby?" I stand there making small talk with a guy I can barely stand.

"Funny story." Jeffery snorts. "Turns out, Angel is farther along than what we thought." He nods.

"Jeffery, I'm sorry, but hearing you were actually cheating on me longer than I originally thought isn't the kind of small talk I want to have this morning." I adjust my bag on my shoulder. "But good luck with all that."

I get a couple steps away before he jogs in front of me and lets out a string of confessions. "Angel and I broke up. The baby isn't mine. She lied."

"Jeffery—"

"I should have never broken up with you."

"You know what? You shouldn't have, but I'm so thankful you did. Because of you, because of your idiotic ways, I went off the deep end, but when I did, I found someone who was willing to jump in for me. He saved me, just like he always has."

I leave him with his jaw hanging open.

And this time when I walk away, I don't look back.

CLOVER

"We're back for a special edition of Hotline Hookup. I'm your host, Austin Montgomery, or better known as Dr. Feelgood, for all you virgins out there in radio-land," Austin croons in his smooth and sexy radio personality voice.

It's funny. I never realized how hot his voice is or maybe I never admitted to myself.

"Our first guest is none other than Unlucky in Love herself, Miss Clover Kelley." He turns his head to me and gives me a smile that makes my panties want to drop. "Clover, say hi to all our Hotliners out there."

"Hey, guys." I wave out of habit, not even thinking they can only hear me.

Austin raises a brow in amusement.

I shrug and stick my tongue out like I used to when we were kids. Seeing the look in his eyes turn from humor to desire reminds me how much things have changed since those days.

I've done four of these interviews already, and they never get any easier. I either bump the mic, wave when no one can see me, or run over on time. Needless to say, radio is not my thing.

"For all of you listeners who are just tuning in, Clover is a self-proclaimed goody-two-shoes who was looking to trade her halo for a pair of horns after a nasty breakup. Clover," Austin's gorgeous eyes turn back to me, "how's that going for you?"

"It's been pretty interesting to say the least."

"Dating is no joke," Austin agrees. "I'm sure all our listeners will agree too." Turning his attention to the board, he fiddles with some knobs.

"So, Clover, tell us how the final date went." He winks at me, knowing exactly how it went, or didn't go.

I smile in response.

"Well, as you all know, I went on my final date with stand-in Owen Decker, Hotline Hookup's most eligible bachelor."

"Did you catch that? She said bachelor."

"I did." I roll my eyes at Austin trying to be all alpha.

Tree claimed, Spot, lower that leg.

"Are you saying he's still single?" He keeps going, and my eyes widen, knowing Owen can hear, even though I'm pretty sure his mind is elsewhere right now. Mal's coming back next week, and Owen isn't very pleased about it.

"I am." My head shakes in response as I answer his question.

Austin is getting a kick out of this. Even though nothing happened between me and Owen and Austin got the girl, there is a part of him still irritated he even tried.

"And how about you? Are you still single after…help me out here, Clover, how many dates have you been on?"

I laugh at his annoyed expression. "Well, Austin, counting the speed dating round, I've technically gone on fifty-three dates."

"Talk about playing the field. Right, fellas?" I look away, fighting back laughter.

"I tried."

"Well, the listeners are dying to know, as well as myself, did you get lucky?" Austin's lips curl up in a devilish smile.

We both did.

"I did—indeed." I chuckle.

"Tell us, which one of these lucky guys captured your heart?"

I lean into the mic. "None of them."

"None of them? Hmm…and you call that lucky?" Austin plays along with our cryptic little game.

"I do."

"Please, do explain."

"Well, while I was searching for love, it found me in the most unexpected way."

"Interesting. Is it with one of our listeners?" Austin prods.

"Hmm, yeah, you can say that." Now it's my turn to wink at him.

"Does *he* have a name?" He licks his lips.

"He does, but this one, I'm going to keep private." I bite my lip. This little game is taking a naughty turn.

"Well, damn, I thought we were going to pull this out of you." Austin pats me on the leg and mouths that I did good. "Before you go, how about one last tweet?"

His hand moves higher on my leg, and my thighs clench.

"Sure." I shrug. "But first, I want to thank all the listeners who followed me on this journey. Your tweets and replies kept me going through the bad dates and entertained me through the good."

Austin nods in encouragement.

"And to all the gentleman who applied—thank you for making this lonely girl feel special after a crazy breakup."

I look at Austin to signal I'm finished. He gives my leg one last squeeze before releasing it to turn a dial, and music starts fading in.

"There you have it. Hotline Hookup is in the dating business. If you think this is something we should try again, head over to our website www.hotlinehookup.com and check out our latest poll."

"This is all for us right now. Stay tuned for our regularly scheduled program this afternoon. We are talking about first kisses and what not to do. Until then, I'm Dr. Feelgood, signing off."

He turns my chair toward him and scoots me closer.

"That went well." He smiles before capturing my lips with his own.

Before the kiss goes from PG-13 to R, someone taps on the glass and an intern walks in, reminding us both we're not alone.

Grabbing my phone, I do the final tweet while Austin shuts his stuff down.

Clover Kelly @UnLuckyInLove_13

Unlucky in love? Not anymore. #taken #unluckyinlove #hotlinehookup #illnevertell #shhh #cloTin

"I hope you don't care that I kept this little thing between us a secret." I smile as he takes my hand in his and I follow him to the door.

"Little?" He pulls me against him as we pass through the doorway. "Maybe you need a reminder." His breath tickles my ear. "Eggplant emoji? Porn peen? Ringing any bells?" he teases, using my words against me.

"You know what I mean." I kiss him and continue walking, pulling him with me. "The world can have Dr. Feelgood, but Austin Montgomery is all mine."

"I like the sound of that." He smiles and struggles to keep up.

"Me too."

I went from UnLucky in love, to lucky and in love with my best friend. All it took was fifty-three bad dates, a douchebag ex, and a non-Google dick pic to make me realize what I was looking for was right beside me all along.

EPILOGUE

AUSTIN

18 months later

Pacing around, I'm anxiously waiting for Clover to get home from showing a house. She's still so dedicated to helping everyone find their happy-ever-after home. She sure found ours. I let her pick.

It's been almost a year since we took the plunge and moved out of my apartment and into our forever home. I could care less about the house. My home is where she is.

Speaking of my hopefully soon-to-be fiancée…

"What's taking so long?" I sigh aloud. She should be here by now.

"Baaaawk! She's not coming! Baaaawk!"

"Seriously, Kramer?" I stare at Clover's bird, who by default is now my bird.

He's wearing a little bird tuxedo that I found online, and for the last hour has been alternating between moral support and singing the tune of the wedding march. Hopefully, he won't blow my cover.

I've spent the morning getting the house ready, following the binder checklist very carefully.

Romantic music—check.

Candles—check.

Fresh flowers—check.

Champagne—check.

Brownies, only edges—check.

I mean, she did make the list when she was twelve, but I love brownies, so those stayed.

"Runaway bride! Run. Run. Runaway bride. Bride," Kramer adds as I look out the window for a sign she's home.

"Thanks, buddy." I reach down and pat his little Mohawk. "You ready?" I exhale. Of course, the bird is ready, and honestly, I am too. I just hope she feels the same way.

"Spots!" I call out to Kramer.

When I did a test run earlier, he took his place behind me, and to my surprise, he did it again.

"Good boy," I praise.

"Polly! Polly want a cracker. Polly!" Kramer squawks.

"Shh." I turn around to calm him down.

During one of our many dress rehearsals, I may have bribed Kramer with crackers and berries to con him into participating. *Wrong move.*

The door flies open. "Austin! I sold four houses today." She fusses with her bags, trying to get them in.

This wasn't part of the plan.

"Let me help." I jog toward her, hoping Kramer stays put. "So, this is why you're running late."

"Late?" She spins around and looks up at me. "Oh my God." Her eyes go wide. "Is tonight the awards show?" She begins to panic and digs through one of the bags, pulling out a sexy soft pink number.

My favorite. It matches the softness of her lips I'm dying to taste. Later. Focus.

"Clo—" I try to grab her attention.

"Give me forty minutes to get ready." She glances down at her phone. "Or maybe an hour."

"Clo—"

"Huh?" She glances up for a second, but continues to fiddle with her outfit, tearing off the tags.

"Clover?" My fingers tug underneath her chin. Her eyes finally meet mine. "Hi."

"Hello?" She looks at me with a puzzled expression.

"Welcome home." I drop my hand, stepping backward.

Her gaze follows, and slowly, she begins to take in the setting.

"The award show isn't tonight." She takes a step forward.

"Nope." I shake my head and smile.

"Austin, what's going on?" She takes in her surroundings.

"Just a little trip down memory lane." I reach behind me and grab her old binder.

"No." She shakes her head. "I told you, I'm not that person anymore."

"I want you to open it." I stand in front of her, holding the binder that contained her hopes and dreams—everything she worked so hard to become.

"Clover, sometimes life gets so crazy, we forget all the little things we did when we were young." I clear my throat. "This planner is what made you who you are." She takes it from me and smiles as she flips through it.

"Some of us were more excessive than others." She chuckles, flipping page after page.

I let her have a few moments to take it all in while I work up the nerve to ask her to be mine…*forever.*

"Du-dun-ta-da. Du-du-dun-ta-da," Kramer chimes in at the wrong time, hitting all the wrong notes.

Clover looks around. "Where's Kramer?"

At the sound of his name, he peeks his head out.

Traitor.

"Du-dun-ta-da. Du-du-dun-ta-da."

"Whatcha singin' there?" Clover coos. Her eyes go wide before she looks back up to me confused. "Is he wearing a tux?"

"Yeah." I push the book toward her. "Now, continue."

Rocking back on my heels, I hold my breath, waiting for her to see the revisions.

"Okay. Okay." She giggles, then flashes me one of those *stop bossing me, I'm the boss* smiles.

And she is. She owns me, heart and soul.

"What's this?" She comes up on one of the little adjustments I've made to her binder.

Her tear-filled eyes flit between me and the book and back again.

"You did this?" She sniffles and holds the binder to her chest before looking back down at a scrapbook of all our memories, including the new photos I added, and a very special ending.

As realization dawns on her gorgeous face, I drop to one knee.

I reach for Kramer who has the ring around his neck. As usual, he has a mind of his own and tries to take off.

I nearly do the splits as I struggle to hold on to his foot and grab the ring before he can completely derail my plan.

"Okay, this didn't go as planned, and you know what, I'm okay with that." I rise to my feet.

"Austin." She sets the book down and covers her mouth in shock.

"You thought this binder was flawed, but I happen to think it's perfect. Those hopes and dreams are what brought us together and made us realize what we had."

For once in her life, Clover remains silent. Shocked even.

"Will you marry me?" The words tumble out before I have a chance to overthink it.

"Yes." She sets the book aside and jumps into my waiting arms.

"Yes?"

"Yes!" She laughs and cries at the same time as our lips crash together.

Turns out, we both got lucky…*in love.*

WHAT'S NEXT

Cant' Wait for Cary Hart's Next Book?

Let her know by leaving stars and telling her what you liked about UNLUCKY IN LOVE in a review!

Plus sign up and know when her next release is happening.
Cary's Newsletter: **The Pulse**
or
Follow her on her website: **www.authorcaryhart.com**

Need to Find Cary? Send her an email:
caryhartbooks@gmail.com

BOOKS BY CARY HART

THE HOTLINE COLLECTION

UnLucky in Love

BATTLEFIELD OF LOVE SERIES

Love War

Love Divide

Love Conquer

SPOTLIGHT COLLECTION

Play Me

Protect Me

Make Me (Coming 2019)

Own Me (Coming 2019)

THE FOREVER SERIES

Building Forever

Saving Forever

Broken Forever

STANDALONES

Honeymoon Hideaway

ACKNOWLEDGEMENTS

Cary's SweetHarts, Readers & VIP's – muah! You guys rock my world! Thank you for reading my books. #ThisOneIs4U#SweetHartsFoLife #LoveYouHard

Brittany – you saved my life a time or two. Thanks girl. #coffeesaveslives

Stephanie – you whore! I finally got it done! Time to Netflix #TacoWhore #HippyShit

Jessica – Finally! Finally! Finally! The end! I did it! Go me! Thank you for being my biggest cheerleader! #WooHoo #Squirrel #BetterNextTime

Monica– you said don't worry. You told me it can be done. I believed you and you were right. Thank you for putting up with my crazy. #LapItUp #Echo #RealAF #LifeSaver

Marla – Thank you for glittering my shit up! XOXO #LayVsLie #TowardsorToward

Tracey – you were there for me every step of the way. I couldn't have finished this book without you. Thank you for taking this journey with me. #MadLove #ForeverFriends

Mom – your my mom, my business partner, my best friend. I love you SO much. #ImTheFavorite

Bloggers – You guys are amazing. Thank you for taking the time out to do what you do so it makes it easier to do what we do. Geesh...that was a mouthful. Big hugs, guys. Big hugs! #PimpItRealGood #

Let's not forget Spotify –thank you Spotify! I will never leave you! You are my forever! #MusicIsLife #Inspiration #FeedMySoul

Last but not least... To my husband and kids – I love you guys so much. Oops, I did it again!

#LoveYouToTheMoon #SummerIsFinallyHere

ABOUT THE AUTHOR

Cary Hart hails from the Midwest. A sassy, coffee drinking, sometimes sailor swearing, Spotify addict, lover of all things books!

When not pushing women down the stairs in the fictional world, Cary has her hands full. Soccer mom in all sense of the word to two wild and crazy, spoiled kiddos, and wife to the most supportive husband. In addition to writing full time, she enjoys binge watching Netflix, laying around in her hammock and baking up cookies for her family and friends.

Cary writes real, raw romance! In her stories the characters deal with life's everyday struggles and unwanted drama, they talk about the ugly and they become the broken. Everyone deserves a happy ending, but sometimes before you can appreciate the light, there has to be darkness.

Growing up, if someone would have told her she would become a writer, she wouldn't have believed them. It wasn't until she got her hands on her first romance novel, that the passion grew. Now she couldn't imagine her life any other way - she's living her dream.

For more information on any of these titles and upcoming releases, please visit Cary's website: www.authorcaryhart.com

READER NOTES

READER NOTES

READER NOTES

Made in the USA
Lexington, KY
28 July 2019